DEAR ROOMIE

A ROOKIE REBELS NOVEL

KATE MEADER

This novel is a work of fiction. Any references to historical events, real people, or real places are used fictitiously. Other names, characters, places, and events are products of the author's imagination, and any resemblance to actual events or places or persons, living or dead, is entirely coincidental.

Cover design by Qamber Designs

Editing: Kristi Yanta

Copyediting: Kim Cannon

Afoot and lighthearted, take to the open road
Healthy, free, the world before you
The long brown path before you,
Leading wherever you choose.

— WALT WHITMAN

1

If Reid Durand had a motto, it was this: keep your personal life personal.

Simple, attainable, crucial. Walking into the coffee shop, this maxim seemed especially relevant. Although a few customers were seated, there was no sign of any of the baristas except for someone talking loudly behind the staff-only door.

More like shouting.

"*You can't just make a snap decision like that!*"

A pause, then, "*But my stuff is there. And now I can't access it!*"

It all sounded very dramatic, but really such drama shouldn't be brought to work. People needed to separate the personal from the professional. Better yet, don't bother with the personal at all.

"Hello?" he called out on the off chance this person might want to do what she was paid to do: serve customers. He dropped his gaze to the counter, longing for a bell like in an old-fashioned hotel. He didn't like to act all lord-and-master but this was a business, was it not?

The noisy person who wasn't doing her job had moved away from the door, so he couldn't hear her exact words. Every now and then melodramatic snatches would float through to the front.

"Locks ... Promises ... Sentimental value."

Another customer came in, an older man with one of those reusable mugs. He stood beside Reid and looked behind the counter rather comically as if someone might be hiding.

"No one home today?" All that was missing was a nudge and a wink.

The argument was becoming more heated. *"He fucking promised I could stay!"*

The new arrival turned to Reid and said rather obviously, "This is ridiculous. They have people waiting here." His eyes widened. "Hey, you're Reid Durand! Great game the other night. That goal from Foreman was something else."

Sure. The *incroyable* Cal Foreman, Reid's rival for the coveted right-wing position on the first line.

"You'll need to get in there more if you want to catch your brother." The fan—of players other than Reid—nudged with his elbow. And winked. "*He* was the top goal scorer last season for the Hawks. Your father must be so proud."

"Stepfather."

"Right. Stepfather." The guy went on for another minute about the Hawks-Rebels rivalry and how that was really going to take off now that the Durand brothers were in the same city at last. Finally, the fanboy gush petered out because Reid refused to keep it rolling.

They both looked toward the back area.

The door remained stubbornly still.

"This is a disgrace," Captain Obvious said. "I have a good mind to call the corporate office and tell them all about it."

"Uh-huh." *If it means you stop talking to me.*

"You know? I think I will. I don't have time for this!" Unpocketing his phone, he nodded at Reid. "Nice to meet you, Durand. Good luck for the rest of the season."

Reid breathed a sigh of relief when he left.

The peace didn't last, and not just because the woman auditioning for a Daytime Emmy in back was in full flight. (She had moved on to bargaining. *"At least let me get my belongings!"*)

Reid's phone rang with a call from ... well, if it wasn't that famous brother of his. Usually he would let it go to voice mail, just to annoy him, but Bastian had been making such an effort since Reid moved to Chicago two months ago. Reid really should answer before his younger brother tattled to Mom.

"Yes?"

"Holy shit! It can't be. Is this *the* Reid Durand?"

"Oh, shut up. Sometimes it's better to answer so you don't have a fit, wondering if I'm safe in the dangerous suburbs."

Bastian chuckled. He was an easygoing guy who found humor in everything, especially his grumpy older brother.

"So I'm calling to invite you over to mine for cards. And before you say you're busy, remember I know your schedule and I also know you don't have any friends."

"I have plenty of friends."

"Name one."

He growled. "When?"

"Probably Thursday. The guys are dying to know if you're an asshole off the ice as well as on. I told them you're even worse."

"Then I'll try not to disappoint them." Hanging with Hawks players? That might be useful.

The door to the staff area crashed open and someone emerged at last.

It was *her*, the smartass barista with the pink-blond hair.

His pulse rate quickened because ... he wasn't sure why. Her hair? He supposed that was it. He didn't usually have opinions on hair. Hair didn't usually rate with him at all. But something about this woman—and her hair—gave him a subtle lift. Perhaps because it signified a push against the grain. He shouldn't appreciate that, but then we're often drawn to an opposite. Yin and yang, metal to magnet.

She pushed a few stray tresses back, tucking it beneath the ball cap all the staff here wore. Her features were set in granite, yet she seemed to become more grim and annoyed on seeing him. As if *he* was the source of her problems.

Each time he came in here, his gaze was drawn to her. A couple of times, he had thought about talking to her.

He had wanted to talk to her.

Which was strange because he never wanted to talk to anyone.

Of course, that wanting had made him suspicious, because if he had the desire to do something that would have no immediate benefit for him, if the act of talking with an interesting-looking woman was so appealing, then it was imperative that he shut it down. If it didn't help his game, he didn't want to know.

He wasn't one for feelings or instincts, but he had the strangest sense about this woman. The pull he felt toward her made him want to step outside his zone.

So last week, he had dipped a toe into treacherous waters. He talked to her ...

... about his drink (their common ground)

... which he assumed she made incorrectly (she had recited the drink name differently)

... only she hadn't (but she found it amusing that he would think so)

... and that was the sum of that.

Sometimes he stayed on his phone so he wouldn't have to make small talk with retail employees. Better rude than awkward. In this moment, he had a feeling it would only make Coffee Shop Girl's day worse and something lurched in his chest at the thought.

"I have to go," he murmured to his brother.

"Okay, I'll text—" Reid had already hung up.

"Hi, can I interest you in a pumpkin spice latte today?"

This pumpkin spice shit. They were likely obliged to offer this nonsense to everyone regardless, all part of the great American upsell. She should really start with an apology for the length of time she had left him waiting.

"No, I would like an—"

"Yeah, yeah, I know. Extra shot Americano, right?"

An abrupt response, but she was having a bad day. He knew what that was like. Sometimes he took it out on people at his place of work.

"Yes, that's it."

She nodded tersely and rang it up. He paid with a credit card tap and watched as she headed to the sink to wash her hands.

He usually dropped money into the tip jar and today was no exception. He didn't have a five, so he left a twenty and pushed the tip box back to the edge of the counter because he didn't trust the next customer not to help himself. The world was filled with greedy assholes.

Coffee Shop Girl dried her hands and stepped up to the

bar to make his drink. She kept her head down, the bill of her cap covering her eyes.

No matter. Reid knew their color.

A silver-gray, a mercurial shade that reflected the chrome of the bar and usually made her eyes dance. She told stories with those eyes.

Each time he came in here, she was usually laughing at something, maybe a co-worker or the chatter of a customer. Her eyes would light like silver suns, the eyes of a woman who enjoyed life. But with him, the amusement usually faded—or it was replaced by something else.

Something cooler.

She didn't like him.

He was used to men not liking him, usually because he made sure to strike first, to establish dominance. Setting a tone with his rivals and opponents on the ice was imperative, even with his teammates so they were assured he was here to play. That he meant business. But with women, he usually encountered a different response. Women enjoyed his surliness. He didn't go out of his way to hone that aspect of his personality. It just happened that way, and the results usually benefited him in the bedroom.

But this woman was different. Today, she was in a bad mood, not even faking her effort, which was fine. He didn't care for that phony "customer is always right" business.

He stepped in a little closer, drawn to her forbidding body language, wishing he could do something to alleviate it. With her shoulders tense, she kept her head down, focusing on her task. He remembered the feeling that accompanied that look. Those emotions weren't easily forgotten.

"Is everything all right?"

Her head snapped back, her shock so sharp that she

knocked the cup in her hand sideways. The espresso went spilling across the counter in a muddy mini-wave.

"Oh, shit!" She clamped her mouth shut, then opened it slightly, just enough to murmur, "Sorry." There was a reluctance about that apology.

This woman was a rebel at heart.

"I startled you."

Blinking, she seemed to shake herself from a dream, or a nightmare where Reid Durand, the NHL's poster boy for assholes terrified her with a general query about her well-being.

"No, not at all. Well, yes, you startled me." She threw the cup in the trashcan beside the bar and wiped the counter down. "It'll just be a second to re-do it."

"It's fine, take your time. You're on your own here today?"

"Yeah, my manager stepped out for a moment to get some nickels and dimes from the currency exchange. Abolish all cash, that's what I say!" Chuckling softly, she met his gaze. "Most people pay with credit cards these days anyway, but there's always someone with Benjamins burning a hole, I suppose."

Deftly she worked the machine as she talked, more at ease than before. Obviously this was her natural state, an easy way with strangers. Good for someone who worked with the public.

Thank God he had skills on the ice. He'd never survive in customer service.

"You were talking to someone on the phone earlier?"

She flushed, and Reid's sex-starved brain was filled with lurid images of her pale skin blooming in places unseen. "You heard that?"

"The whole state heard."

She bit her lip, an astonishingly attractive gesture that

hit him right in the gut, or rather somewhere lower. It had been several long, lonely months.

She leaned toward him, the movement making her shirt gape, giving him a view of abundant cleavage. Her name tag read: Kennedy. "Sorry for inflicting that drama on you. Lodging problems. And sorry for leaving you hanging out here. And then spilling your drink. Just sorry all around."

"That last part was my fault. For making you jump."

Straightening, she placed the cup under the hot water spigot and started to pour. "Yeah, it *was* your fault now that I think of it. You're usually such a grouch that the question about my state of being scared the bejesus out of me."

"A grouch?"

She sleeved the cup, topped it with a lid, and placed it on the counter. "Are we going to pretend you're not usually doing your I'm-too-important-to-be-nice act whenever you come in here, *Reid D*?" That was the name he usually gave, though not today. Either she remembered or she recognized him from TV. "I've never seen you be pleasant to anyone except Mia."

So he wasn't at his most charming when he came in here. Unable to enjoy the fakery of the social contract, he rarely made a good impression. His mother had despaired of his grim schoolboy photos. Reid objected to being told to smile by anyone, even professional photographers.

Unsure how to respond—and he was never unsure, but now was doubting his entire life strategy—he passed over the dig about his attitude.

"You're friends with Mia Wallace?" Mia was a hockey player, sister to Vadim Petrov, captain of the Chicago Rebels. On occasion, he had run into her here with that plastic woman who was always making eyes at him.

"More like acquaintances. I walk her dog and make her coffee."

"You walk dogs?"

"Sure do. You looking for a dog walker?"

He shook his head, feeling a hollowness in his chest that made no sense. "I don't have a dog. I travel too much to be able to keep one."

"Sorry to hear that. Sounds like you could do with the company."

That was quite the assumption. Not incorrect, but quite the assumption all the same. He had the strangest urge to ask her out for a drink he couldn't have and a meal he couldn't eat that would lead to a fuck he couldn't indulge in. This season was too important and a woman like this had the capacity to derail all his plans.

"You're one of those know-it-alls, aren't you?"

She touched her throat as if to say, *who, me?* and followed up with a cute kick to the corner of her lips. Really fucking cute. Damn. "I'm just excellent at giving advice. Ask anyone here and they'll tell you I'm a whizz at it."

"Hmm. So what kind of advice do I need?"

Those silver eyes took inventory, but he got the impression she wasn't seeing what everyone else did: Canadian hockey player, the oldest Durand boy, the crank who hated small talk.

Well, look at him now.

This woman saw something else, maybe something he couldn't see for himself.

"To lighten the fuck up."

He snorted. Okay, maybe she saw exactly what everyone else did.

She grinned and then she blushed, as though she realized that might be considered inappropriate to say to a customer. It probably was, but Reid didn't care. He valued honesty above all else, even from his coffee supplier.

A movement interrupted his sightline, someone coming in through the back door and tying an apron. The manager, the one with the simpering smiles. Her gaze split between the two of them, before finally dialing up a fake grin.

Feeling lighter of heart, and with a nod at the pink-haired pixie, Reid picked up his drink and stepped away to doctor it to his liking.

2

"AND NOW BREATHE IN ... and out ... and assume corpse pose."

"Get the mirrors out," someone called from the back. It sounded like Mrs. Goggins. "Check if they're still with us."

To the soundtrack of a coven's cackles, Kennedy Clark jumped up to walk around and check that they were indeed still with us. She hadn't lost a client on her watch yet, but she wouldn't put it past one of them to give up the ghost just to spite her.

She dimmed the lights of the activity room at Larkvale Senior Living, so that the last five minutes could be spent in a womb-like shroud. It was the best way to have the students center themselves after yoga practice.

"Try to empty your mind of all that worries you. Let it all slip away."

Except your life force. Please hold on to that.

If only letting her own worries dissolve were that easy. Kennedy needed to find somewhere to live. She'd had a nice, rent-free deal for the last few months but all good things had to crash and burn. She just hadn't expected it to end with no notice, changed locks, and a banker's box of memories in the trunk of her car.

Now would be the moment to call it quits and head back out on her travels, yet she wasn't quite ready to move on, not when she'd only arrived a few months ago to be nearer to the person who was currently not doing what she was told.

"Edie, you're supposed to close your eyes and assume corpse," she said to the woman looking up at her like a cheeky cherub. "This is the time to relax."

"I'll relax when I'm dead. In real corpse pose!"

Oh God. When Kennedy had volunteered to give this class to the seniors at Edie's residential home—had to put that yoga certification to some use—she hadn't expected that the most troublesome student would be the woman who was the closest thing she had to family.

Edie Dobson had moved into the senior's home about six months ago, though to hear her say it, she was pushed headfirst by her son, who lived in LA and never came to visit. Kennedy had been in Malaysia when she heard about Edie's health troubles, so by the time she returned to Chicago, it was a done deal. Not that she could have changed the situation but she would've preferred to be here to put Edie at ease and help her settle.

Thrilled to have Kennedy back on US soil, Edie had offered her use of the house on Primrose Avenue until it was sold. Now it was and squatter's rights weren't a thing. Neither was Kennedy sure she could tolerate another night sleeping in her car.

Almost five minutes had passed and the inmates were getting restless, so Kennedy raised the lights. "Okay, everyone, great session! I'll be back on Friday but in the meantime, try to remember to stretch when you get out of bed in the morning. It really helps to keep those bones limber."

"Watch you don't fracture something in the meantime," Edie offered.

"No one will fracture anything if you're mindful of your body and its limits," Kennedy called out. "Just don't push it into anything that feels painful." To Edie, she hissed, "I could do without the colorful commentary. You're scaring people."

Edie held out a hand for a boost upright. "Let's hit the juice bar."

A few minutes later, they were in the sunroom with the Jamba Juice smoothies Kennedy had brought and refrigerated in the community kitchen during the class. Larkvale didn't have a juice bar, of course, but Edie liked to refer to their post-yoga meet-ups over smoothies as such. Adorable.

Seated at the big window overlooking the blandly perfect garden, they took a few quiet moments to drink their smoothies and settle in.

"Did you drive by the house on the way over?"

"I did. They've already painted the front door a teal color."

"The red is gone?" Edie's lip curled in disdain. "I hope it chips."

Kennedy chuckled. "My kind of petty."

Edie's son, Louis had closed on his mom's house a week ago and put the money in trust for her remaining days. Which was fine—Kennedy wasn't here to claim a cut of the woman's cash. She just wanted to be close to someone who cared. She could have taken a different route to avoid passing the house where she'd lived for three years until she was eighteen, then the last three months while she tried to get her shit together, but she had been parked on a side street two blocks over and it was the shortest way from point A to B. Also, she liked to think there was something therapeutic about driving by. Each change the new owners made took her a little further away from that time, the most heartbreaking period of her life.

After her parents died when she was fifteen, she had moved in with Edie, her grandfather's second wife. Papa John (yep, that's what he went by) had passed a couple of years before, but Edie had stepped up and given her shelter. Took her into her home and her heart.

Kennedy could never truly repay her, but since Edie's strokes (*they call them mini strokes, so not serious at all, Kennedy!*), she could be here to make sure she was as comfortable as possible.

"So how's the new roommate?"

"Great! But the landlord's the worst." Edie would freak if she knew that Kennedy was living out of her car. "*Still* hasn't fixed the shower. Do you mind if I take a quick one in your room before I leave?"

Edie waved her assent. "I'm glad you were able to find a place so quickly."

Kennedy kept her smile pinned on. She had an appointment with a guy she'd found online this afternoon. The place she'd looked at yesterday had a meth lab vibe. Today's option couldn't be worse.

"Yeah, me, too. Pity you're so entrenched here. We could get our own place together." She was only half-joking. She knew that with Edie's health concerns this was the best place for her, but what she wouldn't give to have somewhere to cushion her fall.

This wasn't Edie's problem, however. She had been on

hand when Kennedy needed a place to land ten years ago, and Kennedy had no doubt she'd dip into her savings to find a place for the girl she treated like her granddaughter. But when it came down to it, Edie didn't owe her a thing. She'd already given her use of her Ford Focus—now her castle—and Kennedy wouldn't take another cent from her.

Edie raised an eyebrow. "Us as roommates? And what happens when your feet get itchy? Off to Taiwan or Thailand or wherever your mood takes you? No, I was resistant at first but I like being Queen Bee here. It didn't take long to ascend the throne and boot that Ginny van Patten off it!"

Ginny van Patten was the head inmate at Larkvale, or had been until Edie arrived and usurped her. A fierce rivalry was born.

"Just an idea. You're right. I'll want to travel again soon." She especially didn't want to be here during any Snowpocalypse when the wind off Lake Michigan would cut through her bones.

"I've had another idea," Edie said after a healthy pull on her straw. "For the bucket list."

"Oh, yeah? Spill."

Edie took out the notebook she carried with her everywhere. Since finishing up her rehab stint and taking up residence at Larkvale, she had been adding to her bucket list. She pointed at the last addition: *See a male stripper.*

"Surely you've already done that."

"No, I have not. I was a married woman."

"Never stopped anyone." Grinning, she took the list from her and gave it another eyeball.

Go ice skating.

Get a tattoo.

Learn yoga.

Do karaoke.

Go on a scavenger hunt.

Solve a mystery.

"I'd like to say you could cross off the yoga one but you're one of my worst students." She also suspected Edie added it to give Kennedy something to do while she remained Stateside. "Some of these are dangerous. Ice skating? You could break a hip."

"I'm not an invalid."

"I know you're not." But she had given Kennedy a helluva scare. Edie had always been the strongest person Kennedy knew, and it was hard to see her at less than a hundred percent. Edie was all Kennedy had left except for an uncle in Texas, who had never shown any interest after her parents died. The fire had destroyed everything, burned Kennedy's childhood and the future of her family to ash, and her only remaining blood relative wasn't willing to step up.

Edie was. Edie treated Kennedy like a granddaughter.

That was how she introduced her to everyone. *Have you met my granddaughter?*

Pressing back the threat of tears—she was so emotional these days!—she refocused on Edie and her damn list.

"There's nothing wrong with living life to the fullest. I just want to be sure you also have longevity in there. I'll do some research on tattoo parlors and see what I can find."

"You should do research on your own list," Edie said. "Give you something to look forward to."

Kennedy's list would be comprised of one item: live another day.

"Bucket lists are for things you've left hanging." Kennedy wasn't even a fan of the fact that Edie had one. It had the stink of a death countdown about it.

"For people like you, they usually involve sex."

Good thing Kennedy had finished her smoothie or she might have choked on it. "At my age?"

"You're twenty-five, hardly on the shelf just yet, honey. I'm sure there are lots of positions you might want to try."

"I'm going to *very* obviously change the subject here. Are you flying out to LA for Thanksgiving or is Louis coming here?"

Edie screwed up her lips in horror. "Whatsherface has already told him she wants to go to Mexico." Whatsherface was Louis's third wife of four years, and would you have guessed that Edie wasn't a fan? Neither were she and her son all that close.

"I'll be here, so I can stop by. A lot of the dog walking clients go out of town so I might have a couple of canine friends with me."

"I worry about you. Not settled. All these different jobs."

"I like my freedom. I don't need a lot to get by." For the last seven years she had stayed on the balls of her feet, ready to make a break when she got bored or reflective or close to anyone.

Though that last one rarely happened. As soon as she saw the telltale signs—a softness in a guy's expression, a tight hand caging her body in that sleepy post-orgasmic state—she was out of there as quick as her wanderlusting feet could carry her. Constant movement was an art, and now she was saving up to ensure there was always a destination.

Edie leaned in. "I'd like to see you happy ... before I go."

Kennedy rolled her eyes at this obvious play on her emotions. "Where are you going? The spa?"

"I might be in excellent health now but when it's your

time, it's your time. And I'm definitely closer to the end than the beginning."

"Keep up the smoothie diet and yoga classes and you will live forever."

"I'd mostly like to see you with a nice man. Or a woman. Whatever makes you happy."

Edie added a maudlin smile, the one that said Kennedy's act might have fooled the masses but Edie Dobson was not one of them. Buddha said that attachment was the root of all suffering, and Kennedy embodied that philosophy to its core.

That didn't mean she couldn't have a little fun. She was a hit it and quit it kind of girl, and used her rolling stone status to ensure no mossy entanglements. There was always some cute Australian backpacker or a nice British digital nomad type available to service her needs. These days in the Chicago burbs with that cold air whipping off the lake, pickings were slim, however, especially when you spent most of your time with the elderly, cute puppies, and entitled coffee shop customers.

A sudden image of cheekbones and a forbidding scowl flashed before her eyes: Mr. Extra Shot Americano, or Hot Jerk, as she had dubbed him. Six-two, midnight-dark hair, denim-blue eyes.

Kennedy wasn't prone to hyperbole, but even she recognized the zing in the air when this guy was on the premises. "Reid D" was the name he gave, usually with a haughty arch of his eyebrow as if they should have memorized it by now. As if they didn't see a thousand faces a day and his was the one that should rise above the ho-hum invisibility of the coffee-loving crowd.

So what if it is was a handsome face.

A gorgeous face.

For Kennedy, it was ruined by the scowl of the beast.

He rarely responded to anyone's attempts at small talk. Half the time he looked at his phone while he placed his order, not even offering the common courtesy of eye contact. Elena, her co-worker, said he played professional hockey and had recently been traded to the Chicago Rebels, the local NHL franchise. (Traded, like he was horsemeat or a stock exchange commodity.) Color her unimpressed.

But yesterday, Hot Jerk hadn't lived up to his moniker. It was weird hearing him speak complete sentences in that deep-chested tone that belonged to a bass or someone who did voice overs for insurance company commercials. Like he was auditioning for *Terminator, the Musical.* (*It doesn't exist, you say? Someone really ought to make that.*)

When he had curled his hand around the cup, Kennedy took notice. Oh, did she. Big, strong, with long fingers. An artist's or a piano player's hand, she would have thought except for the athlete thing. She spent a lot of time looking at hands while modeling for an art class over at the community college.

Shaking off thoughts of hot scowls and hotter hands, she refocused on Edie.

"I'd rather play the field. You know, like you're doing here." She gave a subtle nod to one of the other residents, a dapper gentleman who paid a lot of attention to Edie any time Kennedy came to visit.

Edie perked up as if the residential aide had swung by with the dessert cart. "All right there, George? Have you met my granddaughter?"

"This is your granddaughter? She looks like your sister."

Kennedy rolled her eyes while Larkvale's own Casanova in high-waisted pants ambled away.

Edie whispered, “He let me have the last chocolate chip cookie after dinner last night.”

“Go Edie, go Edie ...” Kennedy sang and did a little shimmy in her chair.

“We’ll see,” Edie said smugly. “Looks like I have a better chance of scoring these days than you do.”

Harsh, but as was often the case when our elders spoke, not entirely wrong.

3

REID LIKED to get to the practice facility ninety minutes before he needed to be on the ice. Some players used that time to warm up, some for assessment by the trainers. Some liked to spend it joking around with their teammates.

Not Reid. Sure, he suffered aches and muscle pulls like everyone else. No elite athlete went a day without nursing some kind of injury. Playing through pain was ingrained in them all. Neither was he the kind of guy who spent time in the pockets of other players. This wasn't play, it was his job. When he wasn't checking in for a physical, he was in the viewing stand of the practice rink for at least an hour before he needed to dress. It was quiet and Reid liked the quiet.

His phone burned in his pocket, the message from Henri a sword about to drop, left while Reid was driving to practice. Typical from the man who liked to rant uninterrupted and enjoyed the option to leave a voice mail to do so. Then he would bemoan that Reid hadn't picked up in the first place.

No way to win that argument.

Now Reid listened and tried to parse the tone, though

really he knew him well enough to understand exactly what was in his head. Henri Durand, NHL legend, the Monster of Montreal, and Reid's stepfather, wasn't exactly a closed book.

Neither was he happy with Reid's play at the home game against New York two nights ago. This was par for the course. If Reid had a good game—and a good game for Henri was at least two points, preferably solo with no assists—Henri called immediately. Any praise was invariably brief, because Henri preferred to spend the call discussing Reid's mistakes.

Sitting in the stands with no one but the ice to eavesdrop, he decided it would be better to get it out of the way.

"You at practice?" Henri barked when he picked up.

"Starts in a few. What's up?"

"What the fuck was that on Thursday?"

"I can't control what Coach does. He's experimenting with the lines, switching me up with Foreman."

"If you were making more of an impact, he would be putting you in more. You know that."

Reid gripped the back of the seat in front of him and watched dispassionately as his knuckles popped white against his skin. *One, two, three ...*

Henri crashed through Reid's answering silence. Something about Coach Calhoun being an asshole, the incompetence of the Rebels management—what did anyone expect with a team run by women—and Americans not knowing their asses from their elbows. The usual.

"You want a multi-year contract, don't you?"

What a stupid question. Of course he did. He hadn't made enough of an impression to stick with any team, and the Rebels was his fourth in five years. But did he want to be in the same city as Bast, constantly compared to his more talented brother, always falling short? The goldfish bowl was more pressurized here.

He grunted in response.

"How much gym time you getting in?"

Reid went through his regimen, though Henri knew it off by heart.

"That's more than your brother. Careful you don't overdo it."

Reid's fingers made dents in the seat back. Asking him to take it easy now was a little like pulling the steak away from the rabid, starving dog. He was a product of Henri's masterplan.

When Reid was eight years old, he had to decide whether to make hockey his life. Bastian was six and already committed but Reid was still unsure. He didn't take the same joy from it as his brother, not that it would have made a difference. Reid had never been the kind of person who needed one hundred percent satisfaction in everything he did. Happiness was never guaranteed so if you could be good at something, could make people proud of you, then maybe that would be happiness of a kind.

Henri had asked him back then, *"You want this, Reid? Because you'll always need to try harder than your brother. You have to want it because it will never come as naturally to you."*

Reid had looked up at the man who married his mother when Reid was two years old, who had thrown him on the ice when he was five, and now was hoping to have sons who followed in his legendary glide. This man was as tough as old skate boot leather. If he was unhappy with you and your effort levels he let you know. If Reid didn't want to play, Henri would have accepted it but something fragile would have broken. The tentative thread of father and almost-son. Reid didn't want that to happen. He might not be as good as Bastian, Henri's biological son, but he could be if he tried.

Today he repeated what he had said nineteen years ago on the practice rink Henri built ten miles outside of Grenville, Quebec. "I don't mind working hard."

Henri chuckled darkly. "Yeah, anything to beat your brother, right?"

I am what you've made me. "I need to go into practice."

"All right. Make sure Coach knows what you can do. When I come down to see you in a couple of weeks, I want a good fight."

Reid shuttered his eyes briefly. Henri would be visiting Chicago for a couple of days capped off by a hockey crosstown classic: Rebels v. Hawks. Both of the Durand boys in the cage together where Henri could assess that plan for world domination.

"Sure, Dad. Gotta go." He went to hang up but his father had already done so. Typical power move.

Fifteen minutes before practice, so he headed into the locker room. One nice thing about the Rebels practice facility was that they built the locker room to be just like the real one. It was a good way to ground the players and keep that continuity between the practice and playing space. Reid headed to his cubby and changed into his gear. Most players were superstitious, employing rituals about the order in which they dressed, the number of rounds of tape on the stick's butt, kissing their holy medals, even for practice.

Reid wasn't superstitious.

Reid was observant.

The Rebels were a tight team. Sure, most sports teams had a band of brothers vibe, but this team was different. More like family, if your family was modeled on some sitcom perfect TV shit.

You had the father figures: Gunnar Bond, Vadim Petrov, even Levi Hunt, though he was newer to the NHL after a stint in the Green Berets. Total badass and a great center.

Then there were the little brothers: Theo "Superglutes" Kershaw, Cade "Alamo" Burnett, both D-men, and Erik "Fish" Jorgenson, their Swedish goalie. Goofballs, the lot of them.

So, all the standard archetypes. What made the Rebels different from other NHL teams was at the top. Owned by the Chase sisters, they had inherited from their father who had been a maverick in the game (read: asshole) and cut from the same ice block as Henri. It should have been a disaster but it worked.

The Chicago Rebels had den moms.

And then there was Cal Foreman, a right winger like Reid, and who, also like Reid, had started with the team this season. In the Rebels family unit, Foreman would be the big brother everyone looked up to—or that's what he aspired to.

Reid didn't like Foreman much, though if pressed, he would have a hard time thinking of an exact reason. The Bostonian was beloved by the team, an all-around stand-up guy. No one had a bad word or was ever on the receiving end of his temper, which was so even Reid wondered how the man managed to score any goals. In his experience, anger fueled competitive play. It was the foundation for winning. Foreman and Reid had roomed together for away games this season, someone's idea of a joke given that they were competing for a spot on the first line.

Foreman adjusted his shorts then took a seat on the bench to lace up his skates. "You come to any big conclusions out there, Durand? Sitting all alone, gazing at the ice."

"Just that I'm going to get to every puck before you in the next hour."

"Visualize it and it'll happen, that kind of thing?" Foreman was smiling, but it wasn't reaching his eyes.

"I don't need to employ my imagination, Foreman. I say it, it happens."

Foreman studied him, probably trying to puzzle him out. Reid knew that look. He'd been on the receiving end of it from pretty much every player, coach, and reporter for the last seven years. People were usually confused about why he didn't try harder to make friends with his teammates. If he made more of an effort to get along with people, surely he'd integrate better, be more of a team player.

Maybe. Or maybe the next time he came across one of his former teammates on an opposing team, he'd let up and go easy on him, all because they were friendly. Not worth the risk.

The game is half won before the puck is dropped.

Words of wisdom from the Book of Henri. His stepfather instilled it in both Reid and his brother but only Reid took it to heart. Bastian didn't need it, not with his abundant talent, but Reid had to rely on other stratagems. If he could earn a slight advantage by getting inside an opponent's head, then he would.

Such as now. "How's Mia?"

Those unsmiling eyes of the nicest guy in the NHL turned to dark slits. "Why do you want to know?"

"After your purchases yesterday, I assumed she was under the weather."

Foreman was currently engaged in supposedly-secret affair with Mia Wallace, sister to the captain who was also Foreman's best bud. Reid had run into Foreman yesterday at the drug store where the man was buying tampons. He didn't need three guesses to figure out who those were for.

Dog food, too, for Mia's Pomeranian, the cutest bundle of fur this side of the Mississippi.

Foreman hadn't liked it when Reid tried to give advice, on the tampon purchase *and* the idiot's love life. *I mean, ya try to be a guy's friend ...* If you wanted to be with someone, why would you let an asshole like Petrov stand in your way?

This was why having buddies on the team was a mistake. Foreman wanted a woman but was deferring to his Russian bestie. So fucked up. All these ridiculous social contracts merely got in the way of progress.

"Don't you worry about Mia," Foreman gritted out. "Just worry about your game."

"Sure, Foreman. See you out there." *Point to Reid.*

Satisfied he'd added a burr to his competition's skate boot, Reid headed out to start practice.

KENNEDY WAS MIXING up a batch of coffee frappe, marveling that people actually wanted to drink this frigid, sugary junk in November, when her co-worker Elena spoke up.

"Your boy was in earlier. Hot Jerk himself in the flesh."

Kennedy should never have shared her nickname for her least favorite customer. Though she had to admit a twinge of disappointment at having missed his visit, especially after their semi-decent connection the other day.

"Did he scowl from door to bar?"

"You know it. But he also—get this—said "thank you" when I handed him his drink. And he kept looking toward the back office door as if he was expecting someone to walk through it."

Kennedy's pulse drummed a little harder. Surely she shouldn't read anything into that.

"He was in on Sunday and he actually spoke to me," Kennedy said. "I'd just got off the phone with the realtor from hell and my damage could be felt in earthquake aftershocks all the way to Navy Pier. He asked if I was all right."

"Really?"

"Yeah, and I promptly spilled his drink because, bam, he opened his mouth." A hot mouth it was, too. His lips were a perfect pink and had a sexy pout to them, even as the eyes rocked ye old Wild West squint. "I told him it was his fault because he's usually such a grouch."

"You didn't!"

"It had to be said. If I can impart a little wisdom while I'm in the serving trenches, then I'll do it. For the little people everywhere."

Elena laughed. "Brave woman."

Not really. She wasn't one for tip-toeing around men, grumpy or otherwise. It had taken her time to assume this armor and she made damn sure it was polished bright.

Elena popped a sleeve of cups from their plastic wrap and stocked the empty spot beside the bar. "How's the house hunt?"

"Ah, yesterday was a bust. The guy wanted me to feed his pet snake when he went on overnight trips. He even showed me the cage of live mice."

Elena looked appropriated horrified. "How long can you last on that sofa?"

"Oh, I'll be fine." She had lied and told Elena that she'd landed at a friend's for the last few nights. Elena wanted to help but she had two kids, her mother on the premises, and a cheating ex to worry about.

Edie was right. Kennedy needed, if not a bucket list, at least a clear set of goals.

An interrupting cough drew their attention. Laura the

manager stood at the door to the office, her mouth set in a grim seal. "Kennedy, could you come in back for a second?"

New to this store as of three weeks ago, Laura had already admonished Kennedy for her pink-streaked blond hair (technically against the dress code but she kept it largely hidden under her baseball cap) and her occasional lateness (Edie's Ford Focus took a while to warm up in the morning, not unlike their caffeine-deprived clientele.) Their previous beloved manager, Aditi had gone on to better things at the corporate office, so now Laura was in charge at Store No. 1436 in Riverbrook, just north of Chicago.

Elena cut her a quick look and mouthed "what?" to which Kennedy shrugged. Every time Laura asked her to come "in back," it was usually for something ridiculous—like the time she'd enquired if her tattoo was "one of those fake ones that she could wash off" because it was "in a foreign language and might be profane." You know, the usual managerial harassment.

Kennedy stepped into the back office-slash-stockroom and hovered near the desk while Laura hit some keys on the computer keyboard. She did that a lot—called the staff for impromptu meetings then made them wait like she was Christian Fucking Grey. Then she would look up, either feigning surprise that the summoned staff member was there or annoyance that they'd arrived as summoned but hadn't let her know.

Today was surprise. *Sure, Jan.*

"Oh, Kennedy, there you are! So, uh, Corporate has been in touch."

"Okay."

"There was a complaint about service here this past weekend."

Kennedy's heart did a dead bounce on the floor. "A complaint?"

"A customer called about the store counter being left unattended because a staff member was on a loud, personal phone call back here. And that staff member was ..." She took a deep inhale. "Swearing."

Kennedy could lie. Or deny. But obviously she was in the frame for this one because she was here "in back."

"I *might* have been talking to someone. Okay, arguing, and I *might* have left a customer waiting for a few seconds too long. But I apologized and he was okay with it." As for swearing, no *might* about it. She had definitely let out a NSFW word when she spilled his drink.

"Apparently not. Because he called and complained, Kennedy. And it's not as if it was just any old customer, is it? That's Reid Durand, the hockey player." Said in a hushed tone like he was the Dali Lama.

The asshole complained after she had been thinking charitable thoughts and musing on his sexy, pouting lips? They'd had a moment! He hadn't left pissed at her, she knew that much.

"According to the email I had from Corporate, his name was mentioned. Not that it matters. All our customers are important, and this is merely one in a long line of examples of where you've disregarded customers. Only a couple of weeks ago, you were disrespectful to him and refused to remake his drink."

There'd been a quick exchange a while back where she had forgotten to say the full name of his drink per company policy when she popped it on the counter. Hot Jerk had taken issue with her possibly missing the extra shot, which she hadn't.

No one *that* good-looking should be that bad-tempered.

As a pro-athlete, he had the world at his skates: looks, talent, money, and the adoration of every person in this coffee shop. But that wasn't good enough. He had to strike a blow for entitled jerks everywhere to keep the 99% in their place.

"I didn't refuse! I assured him I'd made the right one."

"And then made a rude gesture." So she had stuck her tongue out at him when he walked away, which admittedly was childish and unprofessional. "This can't go on. We have to let you go."

Kennedy's heart popped into her throat. "You're firing me?" She hadn't even been here long enough to get the health insurance. That was her whole reason for putting up with this shit. She'd hoped to get an annual physical and have all her plumbing checked before she went traveling again.

"You've left me with no choice. You're disrespectful to customers, you're frequently tardy—"

"Twice!" Since Laura had arrived, anyway.

Laura glared at the interruption. "You don't do your job, and your appearance, while technically within the dress code, has always been shoddy. And don't think I haven't noticed you giving out your dog-walking business card. Touting for customers on the clock? You can pick up your tips and final paystub on Friday."

"Laura, surely we can talk about this."

But Laura's face had cemented to finality, looking like she'd just eaten a sour lemon and was considering asking for seconds. She and Reid D would have beautiful, crabby-faced children.

That was it. No talking, no finagling, no job.

Hot Jerk had gotten her fired.

4

REID FINISHED STRETCHING on the sand of Riverbrook Beach and took off for a run toward the rocky outcrop about a mile off. He didn't usually spend much time running on the beach, partly because this small band of land fronting Lake Michigan just north of Chicago barely met the definition of one. Behind him was a playground, a concession stand and shacks closed for the season. Up ahead a couple walked hand-in-hand, trying to convince themselves that a November day beside a large body of water in the Midwest was romantic. Right.

His jaw still stung where Foreman had hit him.

It had felt good, leaning into the punch, taking that beating as Foreman pounded his frustration into Reid. The hungover idiot had fallen out with his girl at the Rebels charity auction last night and was late to practice after having his ass chewed out by management.

It didn't take much to set him off. Reid merely lit the match of that raw-nerved kindling. If it messed with Foreman's mind and got Reid more ice time then he was prepared to suffer a little bruising.

The worst part was that Foreman tried to apologize. To Reid.

He had almost felt sorry for the guy in that moment. He was a man in love and his world—a world currently revolving around a woman—was imploding. Reid didn't know what that felt like and hoped he never would. How could anyone focus with that kind of distraction? For a man like Foreman, so used to everything going his way, it had to be rough to suddenly find that someone didn't want you.

Maybe Reid would lay off the Masshole for a while. Let that broken heart do its holy work.

The wind made his eyes water. He picked up the pace, overtaking the couple without a sideways glance. Not that they would automatically recognize him, but he didn't want to risk it. Hopefully they would have turned around by the time he reached the rocks and came back.

The sound of a yapping dog, or maybe more than one as the pitches were slightly different, carried on the stiff breeze. He couldn't see any animals but the beach was close to a wooded area, where people probably walked their dogs.

He was supposed to see Bastian tonight. Reid knew he'd been avoiding his brother. *"All the better for our rivalry,"* he had joked, though Bastian had frowned, taking it seriously. And maybe Reid had meant the dig. After all, that was all the Chicago sports press cared about, wasn't it? The Durand brothers, playing hockey in the same city at last. Whoop-de-do. It was ridiculous how the journos assumed they didn't get along when they got along fine.

Mostly fine.

No doubt Henri was responsible for putting a bug in some reporter's ear about his sons' rivalry since birth. Pitting them against each other was merely grist for his grand scheme to make them winners instead of sniveling little pussies.

His words.

But Bast already had his Cup win when the Hawks grabbed the brass ring three years ago. The way he was playing this season he had a good shot at another.

Reid kicked up his legs and moved faster, the water to his right, the rocks his destination. His eyesight blurred with the frigid air, the wind like sharp blades though his running hoodie.

Something snagged his attention. A coat in the water or a piece of carpet. He kept the same pace—or tried to, but the coat insisted on drawing his gaze. Buffeted by the waves, it was covered in frothy frills of surf. Then the oddest thing happened.

It transformed into a face.

With ears.

That's no coat. There was a dog in the water!

About thirty feet out, this dog was valiantly trying to keep his head above the waterline. The beach at this point was more of a break bordered by jagged rocks that extended a shelf of about six feet overhanging the water. Reid could climb over and ... what? Jump in?

The current didn't look particularly strong, but definitely strong enough to cause trouble for a dog and any man who might think taking a dip in sub-zero temps was a good idea.

Why was the animal even here? He looked around. The couple was still far behind. The dog didn't belong to them. No one else seemed to be in the vicinity, but that yapping sound still carried over the wind from the woods. Perhaps his owner was looking for him.

He scanned ahead. The current might carry the pup to

the rocky outcrop about three hundred feet out, where Reid could reach out and grab him.

He went under again. *No no no.*

This helpless creature was fading fast.

Reid stripped off his running jacket, but kept his shoes on because those rocks looked tricky. The last thing he needed was to break his damn ankle. His very expensive ankle. Henri would *love* that.

He climbed over the rocks, feeling his way to the flatter sections until he reached the edge. A voice behind him called out some sort of warning, but he'd already committed to action.

Into the water, and pray there wasn't a murder of jagged rocks just below the surface ready to fuck him up.

He jumped in feet first, rather than risk his hands or head. His feet didn't touch the bottom and he started swimming through the icy water.

The fucking freezing water.

It's Lake Michigan in November. Did you think it would be tropical?

Reid didn't care. He didn't have time to care.

Five feet, ten, at twenty-five feet, he reached the dog who had somehow sensed help was on the way. His head popped out of the water and Reid was sure that was relief he saw in his big brown eye because only one was open.

The pup was smaller than he looked from the shore. He was also a mess. A gash across his head, an eye completely shut. Worse, no eye at all. Anger and sympathy dueled in Reid's chest.

"It's okay, fella. I've got you." He placed his arm behind the animal's front legs, cradling his body. A bag of bones, like coat hangers poking through a sheet. He thrashed in fear, but Reid held on.

Until the little shit bit his shoulder.

It was just a nip, though a touch close to his face. More surprised than hurt, Reid loosened his grip and the pup flailed even more. Reid's legs were getting numb, so he needed to make a decision. He attempted another arm curl around the sodden pup, got a slippery hold, then turned back to the shore.

Only to find that someone else was in the water. Now wait a damn second, Reid only had so much strength. He had this dog to save, he really couldn't be worrying about someone else. Who the hell thought splashing about in the lake in November was a good idea?

This person was swimming toward him. What the fuck?

Distracted by the new arrival—who was actually a strong swimmer and Reid was beginning to realize, a woman—the dog squirmed and started paddling away.

Stupid dog! I'm trying to save you!

The interloper closed the gap. She looked oddly familiar, and even with wet hair he could tell it was streaked with pink.

Coffee Shop Girl.

"Are you okay?" she gasped.

"Am *I*—what are you doing?"

"Saving you!" She grabbed the dog and of course, the little fucker didn't put up a fuss. Just went quietly like he'd been waiting for *her* to come to the dramatic rescue.

"Do you have enough energy to swim back?" She held the dog to her shoulder, skillfully keeping his head above water.

Did he have ... "I'm fine! Hey—does he belong to you?"

She blinked at him as if he was not all there. "He's not with you?"

"No!" They both looked at the dog who Reid swore

appeared to be enjoying the attention. "You—you shouldn't be in here," Reid bit out, his legs wavering, his teeth starting to chatter. "I have it under control."

"Sure you do, Hot Jerk." And then she kicked out her feet and headed back to shore, swimming on her back with the puppy held under one arm, his head above water. Like she rescued animals from freezing lakes every day.

What in all that was fucking fucked was fucking happening here?

Robbed of his chance to be a hero, he followed alongside, keeping an eye out for trouble (and maybe another chance to be a hero). She was a strong swimmer and it seemed best to leave her holding the dog who obviously preferred her rescuing arms to Reid's. Once at the rocks, she held on to a boulder with one hand while treading water.

"I'll get out first," he said, already pulling himself up over the first rock and looking for a foothold that wouldn't have him slipping and hitting his head on the sharp stones.

"Are you okay?" someone called out. The man in the couple he had overtaken earlier—or at least he thought it was him, except now he had a pack of dogs with him on leashes. "Should we call 911?"

"We're okay," he called back. He leaned over and held out his hands for the dog. Coffee Shop Girl looked up, her hair dripping into her silver-disc eyes, like the swim in the lake had invigorated her. "I can take him."

She held the pup a few inches out of the water and he used every ounce of his training to keep his balance.

"Got him?" Gripping the rock, she held tight while the lake rocked her. But she didn't seem to be in any immediate danger. He was glad he didn't have to choose between her and the dog.

Society would have expected him to go the way of the human.

"I do. Back in a sec."

Quickly and carefully, he stepped over the rocks until he reached the grass. He placed the shivering puppy down and got a better look at him. Indeterminate breed, a brown and white streaked mess, plentiful scars, and a history of pain.

He peered up at the couple. The woman had her phone out, but not to call for assistance. She was taking a picture. "Can you watch him for a minute?" Reid growled, annoyed that she was taking this opportunity to snap a stupid picture instead of helping.

The man nodded. Reid turned, ready to yank Coffee Shop Girl out of the water only to run right into her. She had pulled herself out in no time at all, a testament to significant upper body strength.

"Are you okay?" He grasped her shoulders and instinctively rubbed them trying to get warmth into her ice-cold skin, or maybe into his hands.

She nodded, pushing wet strands out of her eyes, and he didn't imagine that slight angle of her body toward his. "F-fine. How's our guy?"

Our guy.

Not waiting for a response, she hunkered to a crouch and ran assured hands over the dog's body. "There, there, buddy, we've got you now. No one's going to hurt you again." She peered up at Reid through spiky, wet lashes. "Do you know what happened to him?"

"No, I just saw him struggling in the water."

She held his gaze, bit her lip, and something sparked between them: a recognition of what had occurred and a simpatico that now connected them. Some fucker had thrown the dog into the water, discarded him like trash. No way did the pup make that decision. If he was with someone, where was his owner?

She reached over a few feet and picked up a piece of clothing. As she rolled it out, he realized what she was doing: giving the dog her coat. Reid should have thought of that. He hunkered down and together they moved the dog onto the coat's fleece lining. She wrapped it around him and started rubbing the dog's body, gently but vigorously.

"You can quit filming now," she said without taking her eyes off the dog.

"I'm—I'm not." The woman lowered the phone, caught Reid's flinty stare, and reddened. *Yeah, you were, lady.*

Reid picked up his phone from where he'd dropped it with his running jacket. "We should take him to a vet."

"Maybe." Coffee Shop Girl rubbed the dog's head. "It's hard to find one open on Sundays, but there's one just off the main street in Riverbrook that has emergency hours. He's actually not doing too bad. Might just need to warm up."

She was right. The dog was definitely perking up, his one eye bright with life and adrenaline.

Reid would probably feel the same if a woman as attractive as this was giving him a rub-down.

"You seem to know a lot about it."

"I work with dogs all the time. Got him?" Pulling herself to a stand, she smiled at the man of the couple and reached for the dog leashes in his hand. "Thanks for holding them."

"Sure, Miss. You were pretty amazing out there." He shot a quick glance at Reid. "You, too," he added.

Yes, let's not forget who jumped in the water first.

Now that the adrenaline of the adventure was starting to wear off, Reid was feeling the chill. Coffee Shop Girl must be freezing as well now that she'd handed her coat off to the dog.

He picked up his hoodie and placed it over her shoulders. "Here, you need this."

"Oh." She flushed an uncommonly attractive hue. "Thanks."

Reid picked up the dog, still wrapped in Coffee Shop Girl's coat. "I'm parked near the beach entrance," he said to her.

"Me, too." She looked at him expectantly.

"We should get him somewhere warm."

"Agreed." She pulled at the leashes. "Come on, guys, let's go."

5

THE FIRST MINUTE walking back to the cars was spent in silence except for the intermittent yapping of one of the dogs in Coffee Shop Girl's care. The bundle in his arms didn't squirm or struggle, apparently accepting of Reid's firm hold. But Reid watched him closely anyway, looking for changes in his demeanor. He seemed content to snuggle in Reid's arms.

No weight had ever felt better.

"You shouldn't have jumped in," Reid said after a moment. "I had it under control."

"Did you? Because from where I was standing it looked like you were having a hard time wrangling this little guy."

"He was scared, that was all. You didn't need to get wet." Or save Reid, which is what she had claimed she was doing. How ridiculous.

"Admit it, you were starting to panic."

"I was not." He stared at her, and she laughed. Ah, she had been teasing him. "I was not," he repeated in a lower voice, so they were clear, teasing or not.

"I'm a good swimmer. I don't know how strong you are but I know how strong I am. It was a no-brainer."

So foolish. No decision like that should ever be a no-brainer.

"I'm Kennedy, since you haven't asked."

"Reid."

"Yeah, I know. Reid *D*."

So she recognized him—he hadn't been sure before. But now he recalled something else. Something from their time in the lake.

She had called him *Hot Jerk*.

Maybe he was mistaken. He couldn't exactly ask if that was her nickname for him. Neither was he sure he wanted to know.

He took a furtive look at her. The clothes she wore clung to her body—a long-sleeved T-shirt over amazing breasts and leggings hugging nicely-shaped thighs. She was short, maybe five feet two inches, but she didn't seem fragile. She seemed strong.

What an incredibly brave woman. A hot, tempting, incredibly brave woman.

"What you did back there—jumping in like that—it was courageous. Foolish, but courageous."

Two spots of color appeared high on her cheekbones. "Anyone would have done it."

"Not anyone. You did it. And this little guy is here because of it."

"You would have been fine."

"A minute ago you said I was starting to panic."

"Yeah, I did, didn't I?" One of the dogs strained at the leash, trying to get ahead of the others. She reined him in gently.

"Who are your friends?"

"My friends?" She looked down at the dogs. "Oh, these beauties! Meet Tiger, Dylan, and Smoky."

"Hallo, boys." He nodded at the dogs who paid him no heed.

"Dylan's a lady."

"Ma'am."

Kennedy smiled, and it was only the most gorgeous smile he had ever seen. How had he not noticed it before?

Oh yeah. Because she never smiled at you *in the coffee shop.*

They reached the parking lot and Reid switched the dog to one arm while he fished his keys out.

"I have a blanket in my car," Kennedy said. Adroitly while still holding the dogs, she opened the door of a battered-looking, older model Ford Focus and funneled the dogs into the back seat. Then she popped the trunk and took out a plaid blanket. As she closed the trunk, he could have sworn he saw a suitcase.

With great efficiency, she placed the blanket in the back seat of Reid's car and stood back while he transferred the puppy to the new blanket and wrapped him up. The dog nuzzled his nose against Reid's hand, a gesture that pleased him to no end. He was an affectionate little thing.

Reid shook out Kennedy's coat, letting the sand fall to the icy ground, and draped it over the passenger seat.

"Your car is warm. Even the back seats." She pressed her palm to the leather.

"I did it remotely when we started walking back. Get in."

"Excuse me?"

He opened the car door. "Just for a second to warm up."

With a quick glance toward her car, she shivered, and that seemed to decide it. She climbed in, he shut the door, then skirted the car to the driver's side. The combination of wet dog, soaked humans, and frigid temperatures quickly turned the SUV's interior into a steamy cave.

"This is pretty nice," she murmured, her hand smoothing over the hand-stitched leather arm rest.

"Feeling a little better?"

"Could be worse. I could still be in that lake." She chuckled, and the tone of it—sort of naughty—mixed with the sauna-like cocoon put his body on lust-alert. Of all the times ...

"So tell me the truth," he said.

"About?" Mon Dieu, there was something about those silver eyes that sent a pulse of desire through him. When he really should be feeling nothing of the sort after that unplanned dip.

"Should I take our friend to the vet?"

She twisted to take another look at the dog. "I think he just needs to get warm and fed. When you drop him off at the shelter, they'll figure out what kind of care he needs."

"The shelter?"

"You said you travel too much to care for a dog."

He had said that. It seemed like a long time ago, but that was only ... a couple of days?

"I'll think of something."

Suddenly her hand was on his jaw. "You're injured! Did you hit a rock out there?"

He placed his hand over hers, only now remembering his ice-dance with Foreman. "No, this was something else. I got into a fight with someone."

"I see." She hesitated, then asked, "Did you deserve to get hit?"

There was that feeling he'd had back at the coffee shop, the sense that she knew something about him. But it wasn't because she had witnessed his abruptness in pressers or heard some coach bawl him out. This was something more innate.

"Definitely."

She grinned, and it made him want to smile back. He fought that impulse, but not the one to keep his hand covering hers. Sentimental, perhaps, but it was nice to have this connection. He usually forewent most human contact during the season.

Not just the season.

"Why do you think you deserved it?"

"I have a habit of provoking people." They remained still, staring at each other, provoking, if you will. That chill he felt vanished in the heat of her touch.

"Now why doesn't that surprise me?"

The grin he had fought finally found residence on his face, his muscles straining slightly at the unusual call to action. Good aim, this girl, calling him out on his emo posturing. Removing her hand from his jaw, he wrapped it in his to keep it warm.

"Are you busy right now?"

"Busy?" Her gaze dropped to his lips.

"I could do with some help." He squeezed her hand, and instantly regretted it because until then she seemed to have forgotten he was holding it. She looked down at their joined hands, almost confused that they'd come so far, then back at his face.

"I have to take care of my charges. Get them back to their humans."

Their humans. He liked that phrasing. The idea of the animal owning them instead of the other way around. There was something liberating in that unconditional love.

But love had no use for practicalities. He needed help,

and while it went against every cell in his being to ask, he recognized it was necessary.

"I don't want to take him to a shelter. He needs someone to care for him. Perhaps you'd want to ..."

"No, I can't. I walk them but then I give them back. My living situation is—it's not suitable for a dog. I don't even have a—" She broke off, her speech and the connection of their hands. Her eyes burned bright with something closer to annoyance.

Just as he was thinking he would hate to be on the end of that, he realized that perhaps he already was. His head was heating up under the force of that death ray glare.

"I need to go."

"Okay. Send me the bill for your dry cleaning."

Her lip curled in disgust. "I knew what I was doing. I'll be fine." She turned around and rubbed a hand along the puppy's body. He lifted his head to acknowledge the affection and made a light mewling sound. "Take care, little guy. I hope you find a forever home."

She opened the door and clambered out.

He followed, wondering what he had done wrong. "Kennedy, your coat."

She stopped half-way to her car and turned.

"I know you're wet, but you'd probably be better off putting this back on."

Silently but still fuming, she walked the few steps toward him and slipped off his hoodie. He held the coat open for her and she pivoted, inserting her arms. With her back to his front, the proximity to her stirred something in his gut. She should have smelled of stinky lake water, but instead her scent was weirdly intoxicating.

Losing it, Durand.

He would have given anything to wrap his body around

hers from behind, to do the job of that blanket around the half-drowned dog. Transfer his body heat, or what little of it remained, to her. Instead he held the collar of her coat. It was frayed, the threads unraveling at the edges, a situation he understood.

"Take care of him," she bit out, almost accusing.

"I will. See you at the coffee shop."

One more glare, then without a word she got in her car and drove away.

6

Reid made it all the way home before he realized he had no food fit for dogs.

Google could probably tell him what human food dogs could eat. Ideally he would have liked to ask Coffee Shop Girl—Kennedy—to come home with him to guide him through the next steps. But she obviously had her own life to run and dogs to walk. She'd also hightailed it out of there whip quick. He'd said something to offend her, so no surprise there.

He pulled up to the resident parking and lo and behold, a recognizable form stood leaning against a car in the space next to Reid's usual spot.

Right-wing Masshole, Cal Foreman.

Please, not another apology. Reid couldn't stand the idea of any man feeling he needed to apologize for something as ludicrous as a couple of punches, especially when he was blameless. Reid had provoked him and deserved to be struck.

He stepped out of the car, wincing at the loud squelching noise as his running shoes hit the tarmac.

Foreman stepped forward, looked him over, and asked, "Been swimming?"

"Something like that." He opened the back door and carefully removed his precious cargo. The dog had been mostly quiet all the way home and Reid prayed he wasn't in some sort of shock. Perhaps he should have gone to the emergency vet after all.

Please give me a sign.

The puppy squirmed a little. Not dead yet.

Foreman closed the gap. "You need a hand there?"

Did he want to be beholden to this guy, of all people? The dog was the priority here. Now wasn't the time for grudges.

"Yeah, I do. Could you …?" He passed the blanket-wrapped package to Cal, who cradled it with an assurance that told Reid he'd made the right call. "I—well, we pulled him out of the lake. I need to get him warm and feed him. I don't think he's eaten in a while."

Without waiting for an answer, Reid walked toward the front entrance to his apartment building, knowing good guy Foreman would follow. He was alert to the sounds Foreman was making, barely intelligible words of comfort as if the dog was a child.

He usually took the stairs because it was just three floors, and today he figured it would be quicker anyway. Once inside Reid's apartment, Foreman placed the dog down gently on the sofa. "I'm guessing you don't have any dog food."

"No, but I can go out and get some." Reid shivered as he spoke. Could he trust Foreman? Now that his teammate was on hand, maybe he'd dogsit while Reid went for a food run.

"Got any deli turkey or corn?" Cal asked. "Those are pretty safe foods for dogs."

Reid didn't realize how relieved he was not to have to leave the puppy so soon until Foreman presented a solution. Sounded like he knew what he was talking about. Probably had a big, friendly Lab when he was a kid. No one had ever told him animals were for winners.

Fuck, not now, Henri.

He turned toward the kitchen but Foreman spoke up before he got a step off.

"I can take care of this. Why don't you hop in the shower?"

Leave the dog alone? Sure, he'd been willing to do so a moment ago when he thought he had to pillage for food, but in all truth, he never wanted to let this puppy out of his sight.

"I have a dog of my own," Cal assured him, evidently reading into Reid's hesitation because he was one of those intuitive types who understood shit and wowed women and dogs with their sensitivity. "He'll be safe for a few minutes."

Reid ran a hand over the mutt's head. All those scars. All that pain. "I will be back soon."

In the shower he let the water chase away the chill in his bones and thought about what Kennedy had said about taking the dog to a shelter. She was right. Reid couldn't take care of him, not with his travel and practice schedule. He could kennel him, but that would mean taking him in and out, with no semblance of stability. A dog like this, one who had been battered, bruised, and abandoned, needed an owner who was all in.

Something pinged in his brain, something Foreman had said. *A dog of my own ...*

Out in the living room, he found the man from Boston on his sofa and the puppy on the rug, next to a bowl surrounded by corn kernels. He had eaten and Reid's heart checked. He would have liked to have seen that; now he felt as though he'd missed out on an important first in the relationship between man and beast. The dog had probably bonded to fucking Foreman now.

"How is he?" Reid sat on the rug beside the dog and rubbed his head. The abject creature raised it slightly, as if craving Reid's touch. It must have been a while since anyone showed him kindness.

"Tuckered out after a snack and the afternoon's festivities."

Reid turned his attention to Foreman, eager to get this, whatever *this* was, over with. "Are you here to apologize?"

"Yep."

"Not necessary."

"I happen to think it is. Sure you were a dick. You *are* a dick. An apology from me doesn't change that, but I shouldn't have lost my temper."

Reid assessed him. "Sometimes it's good to let it out."

"That's what the game is for."

"Pity you don't get enough shifts, then."

Foreman laughed, so good-natured about it all. Just like Reid's brother. "We're having a moment here. Why you wanna be an asshole about it?"

"Someone's got to be in my family."

Foreman studied him, looked like he was about to ask something else, but took a left turn instead of right. "How did your friend end up in the lake?"

"There are no limits to people's cruelty." Reid would happily beat the tar out of whoever had hurt this creature. He peered up at Foreman. "Looks like you've sorted things out with Petrov."

"For the most part."

"And La Petrova?"

"Not sure that's fixable."

"Now who's the dick?" Mia clearly wanted Foreman. Foreman clearly wanted Mia, as evidenced by their back-and-forth in front of the well-heeled fundraiser crowd last night. So tiresome. "That performance last night at the auction? She bid on you to make a point."

"Yeah, the point being that she can buy and sell me a million times over and then pass me off to my ex." Reid didn't know all the details, but that sounded overly complicated and not remotely true.

"You're even dumber than you look."

Foreman merely shrugged. "Mind if I make a sandwich?"

"Yes." He would prefer Foreman left. He had proven useful but now Reid wanted to be alone. His undesired guest refused to take the hint, just walked into the kitchen and removed sandwich fixings from the fridge.

Reid looked down at his new friend—the dog—and ran a hand over his frail body. He needed to get him food, shots, and a roof over his head. Foreman emerged from the kitchen with two plates and put them down on the coffee table.

That was it, the tickle of a thought. "You said you have a dog."

Foreman picked up a sandwich and bit into it. The fucker actually waited until he'd swallowed before he answered. "Yep."

"Who looks after it when you're playing and traveling?"

"I co-own him with my ex. She's in Boston so I only see him when I play there or make a visit."

That didn't solve anything. "That works? The co-owning situation?"

"Sure," Foreman said around his chewing. "But I don't

have to live with her, which helps. If I could have him here, I'd need someone else on deck to watch him." He gestured with his sandwich to the dog. "Thinking of keeping him?"

"I'd like to." Never had a statement about something so important sounded so bland. He wanted to keep this dog with a force that scared him.

Henri wouldn't let him have a dog when he was a kid and now Reid could do whatever he wanted. Maybe he was using the dog to make a point—what exactly, he wasn't sure. He just knew that he would make a good caretaker for this poor thing.

"You could kennel him but a dog like this needs special attention," Foreman said.

"I could hire someone to look after him while I'm away, perhaps."

Her. Coffee Shop Girl. He could hire her.

She obviously had experience with animals, and how much could she be earning walking dogs and working in a coffee shop? Two jobs, probably part-time. Likely, she was barely making ends meet. This would be the perfect solution.

If his heart started hammering like a runaway train, he would swear in a court of law it was because he was excited about owning a dog.

"You should eat," Foreman said. "I make a good sandwich."

Reid picked up the other sandwich, spotting gouda, turkey, lettuce, and when he bit into it, he tasted mayo and a dash of mustard. Usually he wouldn't eat mayo during the season. He didn't even realize he had it but Bastian had stopped by yesterday with groceries, a stunt he had started pulling lately to mess with him.

He hadn't realized how hungry he was until now. "So you make a good sandwich. It's hardly rocket science."

"Ungrateful pup."

That made Reid laugh, which obviously surprised Foreman, whose eyebrows rose in puzzlement.

Feeling unaccountably magnanimous, Reid said, "You need to fix things with Mia."

Foreman sighed. "You're matchmaking now."

"Now? I've been rooting for you kids from the start."

"Asshole." Foreman looked mildly amused, then thoughtful. After a few seconds, he jumped to his feet. "From the start ... Durand, you're a genius."

"I know."

But Foreman was already out the door so fast he left scorch marks on Reid's hardwood floor.

Reid looked at his new roommate, who, on hearing the front door slam, jumped to his feet and ran around the living room, barking.

"Looks like someone has his mojo back. You up for a visit to the coffee shop?"

7

Because the universe hated her, Kennedy's foldable travel hairdryer, which had always been too precious for its own good, chose this moment to crap out. She checked the mirror of the locker room at the Y, sighed at her half-damp and unsexily tousled locks, and decided, *good enough*.

It would have to be.

She'd tried to get a job here teaching yoga when she first landed in Chicago three months ago, but no luck, hence her Frankenstein-ing of various side hustles to make a full hustle. Today she was back—still no magical job—but was forced to pony up the monthly membership fee.

Sixty-nine bucks for unlimited shower access would be a bargain if Kennedy wasn't so broke. While she had down-time, which was looking like a distinct possibility, she could take free Aqua Fit and yoga classes. She might be qualified to teach it, but it never hurt to check in on how other practitioners were dispensing the latest wisdom.

Jumping in the lake was definitely one of her more bone-headed moves. The "rescuer" looked like he was struggling. The "rescuee" looked like he was in trouble. She was a great swimmer and wasn't one for second-guessing, well, anything. Once she decided on a course of action, she went full-throttle into the wind.

Or the water.

Discovering who she was rescuing had been, to say the least, a shock. Hot Jerk, himself. Complainer-in-Chief. Thief of employment.

Yet, back on land, she'd curled into his strong touch like a kitten seeking shelter. His big hands on her shoulders and his warm breath on her neck as he slipped her coat back on set her heart and hormones aflutter, all signs that she was a little too desperate for human contact. It had been a while since she'd had a man-made orgasm, and now it looked like it would be even longer because nothing dimmed the fires of lust better than financial ruin and homelessness.

She hoped the dog was okay. Someone had hurt him badly, then threw him away. Kennedy was a sucker for a dog in distress. With his bright eye and scampish expression, this bedraggled creature had looked a little like her childhood puppy Peanut. At least she was able to save this one ...

Anger flared. Oh, how she would happily do a murder if she ever found the culprit.

Back to her current dilemma. She checked Craigslist again, and while there were plenty of apartments in Chicago, they were mostly out of her price range. She needed to save every penny for her return flight to Thailand in January for the job she'd lined up. Years traveling outside the US had affected her credit and she would never pass the background check. A roommate situation would be better, but the one she visited yesterday had definitely given her creeper vibes.

Never trust a guy with a waterbed.

Now she needed to figure out where she could park her car tonight so as not to draw the attention of any nosey passersby.

Or worse.

Back to the beach, perhaps, site of her great adventure in dog rescue. Did they gate it at night? If that didn't work, she could park at the strip mall close to the highway. After eleven it was completely empty.

The phone rang, and Kennedy's heart rate ticked upward. She had left a message for a room in an all-female collective, so was ever hopeful.

"Is this Kennedy?"

That voice. Either someone was about to sell her car insurance or Hot Jerk had tracked her down.

"Might be."

"This is Reid Durand. We went swimming together earlier."

Cute. But then she recalled not cute. This asshole had cost her a job.

"Is the dog okay?"

"Bucky? Oui, just fine. Shitting everywhere, eating me out of house and home, and generally taking over."

"His name is Bucky?"

He paused a beat. "Yeah, after Bucky Barnes from the Avengers? First I thought I'd do Fury—"

"Because of the one eye."

"Right, but he didn't respond to that. The vet said he'd broken his leg a few times but it didn't heal so well. He's got a slight limp and some other scars." She heard his sharp, angry intake of breath. "And with what he's been through, it seemed ... well, anyway, he responded to Bucky."

Despite her best efforts, a smile played on her lips. She could see the dog as the Winter Soldier: tortured, bruised, in need of his best friend—and saving his best friend from a watery demise. She liked how Hot Jerk had thought that through.

Then she remembered that she didn't like much else about him.

"How did you get this number?"

"Mia Wallace gave it to me. I heard you lost your job."

"Oh, did you now."

He sniffed. "I just got back from the coffee shop. That wasn't me who complained and got you canned."

"But Laura said—"

"That manager chick? What a piece of work. I didn't get you fired but ... it was my fault, all the same." Vigorous yapping sounded in the background. "I have a proposition for you. Could you come over now so we can discuss it? I can't leave him."

Drop everything and attend to the king? Oh, sure! People who looked like that expected everyone else to do their bidding.

Yet he'd figured out Laura. She *was* a piece of work, and it was nice to have consensus on this during a time when the world was against her.

"I'm kind of busy." *Figuring out where I'm going to sleep tonight.*

"And I'm in a bind here," he said imperiously as if his problem superseded all others. "I have to go out of town tomorrow for a couple of days and I need someone to stay with him. It's either that or I'll have to kennel him and I don't think he's ready for that."

Ask and the universe shall provide. She tried to sound as casual as a limp noodle. "For how long?"

"Two days. More like three. I'll be back on Wednesday.

But I need someone to stay with him for the next two nights."

"At your place?"

"Yes, at my place," he said impatiently. Jeez, she was just confirming. "It's an emergency. I asked Mia but she says her dog doesn't play well with others. She could drop in but not stay overnight and I don't think he's ready to be alone yet. I know it's an imposition but I owe you."

Back to that. "I thought you didn't get me fired, so how is it your fault?"

"It's hard to explain. It would be easier if you came over and discussed the details. He already likes you."

She already liked him. The dog, that is.

If she had to place her priorities in order right now it would be a place to stay anywhere but the backseat of her Ford Focus followed by a dog in need of her special skillset. This grouchy grump of a grinch would come in at a very, very distant third.

"Okay, I'll stop by and see if Bucky and I are a good fit. Where do you live?"

KENNEDY EXITED the elevator of one of those luxury high-rises in downtown Riverbrook and walked down the hall just as a door opened. Out rushed a bundle of energy on four legs, barking his head off.

She fell to her knees and reached for him, but he cowered, as shaky as a leaf in the wind.

"It's okay, I'm a friend. We've already met."

She looked up. Hot Jerk stood at the entrance to his apartment wearing a black tee stretched tight enough to give pec-impressions and nipples at the ready, which had the domino effect of placing *her* nipples at the ready.

That's what he wore for visitors? Positively indecent.

The dog turned tail and ran back to his daddy.

"He's a little jumpy, huh?" she said, knowing the feeling.

"The vet says he has ringworm and is malnourished."

"What about his eye?"

Hot Jerk looked even hotter in his fury. "That happened a while back. Maybe a year, according to the vet. Some of the gashes are more recent."

Consistent abuse. Then someone got sick of using him as a punching bag and either threw him in the lake or abandoned him in such a way that he ended up there. Though somehow she doubted this little guy took that jump all by himself.

She walked toward them both, careful about making any sudden movements. Odd, but that strategy seemed appropriate for both of them.

"You going to invite me in?"

He stood back, gesturing with a hand toward the inside. She had run a quickie background check by calling Mia immediately after she got off the phone with HJ. When Kennedy mentioned she was coming over to Reid's to discuss a job offer, Mia had chuckled and murmured, "This should be good."

The bottom line was that she didn't feel in any immediate danger from this guy.

Not physical anyway.

She had also done her Internet due diligence, which was enough to give her *the facts, Ma'am. Just the facts.*

Reid Durand was twenty-seven, Canadian, and considered a bit of a bad boy in the NHL. So those exact words weren't used, but she could infer with the best of them.

Pundits mentioned his tendency to trash-talk both his teammates and his opponents, and his atypical, unCanadian rudeness during press conferences. He had once made a (male) reporter break down in tears. Even the teammates at his old club were less than flattering about his personality. Difficult, ornery, and cantankerous were the nicer things said about him.

The coffee shop behavior was on brand, apparently.

"Let me take your coat." Before she could demur, he had placed his hands on her shoulders from behind and gently tugged. The proximity of him was heady, just as before when he was putting her coat on near the lake. Off, on, apparently it didn't matter.

She only had this one heavy coat, a seven-dollar find at Goodwill. Kennedy's usual clothes were hot weather and yoga appropriate, meaning not appropriate for a Chicago winter at all. He hung the coat up in a closet, which was about the nicest thing that had ever happened to it.

She was kind of regretting wearing this sweater right now, one of Edie's gems, borrowed along with the rest of her winter wardrobe. It had cats embroidered on it with green jewels for eyes. Yesterday she'd thought it ironic. Today, not so much.

She sought out the dog, now nowhere to be seen. "Where did he go?"

"He's in the empty TV box." Sure enough, the cardboard box that had once housed the fifty-inch screen affixed to the living room wall, was breathing. "I think he feels safe in there."

"Has he been like this all day?"

"He was better when I brought him out for a walk to the coffee shop and the pet store but he was nervous at the vet's office. He didn't like the shots." He gave her a twice-over, long and penetrating. "Are you recovered from the day's events?"

"I'm okay. I think I'll just sit here and see if he comes to me." She took a seat on the sofa. "Maybe you can tell me more about what you have in mind."

Reid—she couldn't call him Hot Jerk forever and frankly, the label was fifty percent too nice anyway—sat at the other end of the sofa. He took up a lot of room with his long legs and big chest and no doubt other body parts vying for space on the leather.

"I play hockey for the Chicago Rebels."

"Mia said."

"I'm on the road and at practice a lot. Home games are often an all-day affair though I can come back here in the afternoon for a couple of hours and check in on him."

"It doesn't sound like you'd make a good owner at all."

There it was, the beast scowl, but with something else mixed in: she had wounded him.

"I know he needs a lot of care," he said after a protracted beat. "But I'm determined to look after him. I don't think he'd have much luck at a shelter."

"Oh, I don't know. If you spin the story of how you saved him, do something on Insta or with your team's PR, you're bound to find a good home for him. You see stories like that all the time."

What was she playing at? It was in her interest to have him need her, not to find a way to divest him of this puppy. But she also wanted the dog to have a good life. He hadn't had one up until now. As much as she needed a roof over her head, she wouldn't play along with any puppy-for-a-day scheme.

Reid shifted, placed his hands together and his elbows on his knees. He seemed to be thinking about what she said, actually giving it careful consideration. It made her heart thrum. Having someone listen to you with such intensity was potent stuff.

"I would like to try to care for him first. If it doesn't work, I'll find a solution but I have to give this a shot."

He sounded so serious, like this was his sole purpose in life. His gravity seeped into her and laid claim to her heart.

She felt a cold nose at her hand. Bucky must have sensed they were talking about him and had left the shelter of his cardboard harbor to be part of the conversation.

"Hey, there, it's great to meet you again." She gave him a tentative pat. He stayed put. She rubbed him a little more forcefully. He angled into her touch.

She turned back to Reid, who was watching her and Bucky carefully. Almost like his Terminator brain was recording the interaction.

Three strokes. Dog likes. Store in memory hard drive.

"So are you going to tell me what happened that got me fired but still wasn't your fault?"

"There was another guy."

"Did he have one arm, Dr. Kimble?"

He raised that arrogant eyebrow. "I was waiting for you to finish your rant when another customer came in after me. He was annoyed to have to wait but he recognized me and wouldn't shut up. Then he got annoyed about you again and said he would call the corporate office."

"And how is this your fault?"

"I told him he should do it."

"I see."

He gestured with his hand. "Purely to get him out of my face."

"Well, I can understand how your need to escape some

inconvenient fan worship might be more important than my employment."

He scowled again. "I may have encouraged him but *he* made the call."

"Incitement to do violence to my job prospects. Got it."

Head shake. "I'm making up for it now by offering you a job looking after Bucky. I would need you to stay over here while I'm out of town and stop in to care for him during practices and home games. It would be a full-time gig."

"Until you get tired of him." She was still hung up on the loss of a job she didn't even like though the answer to all her problems was being offered up on a platter.

"I won't get tired of him." Said with a growl and a clear sense of conviction. "I want to keep him and I'll do whatever it takes. True, I won't be around as much as I'd like but when I am he will be left in no doubt that I care for and love him dearly."

Just when she thought this guy had hit the ocean floor of her disapproval, he said something to haul himself above sea level. Looking around, she took in the large apartment filled with furniture but lacking in personality. Of course it was *his* apartment, so it shouldn't surprise her.

"Did you just move here?"

"A couple of months ago."

"From where?"

"Boston, but I'm originally from Canada. A small town in Quebec."

The source of that accent. Would he murmur French endearments to the dog? To her?

"Where would Bucky sleep?"

He stood, stretching to his full height. She was impressed with the whole man package in her immediate sightline. Walking away, even more so.

He barked over his shoulder. "Are you coming?"

Never mind. That rudeness was a vat of ice to her genitals.

She followed him further into the bowels of ~~hell~~ the apartment. He stopped at the entrance to one room and stepped back so she could peer inside.

The master bedroom.

"I have his bed there so he can be close to me when he sleeps." A dog bed lay beside the nightstand. "But if he needs to sleep on the bed with me, then he can. I won't have rules for that."

Spoken as if rules were important—or important enough that an infraction, even by a dog, would have to be pre-approved, if only in Reid's brain. Some people lived rule-bound lives, so it was probably a big deal if this guy was considering breaking one or two.

"And when you're not here?"

"He can sleep anywhere but if he bonds with me, he might like to be in here. Perhaps he'll smell me on the sheets."

He sounded so earnest and her heart melted all over again. Kind of like Data in *Star Trek* striving to attain humanity. "Is he house-trained?"

A rather adorable sheepishness came over him. "He might need some help there."

In other words, there had already been accidents but Reid had cleaned up. The house smelled lemony fresh. In fact, it looked pin-neat with not a hair out of place except for that cardboard box.

The only objection she could make was the potential for hurting this dog further. If Reid couldn't be a more permanent, loving influence in his life, then Bucky might be harmed, though how could it be any worse than what he'd already endured? Reid wanted to try and he had a good point about the shelter—it wasn't much better.

She looked down to find Bucky standing between them. He trotted in and sat in the dog bed.

"When you're in the living room, he'd probably like being there with you, too," she said. "If you don't mind moving the bed around. Or you could buy two."

"That's a good idea. Between the pet store purchases and the vet visit, I've already dropped six hundred bucks on this guy. What's another fifty?"

What, indeed? She kept her smile hidden. Reid's affection for the dog was so stinkin' cute.

"If I was here for a few days, where would I sleep?" Not in the master bedroom. Unlike Bucky, she wouldn't want to get accustomed to the smell of Hot Jerk on his sheets.

"There's a guest room here." He walked further down the corridor and opened the door, gesturing with a hand inside.

She stayed where she was so as not to betray her excitement. A bed was a luxury, especially when you didn't have ready access to one.

"What do you say?" He closed the gap, looming over her. "Will you help me, Kennedy?"

Saying her name should not have affected her, yet her heart sped up. That should have been a warning right there.

"How much does it pay?"

"Name your price."

"Oh, you've gone and done it now."

"You're my only option. Either that or the shelter. I can't leave him alone so you have all the power." He moved past her, close enough to get a scent of him in her nostrils—something clean and woodsy—then went into the bedroom and sat on the bed. Bucky nudged his legs and Reid lifted him into his lap, murmuring soothing dog-babble. The dog shivered before relaxing in his arms.

Bucky wouldn't do well at a shelter. He needed full-time care and these two had already bonded.

Kennedy had all the power, and for someone who had lately felt powerless, that was about as good a reason as any to say yes.

"Let's talk about my fee."

8

REID MIGHT HAVE MADE A MISTAKE.

He lived a life constricted by rules. What to eat. How much to practice. When to sleep. His entire life was organized this way so he could be the best at what he did. Henri Durand expected it, so Reid expected it of himself.

When he was five, his stepfather took him onto the ice for the first time. Bastian was there as well, only three years old, and Reid remembered a hollow ache of disappointment that it wasn't just him and Henri. That his baby of a brother was being introduced to the family business at the same time as Reid. Henri wanted to train them together. He wanted to train them *against* each other, hoping to instill a competitive spirit. They wouldn't just compete on the ice, they would compete in all areas.

All with the goal of winning Henri Durand's approval. To know Henri was to understand that there wasn't enough of that precious commodity for both his sons.

For five years, they trained as a duo, though at two years older, Reid was better for a while. Stronger. Back then he didn't enjoy hockey all that much, merely saw it as a tool to win his stepfather's love and respect.

By the time Reid was ten, Bastian was starting to catch up and fulfill the promise of the Durand genes. It was the great experiment, nature versus nurture. Reid had the training, the need to prove himself, and maybe that was why Henri pushed him so hard. He would never be able to rely on natural talent like Bastian. Every moment on the ice would require focus and hard work. No skating by for Reid.

Henri would hate the idea of Reid owning a dog. When they were kids, Bastian had one, and Reid wasn't allowed to walk him because Bast (a) deserved the companion more and (b) had to exhibit responsibility in owning it. Reid could easily imagine Henri's reaction now, that fleshy mouth curved in a sneer, his barrel chest heaving in disgust.

How the hell can you look after that thing? Your focus will be divided. Remember you can't fall back on a talent you don't have.

Reid didn't think he'd made a mistake because he now owned a dog. It was the other thing: *her*. He was going to allow a stranger stay in his apartment. Introduce an element of randomness to his carefully-calibrated world.

He rarely made a decision so quickly and now was torn between exhilaration at jumping in, feet first—literally!—and unease that he was moving too fast. Last night, the moment Kennedy left with instructions to return the next day at 10 a.m. precisely—it was now eleven minutes past—Reid had called Mia. The conversation went something like this:

"I need a reference."

"Reid, is that you?"

"Oui. I've just hired the coffee shop girl to look after my dog. Can you verify she's not some sort of grifter?"

Mia chuckled. “I can verify that I trust her with Gordie Howe when I’m out of town.”

Mia seemed like the kind of person who wouldn’t take guardianship of her dog lightly. She called the dog Gordie Howe, after the great player. Perhaps Reid should have done that—named his new friend after a legend.

Yet he balked at bringing hockey into it at all. He wanted this to be separate. He had very little in his life that existed apart from his career.

“She’s staying here. In my apartment.”

“Who? The dog?”

“Kennedy.” Just saying her name made him warm.

“Oh, I see. I suppose you could have her pick him up and bring him to her place?”

Kennedy had already said she couldn’t do that. “It’s better the dog stays here with the familiar. He needs special care. I just wonder if it’s a good idea to have a stranger in my apartment.”

It was a bit late to be making these kinds of enquiries. He just needed someone to tell him he wasn’t making a terrible decision.

“I can see that’s kind of tricky. I could visit if you want, see how they’re getting on.” She whispered away from the phone. The next voice he heard was … merde. Foreman’s.

“Durand, what’s the problem?”

“I see you’ve figured things out.”

“You could say that. What’s going on? You want Mia to check in at your place?”

“I didn’t say that—she offered.” The idiot growled and while normally Reid found it amusing to needle Mr. Nice Guy, he didn’t have time for games. “I’m not interested in your woman, Foreman. This is purely for informational purposes.”

"Right, the puppy. How's he doing?"

"Fine." He recalled their last conversation. "You said you share custody of your dog. How does that work?"

"My dog's in Boston with my ex. I see him every couple of months. She sends pics, videos. We, uh, Facetime."

"You FaceTime with your dog?" In the background, he could hear Mia saying something that sounded like "sexy," followed by a muffled sound. Kissing. *Serenity fucking now.*

Foreman came back on. "He needs to know I'm still his guy, so the phone and video contact is important. You're keeping the dog?"

"I am. But I had to hire someone to look after him while I'm away and I'm trying to determine the best way forward." *Neither did I call to talk to you, Masshole.* "I just wanted to find out if the dog sitter can be trusted. I've learned that so we're done here."

"Okay, see you at the bus—"

Reid had already clicked off.

That was last night, and now Reid was second-guessing ... everything. He looked around his place, a bland bachelor pad that he had yet to personalize. This was his fourth city in five years, so he didn't see the point in expending the effort. He wondered if his space would feel different when he returned, if she would somehow imprint *her* personality on it.

There was a knock at the door. Bucky started growling in a menacing manner, or as menacing as this baby bundle of bones could manage.

"It's okay. It's just your nanny."

On opening the door, his heart hitched while his brain immediately set up a counter-argument: *why?* She didn't look any different. Same chin-length blonde hair with that rebellious pink streaks, same sly grin that seemed to know all his secrets, same bulky coat that had seen better days. She rolled a suitcase in behind her.

"Hey, roomie!"

"You're only here for two days. And we're not roommates."

"Ah, wasn't talking to you." She fished in her pocket, hunkered down, and opened her hand to reveal a bone-shaped biscuit. Those actually existed? Reid had always thought they were fake, for cartoons and commercials. He had a lot to learn about this dog-raising business.

Bucky tentatively approached, sniffed the biscuit, and looked up at him for approval. Reid's heart burst.

"Go ahead. It's a treat for you."

The dog licked the biscuit, decided it was safe, and took the whole thing in his mouth, crunching away and spilling crumbs on the hardwood floor. Reid threw a furtive glance at the closet where the Dustbuster was located. It would take just a minute to clean up ...

"Good fella!" Kennedy stood and smiled. "What time do you have to leave?"

"Twelve minutes ago. You're late."

"Okay, let's chat," she said blithely. "I assume I can call you on the regular number. Would it help to have your hotel's as well in case I can't get a hold of you?"

Good. She was asking the right things and focused on the dog. "I have a list here with numbers of the hotel, the team management, and the team's travel staff. I also have the vet's information."

"Got it. And his food and any meds?"

He led her into the kitchen and opened a cupboard. "This is what the man at the pet store recommended. I also have shit bags and his leash." He refused to say the word "poop," though that's what the pet store guy had said, like they were all children. He opened another cupboard door. "This is the ringworm medication and vitamins."

"Hold on, let's look at the food again." She laughed, her silver eyes shining with amusement. "You leave anything at the store?"

So it was a lot, but he wasn't sure how much dogs ate. If he could buy in bulk to save time, why not?

"I'm new to this."

She grasped his arm. "Hey, I'm just kidding. This is great. Really. So is there anything else I can do while I'm here? Clean the bathroom, do laundry—"

"You're here for the dog. You don't have to do anything else. Just look after the dog."

She grinned and his heart blundered around his chest again. What was wrong with him?

She was pretty, but not exceptionally so.

She had a nice smile, but nothing special. (So he had thought it gorgeous before but that was when he had just emerged from a frigid, wet lake and any flash of warmth was welcome.)

There was something indefinable about her, a joie-de-vivre that was very attractive. She was the kind of girl who flitted about, in and out of people's lives, leaving ... impressions. She likely lacked the stability Bucky needed but he had no choice.

"There are a few toys in that box over there." The pet store had some very cute ones. Reid had tested them by squeezing them near the dog's face and the rubber bee was a winner. To be honest, he had yelped excitedly about 90% of them. Clearly, this dog hadn't seen much in the way of simple pleasures.

"Sounds good."

"I'll reach the hotel in Philadelphia at about 5 p.m. Chicago time. I'll call then so make sure you're available."

"Yes, sir!" She gave him a cheeky salute.

Her levity put his back up. "I'm serious."

"Oh, I know."

"Don't leave him alone, if you have to go to the store or something. What about your other dogs?"

"I'll bring him on my rounds tomorrow and see how he does with others. Dog gossiping is important. Lots of butts to sniff." She chuckled, a husky sound that hit him in the balls. "Could you imagine if that's how we let people know we were interested? Wouldn't that be wild?"

Sure. Wild.

She laughed again, clearly finding herself supremely entertaining. "You probably should get going. You're running late." She added a wink so they all knew this was her fault. Ha ha, hilarious.

He headed into the living room, sat on the sofa, and gestured for Bucky to approach. Bending close to keep it between the boys, he murmured his goodbyes.

"Be good, Bucky. Don't make any trouble for Kennedy, okay?"

The dog licked his face.

It shocked some. Delighted more. He looked up to find Kennedy watching him, a soft look in those silver-gray eyes.

Moving toward his luggage, something occurred to him. "You'll have to take him out late. So he can pee."

"Not my first dog-sitting rodeo."

"Don't go too far at night. Stay close to the apartment." The last thing he needed was to be worried about the dog *and* the sitter. "Also, his collar has a GPS tracker. I left instructions about the app you can download and the login information. Not that you should let him off the leash."

Or lose him. *Please don't fucking lose him.*

She smiled. "We'll be careful, I promise. This guy will take care of me."

Reid doubted that—Bucky was a little pathetic—but it was late and he couldn't give it any more of his mind's capacity. "Call me if anything comes up."

"Will do. Oh, and bring me back a cheese steak from Philly." She held up a hand. "Never mind. Just a slice of cheesecake. Or a whole pie. Whatever you can carry."

Was she serious? He thought she might be.

More laughter. It echoed in his ears and settled in his chest long after the door closed behind him.

9

WITH THE DOOR closed and the mean man gone, Kennedy turned back to her canine charge.

"Party time!"

She did a little jig while the dog watched with head cocked. When she didn't stop, he moved away to observe from a safe distance. Wise decision.

"Okay, I'm going to unpack, take a shower, make lunch, and then we can go for a walk."

Bucky barked, perhaps recognizing the word *walk*—clever boy—then milled about doing a little jig of his own. Very cool.

When she said unpack, she meant dump her suitcase in the guest room and unzip it, so it looked like a drawer. On second thought, maybe not the best plan given the uncertainty with the housetrained situation. No way did she want to emerge from the shower to find her stuff marked with puppy pee.

The queen-sized bed looked like the best thing to happen to her in four days. The bed linens were a pearl-gray bordering on blue and felt soft to the touch. She got her nose in there.

Just laundered. Hmm. She tried to imagine Reid getting this organized since they spoke yesterday evening. Perhaps he had a housekeeper-laundress on call. She lay on the bed, just for a moment, thankful that she'd managed to live to fight another day.

The rest of the room was filled with quality pieces—a dresser, a couple of nightstands. No Ikea here. A potted pink Calla lily sat on one of the bedside tables. Of all the flowers for him to choose ... Was that his idea or whoever cleaned his place? Whatever the source, it made her throat tighten and her heart skip back to another time.

The next room over was a bathroom with a toilet and a shower stall. On the utilitarian end of the spectrum and lacking in personal grooming products, this was obviously the guest bath. She wandered back toward the master bedroom.

Reid's bed was king-size (of course) and the room had an en suite bathroom. As soon as she entered it, her world flashed bright. A gorgeous glass-encased shower with pretty Moroccan blue tiles took up one corner, a hot tub the other. Kennedy was a whore for a beautiful bathroom and despite having access to the Y's facilities, she still didn't feel 100% clean. She'd start with the shower and work up to the tub. Make a real meal of it.

She left the bathroom door open while she took a twenty-minute hot-as-she-could-stand-it shower because when she closed it, Bucky whimpered outside. If Reid returned suddenly, she assumed he'd figure out the situation and not try to get a sneak peek.

If anything, Mr. By-the-Rules wouldn't dare.

There was something oddly affecting about his reaction

to Bucky showing love with a face lick, like he wasn't used to doggie joy. He seemed determined to make a go of this dog ownership thing, which was good because she might have a promising gig here. The only thing was to figure out a place to live. It was great to have a temporary reprieve but she'd have to come up with a solution for the next six weeks soon.

She pulled out a pair of leggings and one of Edie's chunky sweaters, and headed out to the kitchen with Bucky following her.

Music: *B-52s*

Mood: *Hungry*

Mantra: *Inhale, exhale*

"How about lunch?" Bucky's bowl was already full to the brim—Reid must have done that before she arrived. A little too much for a dog this size, so she scooped some of it back into the bag and gave her new roomie a bowl of fresh water before washing her hands and starting on her own. On her way over, she'd stopped at Aldi and picked up some sandwich supplies and a few boxes of cheap-ass Mac & Cheese, enough to tide her over for the next few days.

Chewing on her sandwich, she walked the space, opening doors and noseying about. In-unit washer-dryer—nice! The place was unnaturally clean, though, not even a hint of cut stubble in the bathroom sink. A top-of-the-line Dyson stood sentry in the closet along with plenty of earth-friendly cleaning supplies.

There was something obsessive about Reid. She imagined him cleaning like a freak after a bad game (or maybe after a good game, which might be the way he kept the endorphins flowing). People got their kicks all sorts of ways and while cleaning wasn't one of hers, she knew it worked to appease the demons in some.

"Okay, my friend, it looks like we're going to do that walk!"

Bucky looked up from his spot on the living room rug and raised an eyebrow as if to say "now, you're ready?" In that moment, he looked just like Peanut. That same sense of weary acceptance of his human's foibles.

Her heart squeezed in memory. Poor Peanut had loved hiding out in dark places, too, just like this character. She grabbed the leash, hoping to motivate him, when a text came in.

HOT JERK

Is Bucky okay?

Aw, he couldn't have even left town yet. This guy was in deep, which did a lot to soften those razor-sharp edges.

She took a pic of Bucky lying on the rug and sent it.

KENNEDY

He's worn out after lunch. Look at that cute face

HOT JERK

Okay, thanks. Let me know if anything happens.

KENNEDY

Sure. Break a leg!

Shit, that was for theater and probably not appropriate for hockey.

KENNEDY

I meant good luck.

No response. Okay. She returned to the leash and gave it a shake. "Let's go, Bucky!"

After a vigorous run around the park across from Reid's

apartment, where Bucky had cowered in the face of a particularly vociferous blackbird, Kennedy took a moment for her own calm. She had grabbed her yoga mat from her car, and now she rolled it out in a nice roomy spot in the living area and began her warm-up poses. This was usually the only thing that soothed her racing mind.

That, and sex. She would have to do something about that soon. She had gone a couple of months without, a long time for her. There had been a customer at the coffee shop, then a few weeks later, one of the art students she modeled for at the community college. She had no hang-ups about her body or about finding pleasure where she could. She took care of herself, never led anyone on, or made promises. Permanence was not her goal. For the last six years, she'd moved around and made friends all over the world, a network she could turn to in times of need.

Only she hadn't maintained it properly here in Chicago as her efforts to find a place to live attested. She couldn't leave just yet, not while Edie was going through this transition period. To be honest, it suited her. Sometimes, it was fine to take a breather, as long as she kept busy while doing it. Filling her time pushed away thoughts about the past or the future.

Music: *Bon Iver*

Mood: *Serene*

Mantra: *I Am Here, I Am Now, I Am Enough*

Scattering her worries to the corners of the sparse room, Kennedy focused on her body. Breathing deep, filtering out the negative. She caught Bucky's (one) eye as he watched her from his new favorite spot on the end of the sofa.

"Want to join me, boy?"

Head flop. No, thanks.

Her phone buzzed and as she was close to the end of her

practice, she checked it to find a text from Mia followed by a link.

Is this you?

Her gasp on clicking it made poor Bucky jump. The lake rescue had made the news!

Just as Kennedy suspected, that woman *had* been filming. Even without the added wrinkle of a famous—she supposed—sports star doing the rescuing, it was an interesting enough event in itself. Two people had jumped into the lake to save a dog. She would have filmed it, too.

KENNEDY

Yeah. Long story.

Her phone rang immediately. "You and Reid rescued that dog from the lake together?"

"Reid did. I just happened to be there."

Mia wasn't buying it. "You were in the water! In Chicago! In November! No wonder Reid was trying to track you down. There's something almost fated about it."

"What? That's—that's ridiculous." She didn't subscribe to the notion of fate, or not the romantic view of it, anyway. Buddhists believed that we're in control of our ultimate fates, and while not a die-hard adherent, Kennedy subscribed to the tenets that resonated with her, particularly about human life being one of suffering. Physical work, meditation, and good behavior were the ways to achieve enlightenment.

She was usually sorely lacking in the good behavior department.

"He called last night," Mia continued, "worried you're

some fly-by-night party girl who's going to rob him blind. So, uh, don't do that."

"Of course I wouldn't." That Mia even entertained the idea stung, but of course they didn't know her from a hole in the wall. "I'm a professional." Even if she had used that amazing shower. There had to be *some* perks.

"I know you are. I told Reid you're amazing with Gordie Howe." Mia chuckled. "Having a dog might get him to lighten up."

Glad that she'd brought it up, Kennedy asked, "So what's his deal? Is he always so ..."

"Rude, abrupt, grouchy?"

"In a word or three." She might add intense, sexy, and hot as hell. That Reid X-ray death glare when she showed up a few minutes late was its own sex position.

"He's just one of those guys who's uber focused on his game. There's a lot of competition. Also, the players move around frequently so not all of them are here to make friends. That's Reid in a nutshell, but I don't know. I think the grumpster thing is a bit of an act. As soon as people see that video, he's going to be making a whole lot of friends. People love that shit!"

Kennedy didn't doubt it. She saw it now: Reid making friends with women in coffee shops, bars, nightclubs, hotel lobbies, airports ... Not that she cared. She wasn't even sure why she had thought it.

Probably because she had just been thinking about sex. Hot Jerk was attractive, yes, but she liked her bedmates a little less on the cranky side.

Which might make her problem solvable. Looking around, she thought about this big apartment, Reid's doggie day and night care needs, and her own housing dilemma. Surely there was a way to make this work ...

Foreman approached Reid in the Philly visitors' locker room after the game.

"Good work out there."

Reid eyed him, knowing he had played well with an assist. He wasn't the reason they'd won but he hoped his contribution would be noted by the people in charge. He certainly didn't need a patronizing pat on the pack from the likes of Foreman, though. Now they had the dog as their connective tissue, the last thing he wanted was for Foreman to get ideas that this was the start of a beautiful friendship. That was not how to keep ahead of the pack.

"You see this?" Foreman turned his phone around. A video was playing.

Damn, he had known that woman was filming. "Has everyone seen it?"

"Probably." No one was paying them any mind but Reid was on deck for post-game press duties. "Worried it makes you look like a softie?"

Yes. He would prefer to care for the dog without all the baggage that came with caring for the dog.

Yesterday, he had called Kennedy to ask how Bucky was doing the moment he landed in Philly. Fine, apparently. Absolutely fine. He had wanted to switch to FaceTime but felt weird about it. Kennedy would probably make some assumption about his attraction to her—so what if it might be half-true—and wouldn't believe that he wanted to see his dog. He didn't quite believe it himself.

But now he wanted to talk to her and warn her about the video. He needed to find somewhere private.

Back at the hotel, Foreman stopped at the bar for a drink with Petrov and the crew, which gave Reid at least thirty minutes before he pounded in, probably eager to have phone sex with Mia.

Don't think about phone sex right before you call an attractive woman, connard. Focused on his task, he exhaled a few breaths, dialed using FaceTime, and waited.

No answer.

It was 10:30 p.m. in Chicago. Had Kennedy gone out and left Bucky alone? Or taken him for a walk? That wasn't a good idea. The GPS tracker app only worked within a few miles, so he couldn't check on their safety.

He tried again. This time she answered, but she looked a little flushed. It was ... nothing. Absolutely nothing.

"Okay, hold your horses. I'm here!"

"Where were you?"

"The bathroom. I might be able to get away with an audio call in there but not a video one, right?" She grinned, and foreign warmth flooded his chest cavity. Around her he felt weird. "You win your game?"

"I did."

She cheered and fist pumped with a loud "Whoop! Whoop!" Barking soon followed. Reid's heart thumped hard, probably confused as all hell about what was going on. His brother had texted *good game*, as did his mother. Nothing from Henri yet.

This was the first time he could recall someone outside his family or unconnected to the hockey industrial complex, weighing in on his game with such positivity. She hadn't even seen it. He got the impression she wasn't a sports fan.

"Is Bucky okay?"

"Oh, he's fine. We just got in from a nighttime jaunt and the-world-is-my-toilet excursion. Now he's excited because I'm excited. Here, take a look!" She reversed the camera so he could see the dog milling about. He looked so happy, and yet again Reid lamented missing another important moment in person.

Mental headshake. This was absurd. He wasn't missing anything.

"Is he eating and sleeping okay?"

She turned the camera back to her. "Yeah. I put out a little less food today because he'll pretty much eat anything you put in front of him. For a dog his size, we can take the measurements down a touch."

"I thought he'd stop eating when he was full."

"They're like humans in that respect. Not much willpower when confronted with gads of food. It's best to train them on the ideal amounts. It's all about portion control." She smiled, tempering what could have been an admonishment. "Don't worry, you guys will learn together."

"Would it be okay if I ... talked to him?"

Those silver-gray suns lit up. "That's a great idea. Hold on a sec." A moment later, she had reversed the camera again so the next face he saw was Bucky's. Now that Reid was on the spot, he felt foolish and tongue-tied. He wished Kennedy would leave the room, but then this wouldn't be possible without her holding the phone.

Like an idiot, he said, "Hello, Bucky. Just ... uh, checking in."

Kennedy's words of encouragement filled the silence. "It's Daddy. He's calling home. Give him a bark."

The dog kept his thoughts to himself.

She turned back. "You know something? I think your face isn't big enough—ha, bet you never heard that before! Do you have a computer?"

"Yes, there's one in my bedroom."

"Let's take a walk. Come on, boy." A couple of minutes later, she was logged into his computer. (He had to give her his password which he would now have to change the moment he got home. She had made a joke about hoping there was nothing incriminating in his search history.) "Okay, I'm going to send you a video call link, and you can answer back on that." She hung up.

This seemed like a lot of trouble, but everyone was already committed to their roles. He clicked the link in the message she sent and a few seconds later, there she was with Bucky in her lap. The angle was a little different, further away, but then she put Bucky closer to the screen.

The scruffy guy barked. The next sight was a big, moist sliver of pink flesh.

Kennedy laughed. "Oh, boy. I think he recognizes Daddy."

"Did he just lick the screen?"

"He did! He's so excited to see you. Keep talking to him. Oh, I know! Tell him about the game. About one of your goals? Did you score a goal?"

No, but neither of them would know. "I made this great slap shot move off my blade that the goalie didn't see coming. Back of the net, the crowd went wild."

Bucky barked and jumped out of frame.

"Where's he gone?"

"Oh, he got bored. Don't take it personally. Dogs have limited attention spans."

He couldn't get annoyed at that. "So something happened."

"The video? Mia sent it." Okay, that was a relief. She didn't seem upset. "Mia also told me that you're worried I'll throw a frat party or burn cigarettes into your coffee table."

"I had to check, but she gave you a good reference. She adores that dog of hers so I figure she wouldn't take a chance on his care."

"I am trustworthy. And I only had five guests over—hardly a party."

He squinted at her. "I know you think I'm completely humorless but I understand that's a joke." He hoped.

"Hmm, maybe. You'll have to trust me, Reid."

Trust me. Only so far as was necessary.

10

REID SLIPPED INSIDE THE APARTMENT, dropped his away bag in the hallway, and listened for the patter of doggy feet.

Nothing.

Disappointment rocked him. He was certainly playing the fool, living in far too much anticipation of his new friend's affection. The press got a kick out of asking him stupid questions about the rescue, though they were more interested in Kennedy. No surprise there, they were always looking for an angle. Kershaw had taken to calling him Aquaman on the plane ride back, which everyone thought the height of comic genius.

Henri called multiple times while Reid was flying back to Chicago. He had a feeling he knew what *that* was about.

Perhaps Kennedy and Bucky were out walking. She had other clients, and hopefully Bucky was getting along with them. Socialization, she had called it. Something that Reid could do with a little bit more of.

He rolled his bag toward the bedroom, eager to change and take a shower. Maybe he'd check the GPS tracker first, see if they were nearby. In his room, he found his dog, sitting at the entrance to the en suite bathroom.

"Bucky!"

The little guy cocked his head and raced toward him. Thank God he was safe. Reid hugged him and let his face be thoroughly licked. He pulled a dog biscuit from his pocket and held it out for him.

"A little something for you."

Bucky snatched it up and wolfed it down so fast Reid worried he might choke. But no. He had it under control like the excellent dog he was. His bright eye—looking even brighter than three days ago—was filled with joy.

"Hi, there."

He looked up to find Kennedy standing at the entrance to the bathroom in a towel. He had a flash of ink on her upper arm before his grasping eyes realized he was about to turn into a creeper if he continued.

"Hi. I'm sorry—I should let you get ... why are you showering in my bathroom?"

She giggled. "Okay, Papa Bear. Your shower has the extra jets so of course I'm going to use it before the guest one. Well, I won't again because you're giving me that look that says I've overstepped."

"No, it's fine. I just didn't expect to see you." He bent down again and rubbed Bucky's head. He couldn't look at her in that towel, not when he'd gone without sex for four months. Instead he spoke to the dog. "Were you spying on Kennedy?"

Spying? Why had he used that word?

"He was, the cheeky devil. I tried closing the door but he just scratches at it. Clearly has voyeuristic tendencies or abandonment issues." She waved that off. "Sorry, not a dig. I know you have to go out of town to earn a crust."

"Has he been for a walk yet today?"

"No, but I can get dressed and take him out."

He held up a peremptory hand. "No, I'd like to go out with him." He certainly wasn't asking permission, yet somehow he felt as though she was in charge of the dog's welfare.

"Sounds great. I'll start the coffee and we can chat about how it went when you come back."

She headed back into the bathroom and shut the door.

KENNEDY MIGHT HAVE MISJUDGED REID. When he spotted her in a towel, he'd almost looked shy and somewhat apologetic to have encountered her half-dressed, even though she was the one who had taken over his bathroom. The shower was that much better.

Just seeing Reid with Bucky warmed her heart. The big grump turned into a total cinnamon roll around that puppy. Animals, the great levelers.

Fifteen minutes later, the door opened and both of them came into the kitchen. Reid's cheeks were flushed and his eyes were bright, making him look like a windswept, romantic hero just back from a walk on the moors. Very Heathcliff.

If Heathcliff wore a suit. They must have to dress nice for travel, which was weird. Dress codes for sports people made no sense, though she approved because Reid Durand looked amazing in a suit.

Dragging her eyes away from how the those pants clung fondly to his thighs, she managed to eke out, "How did it go?"

"Fine." He went to the sink to wash his hands. His gaze fell to the counter. "You moved things around."

"Oh, yeah, the mugs. That cupboard is kind of a stretch for me so I put a couple on the counter so I can just reuse them. Easier than having to grab a stool."

He nodded, but his eyebrows formed a frustrated V. *Drinking vessels out of sync. Does not compute.* He was welcome to put them back as soon as she was gone ...

... or right now. The cups were restored to their original location.

"Is there anything I need to know?" He poured coffee, asking this with his back to her. When he turned, she got the impression he was trying to school his expression to calmness. That cup move must have really pissed him off.

He was probably not going to love what she said next.

"So don't freak out but yesterday, I had to take him to the vet—"

He slammed the cup down, splashing drops of coffee on the counter. "The vet? What happened?"

She held up a hand. "No big deal. He vomited yesterday afternoon and I was a bit worried that he might have swallowed something toxic because the cupboard door under the sink was ajar. That's where the dishwasher packets are and the box was open." She waved quickly. "But he was fine! The doc took a look and said that the food we're giving him might be too rich. He's not been fed so well for months, so it's playing havoc on his stomach. That's all, I promise. I moved the stuff from under the sink to the utility room for now until we can figure out how to dog-proof the apartment."

He did *not* look appeased. "You should have told me when I called last night."

"I could have but you would have just worried, maybe

tried to get home sooner. It was all under control. You seem to be a bit, uh, emotional about this puppy so it was better this way. Trust me."

"Trust you? Not sure I can if you're lying to me. You should have told me the minute I got in."

"And ruin your reunion? You guys needed to have some tension-free alone time. Now you have, and I'm filling you in on what's transpired. No secrets, just timing, okay?"

His stare burned into her and if she wasn't so sure he was absolutely pissed, she'd be getting a tad turned on. Her nipples tightened along with the muscles between her legs.

Reid Durand, better than Kegels. Imagine having that staring down at you while he was inside ...

Nope. Not going there, especially with Hot Jerk. Not when she needed to ask him a favor.

"If something's wrong, I need to know about it."

"How would you have reacted?"

He bristled, clearly surprised at her challenge. Probably didn't get much pushback in his blessed, all-hail-the-king life. "It doesn't matter how."

"Yes, it does."

"I would have called the vet myself and spoken with him."

"Her, actually."

Blackest of scowls. "I would have been able to assure myself that he was okay. And I gave you the name of a vet I've already worked with. A male vet."

"Who wasn't available. This was his partner in the same practice. All this happened before your game yesterday. Should I have called you then? Right before you went on the ice?"

He folded his arms. Unfolded them. Placed his hands behind him on the counter, gripping hard. Sheesh, this guy needed a massage or anger management therapy or a good bout in the sack. Not that she was offering ...

"If not then, right after."

"So it would have been okay to delay telling you because it was no longer an emergency and you had a game to play?"

"Yes, that would have been okay."

Game, set, and match. The look on his face was priceless. In the way of a bossy alphahole who realizes he's lost the argument but absolutely hates it, he was evidently thinking about how to claw back some territory. "But last night when we spoke after the game, you should have told me."

"What would you have done then? The vet's office was closed so you would have just been worried all night, maybe not getting any sleep, or trying to get a hold of the vet after hours. You saw him yourself—he was fine. Vet Lisa assured me he was okay and I made a call that this information would be best kept to myself until you returned and could see Bucky in person. You have to trust me to make some executive decisions here or this isn't going to work."

Had she just talked herself out of a job?

He folded his arms. Stared. Looked down at Bucky. Back at her.

"I would prefer you keep me informed ... but I understand why you didn't. Next time, just tell me, I can handle it."

"So you can handle the truth!"

Blank stare. Not a fan of the paraphrased Jack Nicholson impression, then.

"Okay. Got it." She fake-wiped her brow. She'd tell him about the multiple peeing incidents later. Bucky's, that is. "Thought I'd lost my gig there."

"I considered it, but you're all I have and Bucky likes you. That's important."

And she liked him. Reid was growing on her as well. She liked that he had bowed to her greater wisdom here and didn't act like a *complete* dick about it. The beauty of compromise.

They stood staring at each other for a moment that turned into two, then three. It should have been awkward but wasn't.

"Cute sweater," he finally said in a tone that implied, *that's hideous*.

She picked at one of the lumps shaped like pine cones on the front. "It's Edie's."

"Edie?"

"My grandmother. I don't have winter clothes so she let me borrow it." It had the comforting scent of her, too. A faint citrus that kept Kennedy connected to another time.

"Why don't you have winter clothes?"

"I'm usually in warmer climes, but Edie had a stroke and moved into Larkvale." At his curious expression, she explained. "It's an assisted living home for seniors. I haven't lived in the States for a while so I came back to spend time with her."

"Is she ..." His entire demeanor went on alert. "Ill?"

"God, no. The stroke was one of those minor ones. She'll outlive us all but it made me realize that I need to visit more often. I've been gone a while."

"Why?"

"Why have I been gone?"

He nodded.

"For the last six years I've been traveling in Mexico, South America, Asia. In fact, by January I'll be back in Thailand teaching English. I'm just waiting on a work visa." One of her first jobs had been teaching English in Japan, and now she would be doing it again in one of her favorite countries. Definitely more stable work than bartending for a few bucks or trying to marshal funds from broke backpackers for a yoga class. "Always chasing the sun, that's me!"

People usually weighed in at this point in her stock explanation with how awesome it was, how jealous they were, how lucky she had it. This time, her cheery coda didn't produce the typical response.

Reid said nothing, just stared. She felt exposed, her skin flayed and burning. She'd yet to decide if Reid's dark-eyed intensity was sexy or serial killer energy.

"I should get going as I have a few appointments. I wondered if you'd mind paying me before I leave? You can Venmo me." She doubted he'd stiff her but if he changed his mind about using her services again, she'd rather have the cash in hand now.

"Mais oui." He took out his phone and started tapping the screen, completely oblivious to the fact her spine had liquefied in the face of spoken French. "We said two hundred a day?"

She swallowed, worried that she may have overpriced her talents.

"Three days, two nights," he murmured. "Plus what I owe you for the vet ... that should do it. Let me know if it's not what you expected."

She checked, her eyes bugging out. "That's a thousand dollars."

"It's a tip for the extra work you had to do, taking him to the vet. You were cool under pressure and then I was less than polite when you explained. There should be some compensation for putting up with a cranky employer."

She liked that he had a sense of humor about it. "Yes, but this seems like overkill." This would pay for her return ticket to Asia and leave her with some to spare.

"And you had to stay overnight away from your home. That's above and beyond. Today's my day off but I have practice tomorrow, 10 to 1, again the next day, then a home game on Sunday night. Are you available?"

Just like that. Rich people were used to buying their way out of their problems. Hot people, too.

Of course, right now, she was ripe for purchase seeing as she had problems of her own.

"Sounds like you need someone here 24/7."

"Yes, it does. Do you live nearby? My schedule is pretty structured and I usually know far in advance where I'll be. We can plan this to the hour."

She wasn't big on all this structured time and she did have other clients. But mostly she had a different problem that only he might be able to fix.

"I can be at your beck and call but I need to ask something first."

"Okay." His tone was suspicious.

She took a deep breath and steeled her spine. "Could I move in here?"

11

REID DIDN'T SAY A WORD. So he wasn't the most talkative of guys, but he definitely had opinions. She had heard them.

Only now, zilch.

"Did you hear what I said?"

He crossed his arms and assessed her in a way she felt to her toes. "Why do you want to live here?"

A thinker before he spoke, apparently. Fine, fine.

"You might recall that lovely argument a few days back that led to a customer complaining at your encouragement and me losing my job?" It never hurt to remind him of his part in her imminent financial ruin. "Well, that was about my living situation. I need to find another place to live for the next seven weeks and the schedule you're describing for Bucky is basically full-time. It would make more sense if I'm on-site and as I also need a roof over my head, I think this would solve two problems with one stone. Or however it goes."

This explanation was met with silence. So he needed more. Reid was the kind of guy who didn't make decisions impulsively.

She geared up for her next argument. "Sure, you don't want anyone living here, especially a complete stranger, but I stayed for the last two nights and I didn't throw any wild parties or anything. The only thing I did that you clearly don't approve of is move a couple of mugs around and use your epic shower. If you set the ground rules, then I won't do anything that pisses you off. Also, I can keep things ticking over here. Get groceries, do your laundry, clean up." She looked around. "You like it neat. I can make sure it stays that way. And you can deduct a room and board fee from my wages."

"Okay."

"I would definitely stay out of your hair when you're around. I have some other commitments I can work around so I can be gone when you need space or stay in my room—"

"I said okay."

"What?" She stopped pacing—only now realizing that she *had* been pacing—and gave him the Reid treatment. A burner of a stare.

"I said you can stay here. Perhaps not forever, but we could try it while you're looking for another place."

She would be gone by the end of the year and if she played her cards right, she could stay here that entire time. Resolved to keep that to herself for now, she rushed forward and threw her arms around him. "Reid, that's amazing. Thank you!"

When he didn't return her affection, she stood back. "Sorry. Not a hugger. Got it."

Color flagged his cheekbones and something funny happened to his nostrils. Wow, he had *not* enjoyed that.

"I'll definitely look for another place," she rushed on to

cover the awkwardness. "And I should be able to rearrange my yoga classes around your schedule."

"You teach yoga?"

"Occasionally. These days I'm teaching it to the old folks at Larkvale Senior Living."

"And you walk dogs? And serve coffee? Well, you did." Maybe he was rethinking the offer to let her stay. Some people were distrustful of in-your-face poverty, thinking it signified laziness. Nothing said poverty more than multiple part-time gigs.

Best not to tell him about the art class modeling. "Yep. I like to keep busy which is why I will not bother you when you're here. You won't even know I'm on site except for your neater-than-neat apartment."

"You don't have to convince me," he said, though he sounded far from convinced. "I said yes."

He had. So why was she still trying to argue her case? Likely trying to persuade herself this was a good idea. She had little choice. She just needed some breathing room while she waited for her work visa and ensured Edie was in a good place.

"We should talk about rules," Reid said. "And money. Also, I'll need to talk to my accountant about taxes."

Taxes? She was trying to make a buck, not hand it off to Uncle Sam.

"You want to get the government involved?"

He looked at her sharply. Of course he would want the government involved. This guy was not a rule breaker.

"I prefer to keep it all above board." His pretty mouth set in a grimace.

"Sure. Whatever works." She couldn't tell him to break the law. As it was, he was doing her a huge favor. "What rules did you have in mind?"

"I would prefer if you didn't invite people over."

"You mean lov-ahs?"

He scowled. "I mean anyone. During the season I need to focus. I can't do that if there are people here."

Pesky kids playing loud music.

She had no intention of inviting people over yet she felt an unbearable urge to poke at him. "Will you be able to focus while *I'm* here?"

"You just said you'd be out a lot or spending the time in your room. That would probably be best."

A giggle bubbled from somewhere deep, flirted with her lungs, and threatened to climb her throat. By the grace of the housing gods, who clearly recognized a mortal woman in need of a roof over her head, she managed to keep it at bay.

"Got it. And don't worry about food. I'll buy my own and I won't steal yours."

He shook his head. "I don't mind about that. You can order anything you want and charge it to my account. I usually get stuff delivered so we can share a cart in the app. Room and board included in your pay."

That was generous. She wouldn't abuse it, though. "I can do some cleaning. Though I imagine you have someone come in." People with money usually had a maid.

"No need to do anything like that. I do my own cleaning. Helps me concentrate." Ha, she had totally called that. He screwed up his brow, like he was concentrating right now.

Maybe on vacuuming.

What was she getting herself into? She'd lived with roommates before and had a high tolerance for crazy. Backpacking solo though Europe and Asia led to fun interactions with new people, several of whom often had questionable habits. She could fill a Reddit board with her tales of whackery in the room- and hostel-mate department.

So Reid was uptight about his living space. She could work with that. This was a pretty sweet gig for someone who rarely let the hardwood under her feet accumulate dust. Six weeks and she'd be gone.

She moved in closer to the fridge. It was covered with several calendars, one that was obviously for games. "What's this one?"

"My workout schedule."

"And this?" She pointed at a different color-coded one.

"Meals. I have certain dietary requirements."

"This rule about having people over. Does that apply to you?" It was his home and she was a guest, but she did wonder.

"I won't have anyone over."

"You aren't dating anyone?"

"I don't date. And I don't fu—uh, screw anyone during the season."

She could feel her eyes go around at his unvarnished statement. When he said he needed to focus, he really meant focusing on ... not having sex.

Wow. "At all? Not even on your away trips?"

"No."

"So you're like the Hockey Terminator or something. Always the mission." Maybe he went nuts once the season was over. An image of him losing his shit, screwing anything not nailed down popped into her head and set her brain on fire.

"You look like you're thinking," he said, his gaze dipping to her mouth. Or perhaps she imagined that because she was looking at *his* mouth.

Get your eyes in order, girl. All this mouth watching could only spell trouble.

"I'm a human, I'm always thinking. So let me get this straight. From October to June, you keep it in your pants? Every season?"

"It's only to June if we make the playoffs. If that happens, hockey's the only thing on my mind. That and my scratchy playoff beard."

Playoff beard? She would be doing some light Internet research tonight for sure.

"So have you ever lived with a roommate before?"

"Sure, in college. And I room with players at the hotels during away games."

"But a female roommate?"

His gaze narrowed. "Worried you're going to be *so* attractive to me I might break my rules?"

"Oh, I'd never presume. I just want to be sure I don't make things awkward while I run around braless."

He did that nostril thing again, a kind of horsey flare.

Heathcliff, it's me, your Kathy, I've come home ...

"Think I can cope. Besides, you're not just a roommate, you're an employee. I wouldn't cross that line."

Was that disappointment she felt? Surely not. Reid was exceptionally handsome. Beautiful, even. But no way would she risk the roof over her head for a roll in the hay.

Even if making this man slip the reins of his tightly-leashed control was very, very tempting.

12

REID WALKED by the guest room—now Kennedy's room—and stopped to peer inside.

A single suitcase sat near the window. That's what she lived out of.

When she said she was heading back to Thailand at the end of the year, Reid hadn't paid that much attention. People were always going to more interesting places than him. He was just a Canadian puck chaser, after all, who had never ventured outside North America.

But the solitary suitcase put her wandering lifestyle into sharp relief. It also made him wonder. She had mentioned lodging difficulties, and at the beach when they saved Bucky, this suitcase had been in the trunk of her car.

Bucky walked in, sniffed at the case, and did a couple of circuits of the room.

"She'll be here soon." Usually he'd be napping. Instead he'd been answering dumb calls from reporters all morning, asking for interviews because of that video. No matter that he kept referring them to the Rebels press office, somehow one of them got his number and thought they could end-run the team org.

He still couldn't believe he'd said yes to Kennedy's request to move in. Happy to have a solution for his dog care problem fall into his lap like a gift from the gods, he had barely questioned it.

Until she had hugged him. His body had gone stiff on the outside, while on the inside … he burned. This might not have been one of his best ideas, but he had the distinct impression she had nowhere to go. Who kept their suitcase in the trunk of their car?

The potted plant was still on the nightstand, the one he'd picked up at the garden center the night before she stayed the first time. Just to make it a bit more welcoming, that's all. Beside it was a small frame containing a watercolor of a flower, a tulip or maybe even the same flower in the pot. Spooky. The initials LC were tucked into the corner. Carefully, he returned it to the same spot.

Yesterday, she had been busy with her various jobs. Apparently she also did personal assistant errands for a few of the dog owners, volunteered at an animal shelter, and worked on solving world peace in her spare time. All right, not that last one, but it wouldn't have surprised him. So she loved dogs enough to want to spend her free time with them. Reid understood hard work but he had a goal: a multi-year contract with the right team.

Why was Kennedy filling every single moment?

He had gone to the gym last night and when he returned, her door was closed. This morning, she left before he woke up at six, and now he was hovering. Absorbing and learning.

His phone rang with a call from Henri. Reid had been dreading this and was only surprised it hadn't come sooner.

"Hi, Dad."

"The lake? You fished a damn mutt out of the lake?"

Reid exhaled a careful breath. "Was I supposed to let him drown?"

"Christ, what if you'd been injured? Those hands and feet are worth money, Reid. And you're making foolish rescues, risking an injury that could take you off the ice."

"It was a calculated risk."

"And there was someone else there! You should have just let them do it."

Well, he didn't, and now that someone was living with him. *Stupid, Reid.*

"I'm fine."

His father grumbled some more before finally muttering, "So, we won't be visiting Chicago next week."

Reid's heart leaped into his throat. "Why not?"

"Your brother has a groin strain and will be out for the game. You'll play each other again in December, so we'll do it then."

Because coming down to see Reid play wasn't enough of a reason. He felt like a kid again, desperate for any slops of affection Henri would throw at him. Even knowing what a dick his stepfather was, he still craved his approval. The man was a legend in the game and to have him care about your career was a great honor, even when it came with a crushing weight of expectation.

He collected his wits and put his shields in place. "Whatever works."

"Call your brother. He's pretty down about being on IR."

Like Reid could make him better. "Will do."

"And Reid? No more dumb dives in the lake, okay?"

"No plans to." He looked down at Bucky who had somehow managed to remain deathly quiet during that call, as if he sensed there'd be trouble if he made himself known. He had a survivor's instinct, just like Kennedy.

Henri hung up and Reid stepped out of Kennedy's room. "Come on, boy. Time to take a nap."

"DYLAN, DON'T LICK THAT!" Kennedy pulled the Boston terrier away from what looked like soup—hopefully—and turned the corner onto State Street in Riverbrook. The smoothie shop was on the corner so she planned to stop there and juice up.

One of her other charges, Sylvester, strained at the leash as he spotted an oncoming dog. Meanwhile, Bucky hid behind her legs, as he had done for the last five days when confronted with new animals out on their daily walks. Still a scaredy cat.

Kennedy recognized the dog in their path, accompanied by a couple holding hands.

"Hey, Mia."

Mia beamed as she approached, clearly a woman in love. Kennedy had never met her guy, but she'd seen pictures of Cal Foreman, one of the Rebels players. Even better in the flesh. God, they made these hockey players big.

"Kennedy!" Mia hugged her, which took Kennedy by surprise. "So great to see you. How are things with Reid?"

Straight to the point, then. "Fine, fine! This is Bucky, Reid's dog."

Cal squatted and petted Bucky. "Hey, buddy, you're looking a lot better since the last time I saw you." He didn't leave Sylvester or Dylan out of the good-boy pat downs either, which said a lot. He stood, a big smile on his face.

"Amazing what a week of TLC will do. Hey, I'm Cal, seeing as Mia has lost her manners."

She nudged him. "I have not! I was waiting for an opening in the man-beast love fest."

Cal wrapped an arm around her waist and pulled her into his side. "That's okay. I know your mind turned to mush when you saw me getting friendly with this little guy." He kissed her and she kissed him and Kennedy had to cough significantly to remind them she was here.

"You guys are pret-*ty* cute, I have to say."

"We were going for sexy," Cal said with a—yep, sexy—grin. "So you're the poor woman who had to stay over at Durand's?"

"I don't know about poor." So she was literally poor but Cal's comment sounded like a dig at Reid. "As living arrangements go, it's a pretty sweet setup. Neither of us is there all that much so we hardly see each other." She looked down at Bucky who was smelling Gordie Howe's butt. Why did dogs do that?

Mia narrowed her eyes. "Hold up. You've moved in with Reid? Permanently?"

"He needed someone on site and it made more sense to just move in for a few weeks while we get Bucky settled. It's really just to make things easier." Now she was wondering if this setup with Reid was supposed to be a secret. He hadn't told her to keep it to herself.

"Sure," Mia said, clearly not convinced. She slid a glance at Cal who returned a speaking glance of his own. All this couple conversation without a word. Kennedy had never enjoyed that kind of simpatico with anyone, probably because she was usually out the door faster than you can say "thanks for the orgasm, buddy!"

"Reid's roomie," Mia said. "That must be fun."

So Reid wasn't exactly a barrel of laughs, but she would never say so. It felt disloyal to even think it. Besides it was different than fun: she hadn't come up with a label yet.

"I do have him to thank for helping me see what a dumbass I was being." Cal smiled at Mia. "About us."

Mia's mouth dropped open. "Really? Was that before or after you beat him up during practice?"

Kennedy cut in. "You're the one who hit him? Whatever for?"

"He was being a jerk. Nothing new, but he poked a spot, knowing exactly what he was doing, and I lost it." He turned to Mia. "It was the morning after the charity auction, after we had that fight, gorgeous girl. Don't worry, it's all good, I apologized. And it's not as if he can't handle it. Injuries are par for the course."

"But not ones that are deliberately inflicted by their teammates!" Mia threw an exasperated glance at Kennedy, then back at Cal. "You should invite him out to make up for it."

Cal's face twisted like Munch's *The Scream*. "Why the hell would I do that? I have to room with him on away games and believe me, he's not interested in making friends. I've already tried the Foreman charm, which is bona fide irresistible. Except to that guy."

What a strange dynamic. Kennedy would have thought it was a complete sausage fest and all the teammates would be great buddies to bond better for performance enhancement. "So you don't get along with Reid?"

"No one gets along with Reid," Cal said. "But he likes it that way. Thinks if he's a dick to everyone it makes him the ultimate tough guy."

"Daddy issues," Mia said cryptically.

"Really?"

Mia glanced at Cal, then back at Kennedy. "His father is a hockey legend, known for being a hard-ass both on and off the ice. Can't have been easy."

"Yeah, Henri Durand coached for a stint at the Montreal Royals while I was there a while back," Cal said. "Guy was an asshole but Reid's his stepson. Not genetic. Developed that sparkling personality all by himself." He frowned at Mia and Kennedy, who were both staring him down. "Hey, don't feel sorry for him. The guy knows exactly what he's doing. No one plays mind games better than Durand."

"You need to be a better teammate, Cal." Mia smiled conspiratorially at Kennedy. "We'll figure something out."

Cal's brow lined like a corduroy swatch. "That can*not* be good."

13

Reid heard the key in the lock and so did Bucky. He ran to the door and sat on his haunches, waiting. Bucky, that is. Though Reid was tempted. Seriously tempted.

He shouldn't be looking forward to a stranger invading his house, shocking his routine, and upsetting his equilibrium. Since Bucky had come into his life, Reid found himself questioning his lone-wolf strategy. Though he wasn't planning on being too friendly, he saw no reason why he couldn't enjoy the company of his new roommate.

Kennedy breezed in, dropped her yoga mat, and fell to her knees.

"Bucky, how are ya, my friend?"

Happier for seeing you, Bucky said with a face lick.

For the last week they'd fallen into a routine. On non-game days Reid was at practice each day, came home for a nap and food in the afternoon, then went back to the gym. By the time he got home, Kennedy was in her room with her door closed, but had left Post-its about Bucky's care. What he ate, when he took his meds, how long they walked around the park. This was the first time their paths had crossed significantly enough to have a conversation.

She looked up and smiled. *Shot through the heart*, as Bon Jovi would say.

"Good practice, roomie?" A smirk accented the label.

"Yep, fine."

She slipped off her bulky coat and hung it in the closet. Beneath she wore tight yoga pants and a long-sleeved tee that skimmed the top of her gorgeous ass. On the front of the tee was an image of Black Widow and the slogan *It Should Have Been Clint*.

So they were both Avengers fans. Lots of people were, but still, it was a nice touchpoint. He managed to drag his eyes away as she headed to the kitchen.

"I was going to make lunch, then I'll get out of your way."

He followed her and leaned against the counter. "Everything okay for the last few days? Settling in all right?"

"Peachy." She pulled out the bread and cheese, and threw the sandwich together quickly.

"That doesn't look very filling."

"Oh, it's fine."

He picked up the sandwich. "This isn't fine. That's not real cheese."

"Sure it is. And please stop manhandling my sandwich."

"I insist you share my food."

Her lips turned up at the corners. "Maybe I don't want to. It looks weird."

"Gouda is weird?"

"No, the green juice and the grain stuff."

"You don't have to eat that, but you're welcome to the turkey and gouda and wheat bread. And all this other stuff Bastian brought—I won't eat it."

"Bastian?"

"My brother. He dropped off some groceries."

The prick knew Reid was careful about his diet, yet here he was stocking the cupboards with beer and Brie and fucking gelato. Kennedy could have it all. She was clearly short of funds, living paycheck to paycheck. Reid was paid a lot of money to play hockey, and while he was good at it, he often wondered if he was worth those millions. Perhaps the person who looked after animals and helped old people get fit should be respected more.

"Groceries that you won't eat." She looked understandably baffled. "Then why did he bring it over?"

"To mess with me."

She crossed her arms over those fabulous breasts. "Explain."

That made him smile. On the inside. "He knows I have a strict regimen during the season. Diet, exercise—"

"Celibacy."

Yep. "So he thinks he can chip away at that."

"And if you cave in on one thing, you'll be on a slippery slope to empty calories and watching *The Bachelor* and celebrating your wins with half a Sam Adams and a puck bunny at the bar."

"He'd love to see it."

"Sports people." She shook her head sadly.

"It's not a sports thing. It's a Durand thing." He scrubbed a hand through his hair. "We're competitive. But you can help me out my removing some of this food from the sightline of temptation."

"Shakespeare couldn't have said it better." She took out a bottle of Boréale Cuivrée, which was Reid's favorite amber ale. That connard. "I'll have one but first, let me see ... He bought sweet potatoes and chili peppers? Sort of weird for someone who's not going to cook them." She did this cute little nose wrinkle and his lips itched with ... he didn't know what. "Do you like curry?"

Reid was very conscious of his gut health. "That might not work with my diet, but make whatever you want for yourself."

"You're opposed to flavor during the season?"

"Plain is better." Plain food, plain sex (with his hand), plain life. "And you don't have to cook for me."

"I can make it healthy. I'd just need to check on the spice situation." She pulled open one of the cupboards but he could have told her the spice situation would not be to her liking. "Tarragon?" She held up the lone spice jar she found.

"It was here when I moved in."

Epic eye roll. "I'll be back in a few minutes."

"Kennedy, you don't have to—" But she was already out the door.

He looked down at Bucky. "You like curry, buddy?"

He decided to help out by peeling a sweet potato. He couldn't remember the last time he'd peeled ... anything. Judging by the way he was hacking at this, there was a good chance he had never peeled a vegetable at all.

Already, the kitchen was showing signs of impact, though it wasn't this irregularly-chopped root vegetable. It was *her*. This woman was an asteroid on a collision course with his life. He could either take a nuclear weapon and blow it up like Bruce and the crew in *Armageddon* or he could wait for the inevitable extinction level event like the dinosaur he was.

He should go to the gym. Coach Calhoun had warned him off over-training but Reid felt this might be a good time to get on a treadmill to nowhere.

Three minutes later, Kennedy was back with arms full of small containers.

"Where did you get those?"

"Carson in 4C. Such a sweetheart! He opened up his spice rack to me so I think we have everything we need." She dumped her haul on the counter, and he winced at the mess. "Prepare to be astonished, roomie!"

How had he thought inviting Kennedy and her great rack and tight yoga pants into his home was a good idea? After a week of hardly seeing her, he had assumed: *I can do this*. But now after ten minutes in her effervescent presence, he was wondering if he'd made a mistake. Neither was she doing anything out of the ordinary. Just being herself.

"How about some music to cook by?" She opened the music app on her phone and soon she was playing—

"'The Rockford Files'?" He looked at Bucky who had started at the discordant sounds of the electric guitar. "That's your cooking music?"

"Hell, yeah! Seventies TV themes are my jam." She flashed him a smile and shimmied her way along the counter. "I had such a crush on James Garner when I was a kid, especially as Jim Rockford. He was always sleeping with the wrong women and getting knocked about by jealous husbands. I wanted to save him."

"You're kind of weird, you know that?"

"Roomie, we are *all* weird." She picked up the mutilated sweet potato. "I hope you're a better hockey player than a prep chef."

"Yeah, I won't be giving up my day job."

"Right—oh, hold on, this is my favorite riff." She went a little loco on the air guitar, pulling an adorable face and nah-nahing along. Then she winked at him and returned to her task of slicing the chicken.

Cooking should be a lust-neutral project. Reid didn't usually get any particular pleasure out of it. Kennedy obviously did, but then she got pleasure out of everything. And Reid got pleasure out of her.

The gym beckoned. It would be better for his mental health. His dick health.

Instead he asked, "How can I help?"

"Dice this pepper. Oh!"

"What?"

"I just noticed these." Tentatively, as if they were a gift, she touched the three mugs he had removed from the cupboard that was too tall for her, and placed on the counter. "You left these here for me?"

"Oui. You need your coffee, don't you?"

"I do. Thanks, that was kind of you." The softness on her face at this one small thing made his heart leap like Bucky when he spotted a squirrel at the park. She uncapped one of Bast's beers. "You sure you don't want one? I still think it's odd that he brought it, knowing you won't drink it."

"All part of his evil plan. He's a devil in disguise."

"Cute. I'm guessing he got all the personality in your family." She took a drink of her beer and he looked away so he wouldn't add a shot of her slender throat to his fantasy list.

"Yeah, that's Bast. Mr. Personality." He didn't want to talk about his brother, so he changed the subject. "Did you grow up in Chicago?"

"No, in a small town in Indiana, just outside of South Bend."

"But your grandmother's here?"

"Yeah. She's pretty excited that I know you. The mere mention of your name sent her into a Reid-gasm."

Not an image he relished. "Tell me about her."

She gave him an odd look, and maybe it was an odd request. Mostly he just wanted to hear her speak. He hadn't expected he would enjoy that. He didn't enjoy people as a rule, so no one was more surprised than him.

So she talked and he listened, and then he ate the hottest curry he'd ever experienced, and took it like a champion because that's what he aspired to be.

14

THE NEXT MORNING Reid was up at five for a run, Bucky at his heels, as he stumbled toward the kitchen to start the coffee. Caffeine was his one vice during the season. His only vice.

But he was steadily working another one into his routine: fantasizing about his roommate. The curry she'd made last night (*only 400 calories per serving, roomie!*) was hot and spicy, and he'd headed to the gym straight after so he could sweat it—and her—out of his system. By the time he returned, she had gone to bed, having left a note to say Bucky had already been taken out.

Reid took him out for another walk because the little con artist gave him the eye.

Now he was up early, congratulating himself on getting six hours sleep. Sure, he'd only woken up three times.

Jerked off twice.

Dreamed about Mrs. Potato Head who insisted he call her Ms. *Sweet* Potato Head.

Woke up with the theme from *The Rockford Files* on a loop in his head.

Damn dog better be worth it.

Probably not, he decided, because look the fuck here, if it wasn't his roommate up before him, hanging in the kitchen with headphones on as she mixed something in a bowl. This should not have been a big deal except she wore a tank top and white panties.

Skimpy.

White.

Panties.

His dick jumped to life, like Bucky sensing his next meal.

He moved into her sightline to let her know he was there, when really it would have been better if he'd stealth-moded his way out of there. That way he wouldn't have seen the subtle sway of her breasts as she faced him, the clearly hard nipples that seemed to point at him in accusation.

Can't look. Can't touch. Can't taste.

These tits are not for you, dickhead.

In the split second as she turned and before she reacted to his presence, he caught sight of that dark patch of hair beneath the almost translucent white fabric, that triangle that hid nothing and tempted him to dream of falling to his knees and placing his mouth right there.

"Oh, sorry, I thought you were still asleep." She waved over her body, almost an apology that only made it worse because now he was even more aware of those curves. The dips and swells, the places he wanted to visit with his tongue. "I only meant to nip out of my room for a second to whip up some blueberry muffins."

Nip. Every word was loaded.

In the half-shadow of the under-cabinet lighting he noticed something else. Scar tissue on the side of her torso, in the sliver of revealed skin between her tank and her panties.

Frustration pierced his chest, barreling through his veins. Dressed in loose running pants and a long-sleeved tee, he was covered up and following the rules. The least she could do was treat him as the stranger he was.

"It's ..." *Fine*, he wanted to say. *This is your home. Dress as much or as little as you please.*

But it wasn't fine. Not when he had weeks and months of sexual frustration to face. It was only the second week of November, far too early in the season to be confronted with this threat to his balance.

"It would be better if you assumed I'm always about to walk into the room."

"Okay, that sounds scary." She giggled and placed the mixing bowl on the counter. "Reid might be here any second. Reid's turning the corner. *Reid's ... almost ... here!*" She raised both her hands to her cheeks as fists and gave a mock, soundless scream.

"Or do whatever you want," he muttered and walked out the door, grabbing Bucky's leash as he went. The jangle was enough to bring him to attention.

"Reid!"

He was heading to the stairwell when she called his name again. Turning, he found her approaching in her winter coat (open, so *covering nothing*), but still in her bare feet.

Concern reared in his chest. "You'll catch a cold."

"Hey, don't walk away when we're having a discussion."

"We weren't having a discussion. I was telling you a rule of the house and you decided it was a joke."

She bit her lip. "I did. I'm sorry about that. I was up early because Bucky peed in the hallway outside my room—"

"What?" He peered down at Bucky who was giving his trademark look of innocence. "I thought he was getting better."

"He is. He does it more when you're away so a definite improvement. I cleaned it up—not a big deal—and then I was awake so I thought I'd start baking. I really wasn't thinking about how I looked and when you called me on it, I probably projected some of my subconscious annoyance at cleaning up after your puppy on you. Also, I have a tendency to push back at authority."

That was a very mature response, versus his very immature, can't-control-his-dick one. All he could do was mutter, "I'm not an authority."

"You are. This is your place. Your space. Your rules. And I should respect that, especially given your particular situation right now."

The no-sex situation. He should have kept that to himself, but now it was here between them like the lust-crazed elephant in the room. He inhaled a deep breath, trying to fill lungs that would rather refuse the air.

"I want you to be comfortable enough to feel at home. I shouldn't ask you to change your habits for me, especially when it's just you being ... you. And especially when you're being amazing cleaning up after this rogue here." He shot Bucky another admonishing look. This time he had the decency to appear shamefaced. "It's my responsibility to be a grown adult and not leer at my roommate. I shouldn't have asked."

She rushed forward and placed a hand on his bicep. The warmth of that touch, the thrill of it, flooded his entire body with awareness. Of him, of her, of what was barely covered by that winter coat.

Of what it might be like to back her up against the wall and lay his mouth on her gorgeous tits.

"No, of course you should have asked. This is your home and I'm a guest. I need to be more considerate of your feelings. Forgive me."

"There's nothing to forgive. This is *your* home now." He placed his hand over hers, trapping it against his chest. It was meant only to acknowledge her apology but the heat of her seeped into him.

It might have been his imagination, but Reid could have sworn her eyes misted over before she quickly regrouped.

"Huh, maybe you're one of the good ones, Reid."

"Don't let it get out. I have a rep to maintain."

She reached up on tip toes and kissed his cheek. *Oh, Christ.* "Your secret's safe with me."

"I should get going." *Before I tear those panties off, and drive into your wet heat, deep and true.* "Come on, Buck. Let's talk about the right and wrong places to pee."

His naughty little pup wagged his tail.

Another fifteen minutes added to the run should do it. And if it didn't, Reid would add another thirty.

"DURAND, MY OFFICE, NOW."

Reid looked up, only to see Coach Calhoun's back leaving the locker room. He ran through the recent practice in his head. He'd acquitted himself well, might even have made a couple of the guys look like idiots, then spent extra time completing drills solo after everyone had come off the ice.

"What've you done, Duracell?" Theo Kershaw grinned the smile that launched a thousand Insta comments.

"Duracell?"

"Yeah, you're like the Energizer buddy out there, but Duracell works better because of your name. Lots of energy to work off."

"Needs a woman," Erik Jorgenson said as he pulled at his pads. "If you had a woman to go home to nap with, you wouldn't need to spend so much time doing extra, unnecessary drills."

Reid had a woman. Or, he had a roommate who was hotter than the hinges of hell, which for a man who went sex-free during the season, was probably one of the worst ideas in the history of bad ideas.

Skimpy. White. Panties.

So now he was reduced to extra drills and long runs and cold showers for the duration of Kennedy's stay with him. He had given her leave to treat his home as hers, and it would likely come back to bite him—or his dick—later.

He headed toward Coach's office and knocked on the door. "Coach?"

"Come in."

Coach Calhoun was a bear of a man, the kind of guy who didn't suffer fools but had figured out how to be gruff without the asshole quotient. He was quick-tempered and hard to please, but as long as you put in the work, he left you alone.

"Good work out there today, Durand."

"Thanks, Coach."

"So did you ever play center coming up?"

"For a short while. I prefer the wing because I get more chances to score."

Coach nodded thoughtfully. "A lot of guys do, but you've got a bit more going on. You're a workhorse out there. Moving around a lot, never idle, figuring out the plays so you're in the right place at the right time. That's center instinct."

Reid had enjoyed his brief time as center at college level, but Henri had encouraged—more like demanded—that he push for the switch because wingers usually scored more goals and generally didn't need to be as strong on defense. Reid had downplayed his proficiency in the center of the rink and focused on his winger attributes. His favorite players had always been the centers, though. Gretzky, St. James, DuPre.

"Thing is, I have a problem here," Coach went on when Reid didn't say anything. "We're kind of short on center talent. Jones's arm is still not in the place it needs to be and Hunt might have to take time out for ankle surgery. Bond's reliable but I need another player. I think you would work well on the front line with Foreman and Petrov."

The dynamic duo, best friends forever, pinkie swears and all that. Reid wasn't sure he wanted to be the meat in their winger sandwich.

Or maybe he wasn't sure he was good enough.

"They have a bond already and I might interfere with their dynamic. Plus I like having the opportunity to score." On the wing, that was all he needed to think about. One-track mind that ended in the net.

"Or you might make them stronger. Some of the legendary goal scorers have played center. Think Gretzy, Crosby, St. James. A guy with your work ethic is capable of filling a lot of holes for us. At practice tomorrow, I'd like to put you at center and see if it works. If it doesn't, so what. We tried."

Reid couldn't say no to that. He had no control here, and sometimes ... that was good. Sometimes it was better to have someone take charge and just put him where he needed to be. It was a small thing, but perhaps it would lead to a big thing. A bubble of excitement tickled his chest at the idea he might contribute in a way that no one had understood before. That someone might need him.

"You're the coach, Coach."

"That I am." He turned to his computer, which meant Reid was dismissed.

Heading back to the locker room, he became alert to the sound of laughter and commotion and ... barking?

Bucky!

Inside he found his dog holding court, surrounded by players who were acting as if royalty had come to visit. Kennedy sat on the bench in front of his cubby, the spot Reid had just vacated, alongside Mia with her Pom.

"Oh, there's Daddy!" Kennedy smiled and Reid's chest tightened. Bucky spotted him and bounded the short distance over to greet his master.

"Daddy?" Tate Kaminski shot him a look. "This dog and ..." He flicked a glance at Kennedy. "Is yours, Durand?"

"Oui."

Mia chimed in. "I was coming over for lunch and ran into Kennedy and Bucky ..."

No one heard the rest because the entire locker room went gaga about Bucky's name and how cute was that, etcetera. The little huckster loved the attention.

"Bucky ..." Kershaw said in a musing tone that Reid knew he was going to hate, "Which makes you Captain ... Canada?"

"Captain Canuck," Cade Burnett said. "That might work."

"Rebels. Assemble!" Kershaw called out, which jump-started a spirited conversation about which Avengers hero might work for each team member.

As he pulled his shirt on, Erik Jorgenson was refusing the Thor label on the grounds he was Swedish not fucking Norwegian—and now Reid realized that most of the guys were shirtless, and at least one of them was still in his towel from the shower.

Jorgenson crept closer to Reid's roommate. "So, Kennedy, you work at the coffee shop, right?"

Kennedy pointed at their tender. "Chocolate mint frappe!"

"That's me." Jorgenson winked, a total hambone. "Haven't seen you there lately."

"I'm full-time with this little guy." Reid could tell she was doing her best not to look at him and oddly, he was trying to do the same.

Because if he did, he might not be able to stop.

Damn this woman and her skimpy white panties.

Petrov latched that aristocratic Russian gaze onto Reid. "You have a full-time nanny for your dog, Durand?"

"Live-in, too," Foreman said, and that was all it took. Every single player gawped like goldfish learning that water was wet.

Kennedy was watching him, not jumping in to explain, recognizing that this was his territory. He shouldn't have to explain a thing to these fuckers but for some reason known only to the hockey gods, he found himself justifying why he had moved a strange (to him) and gorgeous (to everyone) woman into his apartment. Put like that, maybe it needed no explanation.

"The dog needs a lot of care." *As do I.*

Where had that come from? That wasn't Kennedy's job, yet this morning when she touched his arm and gave him a peck on the cheek, he had felt ... appreciated.

Perhaps he was a touch sensitive because of his conversation with Coach. Coach, who had said Reid had skills the team needed right now. Reid, who had never felt needed for anything.

Cade was staring at him, the gears of that sharp brain turning, rubbing the rough bristle on his chin. "But you got someone to move in. For the dog."

"I like my dog." Bucky needed him. Of *that* Reid was 100% certain.

"He's doing me a huge favor, too," Kennedy said. "I needed a place to stay so it all worked out."

"Sounds like it did," Kaminski muttered.

"Oh, not so sure about that," Foreman said so low only Reid could hear. He turned, ready to be annoyed as always with this guy.

The smart mouth Bostonian was considering him with something like pity. *Shoe's on the other foot*, that look said. Kaminski and the rest of them might think he'd lucked out having a hot, free-spirited roommate like Kennedy under his feet—and maybe under *him*—but Foreman knew better.

Reid was in trouble, and Foreman was enjoying the hell out it.

15

It usually started this way. A slight ache at the back of his skull. If he left it any longer and it moved to the front, he knew.

He was getting a migraine.

Since he was fifteen, he had suffered them, usually triggered by stress, sometimes by alcohol. It was another reason to be careful about his diet and his preparation. Anything out of the ordinary might set him on a road to debilitation. Only once had he felt so sick that he couldn't play: during the semis of the Frozen Four in college. His parents had come down from Canada, and Bastian had been there, ready to cheer him on.

That night the migraine had barreled in swiftly, too fast for him to try to head it off with medication. All he'd wanted to do was lie in a darkened room, put a blanket over his head, and pretend the world didn't exist. He had tried to push through it, getting dressed for the game, taping his stick, running through his mantras.

You are better than anyone here.

You can overcome anything they throw at you.

You deserve this.

Only when he vomited in the locker room did he realize that no amount of positivity-boosting self-talk could get him into that game.

Henri hadn't spoken to him for a month. The team made the final and two nights later, Reid was back in action and even scored a goal, though they lost in the end. His stepfather wouldn't come down for that game, too disappointed at Reid's failure the game before. Too disgusted that the boy he had trained to be champion would let "a girl's problem" fell him.

Reid would never give Henri an excuse to doubt him again. He watched his diet, was a slave to his exercise regimen, kept his entire life on an even keel so there would be no interruptions. He hadn't told the Rebels team doc or Coach Calhoun. Better to play that by ear. No one should perceive weakness in him.

But today he could feel it on the edges of his brain. He stood too quickly from the sofa, and a stab of pain slammed through his skull. He needed quiet and dark and ... his dog.

"Come on, boy," he whispered. "Time for a nap."

Bucky trotted after him and Reid dithered over leaving the door ajar in case the dog needed to get in or out. He couldn't be expected to sleep on Reid's schedule, after all.

At times like this, he wished he didn't have a roommate. Would she make noise? Would she close the door if she saw it open?

Best to give her a heads up. He walked to her room and raised a fist, his ears alert to Dolly Parton being far too nice to that Jolene chick. *Bust her up, Dolly.*

The door was yanked open abruptly.

"Hi!" As if she was surprised to see him. "Listen, about yesterday at the practice, I'm sorry if I made things awkward for you. I wasn't sure how much you'd told people about the living situation and I understand if you want to keep that private."

"It's no big deal." True, he didn't like people knowing his business but he couldn't keep Kennedy under wraps, as much as he'd like to. "They're huge gossips and would jump to conclusions anyway. As far as they're concerned we're banging six ways from Sunday on every surface in the apartment."

"Yeah, pretty crazy idea. Hot hockey player, gorgeous dog-walker, close quarters. Who'd jump to a conclusion there?" She winked, eminently amused with herself. "Happy to be your cover, roomie."

"No—I mean I'll put them straight."

"I don't care what they think, to be honest." Her eyes were bright lights, obviously enjoying the notion of fooling his teammates. "Oh, I'm sorry. You wanted to tell me something?"

"I'm going to take a nap in my room."

She nodded, confused. "Okay."

"I'll leave the door open for Bucky to come and go but I'd appreciate if you didn't make too much noise if you're walking by."

"Oh, right! Sorry, am I making too much noise now?" She moved away from the door. "Let me turn this down."

He peeked in. No efforts to make it more personal except for the watercolor still standing on the nightstand beside the potted plant. He wasn't sure why that bothered him. Did he truly want her to make the place her own?

"No, it's fine. I'm just letting you know."

She held his gaze for a moment. "What's wrong?"

"Nothing."

Pulling the door open fully, she closed the gap, her hand

immediately stretching to touch his jaw. He did everything in his power not to lean into it. He could get to like that too much.

"No, there is. You look pale."

"I have a headache, that's all. I get them sometimes so I'm going to lie down."

"What kind of headache?"

"A migraine." He should withdraw from her touch, but to be honest it was making him feel much better. "I've had them before. It's something that goes away with sleep."

"Did you take something for it?"

"I will. I just wanted to give you a heads up about the open door to my room."

"Sure. Should I wake you at a particular time? I have to head out soon, but I can call you later and make sure you don't oversleep or anything."

"Don't worry about it. Just go about your day." *But without making noise.* That was all, pretty simple.

"Got it."

ON TIP TOES, Kennedy crept past Reid's open door, then stopped to listen. A triangle of light from outside created a geometric spotlight for her to stand in and she quickly stepped outside it, not wanting to disturb him.

Why are you standing there in that triangle of light?

Oh, me? Just watching you like a creeper.

Normally she wouldn't worry about something like this. Just a migraine, after all. But Reid had appeared so pale. Migraines were debilitating for some people, and it was strange to see the usually robust rock of an athlete looking like he'd been clobbered with a hockey stick.

He was laid out on the bed, positioned on his stomach, with Bucky by his side. He looked peaceful and untroubled. And hot, of course, as in unbearably handsome.

Bucky hopped off the bed and rushed by her, as if he'd seen a mouse. So highly-strung.

"What's wrong?" A sleepy voice called out.

"Nothing. Go back to sleep."

He raised his head. "Is Bucky okay?"

"He's fine. He just ran out like he was chasing something." She backed into the shadows. "Sorry, I'll leave you alone."

"Kennedy," he murmured, his voice sleep-rusty. He patted the bed. "Come here."

"I should let you rest. Give me a shout if you need anything."

"I thought you had to go out."

She stepped inside. "Class was canceled. I'll be on hand to look after things."

His eyes fluttered closed, then opened again. "My head hurts."

"It does?" She moved forward quickly, laying her palm on his forehead. Not clammy or feverish. "More than before?"

"No, the same." He grasped her wrist. "Stay and talk to me. But not too loud."

"It would be better if you slept." But *she* might feel better if she talked to him. Make sure he wasn't delirious or unusually groggy or even nauseous. She had no idea why she felt such anxiety.

Her mom used to get migraines. Sometimes they'd be cooking together and they would strike her like a two-by-four. Kennedy had always felt so helpless, hating to see someone she loved in pain and desperate to do anything to relieve it.

She sat on the edge of the bed, though Reid still held her wrist. He moved his thumb over her pulse point and stroked. Her heartbeat reacted predictably.

"Talk to me, roomie," he murmured.

"You're sick."

"I want to hear your voice. Tell me something no one else knows about you."

What a curious request. She thought about it for a moment, digging into her repertoire. "I can recall the plot of every *Columbo* episode. Just name the actor-murderer and I remember how the deed was done. Assuming you know your *Columbo*." *Columbo* had been her dad's favorite TV show. The man had a killer Peter Falk impression.

"I remember some of them. Mr. Spock was in one, I think."

"Ooh, Leonard Nimoy! A particularly deadly episode with three murders. Dissolving suture, tire iron to the head, forced drug overdose."

"Dick Van Dyke?"

"Fake-kidnaps his nagging wife than shoots her."

"Damn, that's quite the talent. I can't think of any more *Columbo* episodes."

She was impressed he even remembered those. Not everyone was as tapped into the seventies TV oeuvre as Kennedy. Those afternoons after school, watching reruns with her dad, were among her most cherished memories. They would hang in the den while he expounded on why *Barney Miller* was the most underrated sitcom ever or how the true stars of *Starsky & Hutch* were Antonio Fargas and the car. Benjamin Clark had opinions, kind of like Reid.

"Everyone's got a hidden talent," she said, putting those memories back in their box. "What's yours?"

He frowned, or maybe it was his hurting head getting the best of him. "I'm only good at hockey."

"That's not true. You're amazing with Bucky. Your vegetable chopping skills are coming along by leaps and bounds. And no one, I mean no one, can wither like you can."

"Wither?"

"The withering look. The one that makes someone want to shrivel up and die." Really it was an incinerate-all-panties look but she couldn't say that.

"I should use that in the games. Wither the competition."

Incinerate all jock straps? It could work.

She thought of something that might resonate more. "If you were a superhero, what powers would you have?"

"Telepathy."

"Because?"

"I usually can tell what my opponents are thinking, but I'd like to know for sure. It'd give me an advantage on the ice."

Sounded awful. "I'd hate to know what other people are thinking. You'd have to be really thick-skinned and not care that someone called you a bitch because you drove too close to her side mirror or that so-and-so you thought was your friend hates you for a reason you can't fathom."

His eyebrow clearly disapproved of her weakness. "I don't care what people think of me, but I'd like to know why someone hates me. All stuff I can use."

Of course Reid would see the benefit of that. "Okay, your turn."

"What's one thing that people wouldn't believe is true about you?"

Good question, Mr. Durand. "That I have an IQ of 154."

"Smarty pants, huh?"

Not always—witness her presence in this room—but she tested well. "Hard to believe, right?"

"Why do you think people wouldn't believe that about you?"

"People take one look and make a call, don't they? My hair, the way I dress, my attitude, my jobs. Those are all ways we judge people and some people might say I'm not that smart if I'm always broke and scrounging for employment."

"There are different kinds of intelligence. The kind that gets you a well-paying job is different than the kind that has given you skills to adapt and survive. Or whatever intelligence is needed to look after animals. I don't have that. I'm trying to learn it, but it's a skillset I have to acquire rather than something innate like what you have."

What a nice thing to say. She knew she had other kinds of intelligence. She'd never considered herself book smart, but she had emotional smarts and chameleon skills, advantages not always appreciated in our money-making, beauty-obsessed world.

They stayed there for a moment, drinking each other in, and she wondered if this was a good idea. Talking with Reid, even a sick Reid, was sexy.

She wanted more. "What's your most prized possession?"

"Bucky." No hesitation. If that didn't get a girl's hormones popping, then nothing would. She could make a smart-ass comment about ownership of another creature being patriarchal or colonial, or that the Buddha thought you can only own your words or actions. But she knew what he meant. He and Bucky belonged to each other.

"What about you?"

"My independence." He maintained the stroke over her wrist, a sensuous encouragement to elaborate. It worked. She hadn't shared this much in years. "I love that I'm not tied to any one place or feel trapped in any way. I'm a one-woman show and I make my own path."

"But you have your grandmother."

"She's my closest relative, I suppose. Not by blood, but we have a close bond." She lay alongside him, leaning up on her elbow.

"If she's not a blood relative, how do you know her?"

"She was married to my grandfather."

He nodded, not questioning further, though she almost wished he had. Now that she'd opened up some, she wanted to tell him about her parents, how she missed them so much the ache still throbbed in her heart all these years later. Why she felt this constant urge to move. To keep busy.

But she shouldn't make it all about her when she was merely a guest in his home and his life. Instead she returned the conversation to him. "How long have you had these migraines?"

"On and off for years. It's not anything serious but sometimes it knocks me out. That's why I'm careful about my diet, my regimen. A lot of things can trigger them."

"I should let you sleep."

"I've lost my sleeping buddy. Stay a while."

Shifting her position, she lay her head down on the pillow, facing him. Usually when they spoke on their ships-passing moments in the kitchen, she was conscious of how much taller he was, at least a foot. Meeting him at eye-level in the intimate half-dark was more comforting than she expected.

He released her wrist, but she didn't take her hand back, not when she was this close to him. She brushed his hair from his forehead and softly stroked the side of his head.

"Does this bother you?"

"No, it's nice." His eyes flickered like butterfly wings. He must be trying to stay awake.

"Go to sleep, Reid."

Thankfully, he did.

16

KENNEDY AWOKE from a lovely dream where someone was lapping at her with a warm and wet—oh, crap! This better not be some sitcom quality deal where she found the dog licking her face.

She peeled open her eyes. Just a dream, thank God, no actual face licking. The room was dark, though a sliver of light had snuck through from the hallway, shining on the spot where Bucky would usually be. He must be off, snacking.

Her body felt lethargic, weighted, and it took her a moment to realize why.

A hand was splayed between her breasts, not favoring one or the other, just lodged in neutral cleavage territory. Reid's hand along with Reid's nose in her hair and Reid's … oh, a lot more Reid. They were spooning and the big spoon was made of stainless steel.

The little spoon turned her mouth to the pillow to muffle a moan of lust.

He was asleep, his body settled against hers, his breath soughing in and out against her neck. She turned over, gently, so as not to disturb him, only realizing now that at some point she had crawled under the covers.

She met a pair of sleepy, come-to-Mama blue eyes. Her roomie was awake.

"Hi," he said.

"Hi yourself. How do you feel?"

"A little groggy, like I'm hungover though I haven't touched a drop. Definitely better than before." His hand had remained in position, though now it was flat against her back, like it never wanted to leave. "You stayed with me."

"I had to make sure you were okay. Sorry if I came off as intrusive."

"You didn't. You have a soothing touch. I think you've missed your calling." He moved his hand from her back—and she almost moved it back, it was that comfortable—and pushed her hair from her eyes. "Sorry about before, touching you. It's been a while since I've been this close to anyone. My body can't help it." He withdrew his touch, appearing to second-guess any discussion of his seeking hand or errant erection. "I've made you uncomfortable."

"Not at all. If it helps you sleep better."

His brow furrowed. "You mean you'd cuddle up with me for sleep quality reasons?"

"I—I liked it. I guess I miss that affection. It's been a while." So much for Ms. Independence.

His hand curled around her neck and she bit back another moan."Why has it been a while?"

"It's hard to separate it from sex. Sometimes you want sex, but other times, you just want to be touched."

"And what do you want right now, Kennedy?"

So many things. But to ask was to place him in danger of crossing the lines he needed to remain for his season goals.

"It's okay. I can't expect you to—"

"Just tell me." He moved closer, his mouth mere inches away, his breath fanning her lips. "You helped soothe my head. Maybe I can return the favor."

That favor would make her body combust.

Her lips parted, her tongue darted out. It might have looked manipulative or teasing, which was not her intention. She just wanted to make out with the guy.

Instead she said something far more shocking. "To be held."

"I can do that. Come closer." No hesitation, not even enough to create an awkward pause.

Deciding for once not to second guess her instincts around Reid, she moved into the soft cage of his embrace, her head in the crook of his neck. His lips brushed her temple and her entire body trembled with pleasure.

"You okay?' His breath was a hot puff of sensation against her hair.

She moved her head slightly, angling back up to look at him. "Not sure."

"Not comfortable?"

She wouldn't say that, only she was caught between tenderness and lust, the worst place on Planet Kennedy. What had she been thinking? Maybe that holding her would be less awkward for him and his celibate self rather than how this would truly work in practice. Now she was realizing that she didn't need—or want—tenderness.

She wanted those perfect, firm, forbidding lips.

She wanted his hands on her body, his chest smashing her breasts, his cock driving inside her. But she would bargain with what was possible. Baby steps.

Tentatively, she stroked his bottom lip with her thumb. He gripped her wrist and pulled it away.

She had gone too far.

In the velvet shadows, she saw his blue eyes dim, darken, *smolder*. He raised her wrist to his lips and dropped a gentle kiss there.

It was the most erotic thing to ever happen to her.

He continued in this vein, his eyes never leaving hers, his lips exploring the soft skin at her wrist, exciting the pulse point and setting every other part of her on fire. Sensuality and tenderness in one devastating package.

"Reid." His name sounded savage on her lips, a desperate plea for him to stop or escalate. One of those two things had to happen, anything to counteract the maddening sensation of ... not enough.

Something between a groan and a growl emerged from his throat before his mouth met hers. After their conversation—so gentle, so quiet, so reasonable—she would have expected more of a tease. But not Reid. He was all in. He held her jaw and moved his lips expertly over hers.

The kiss blew up.

A complete and utter exploration, his tongue twining, seeking, undoing. It was the kind of kiss she would dream about if she dreamed of such things. She'd given up on romantic fantasies long ago. Instead, she usually took what she wanted when it came to men, skipping the build-up because she needed immediate gratification.

Attachment is the root of all suffering, so said the Buddha. Letting herself stay still, put down roots, try to mimic even for a moment what she once had with her long-gone family, was impossible. Because that's what she would be doing: faking it. Trying to reclaim a sliver of joy from the past, then worrying every moment if it could last.

Instead, she lived in the now. Took what she needed and moved on.

This kiss was more than the lead-up to something. This

was the main event. They could go no further, and even if she wanted to, she wouldn't do that to him. He had his reasons and she would respect them.

Probably shouldn't have started this, a voice said inside her head, or she insisted that was the voice's location.

She pulled back, her eyes steeling open to meet his. "That was nice," she murmured.

"Nice?" He smirked because she'd just made the understatement of the millennium.

"You're a good kisser. What do you want, a medal?"

"A medal wouldn't cut it. I want ..." He leaned in. "More."

Her entire body shuddered with bone-deep sensation. That was exactly how she felt. How she needed. It was so good to meet someone who felt the same way, even if it was a small moment of connection.

He gave it to her good, and this time, she responded with more hunger. His hand moved to her back and pulled her close, coasting down to her ass and squeezing.

Music: Making our Dreams Come True, Laverne & Shirley (in her head)

Mood: Horny

Mantra: I am here for you

This was a kiss that lingered, that teased, the ultimate foreplay. She moved in, angling for the weight of him but he maintained a rigid control. As if he had decided this would stay inside the lines.

Well, screw that.

She dipped a hand to his shoulder, needing to feel the heat of him through the fabric of his tee. Fluttering her fingertips over his collar bone, she placed the heel of her hand to his pec. Further down, a brush over a cotton-covered nipple.

Still the kiss went on, changing direction, his lips slanting and seeking more avenues to pleasure.

She rubbed against his nipple. He moaned into her mouth, and she cheered at finding a weak spot in a man so strong.

"Don't you dare, roomie," he murmured, moving his lips to her jaw.

"Dare what?"

"This goes no further." He drew back, taking her wicked hand and placing it above the comforter.

"That's enough for you?"

"It has to be."

She touched his cheek, tracing a thumb over his cheekbone. "Such a tease."

"We'll agree to differ on how true that is. No more kissing, Kennedy. But if you need to be held, I'm available for that."

Oh. He had her number. That moment of weakness in him had revealed a bigger weakness in her. She would need to be careful about that.

"I should go check on Bucky," she said.

He didn't respond, just watched her as she stole out of his room like a thief in the night.

17

REID OPENED the front door and sent Bucky in ahead of him. It wasn't as if he was lingering outside but Reid liked to be sure he was safe and warm. He hoped Kennedy was being careful, too. He would add it to the ever-growing list of things he needed to tell her.

Don't leave your shampoo in my shower. It smells of you.

Don't smile at me when I come home from practice. It makes me feel ... weird.

Don't give me that look—you know the one I mean—that tells me you're still thinking about that kiss. We both know it was a mistake.

So it was the best kind of mistake, the kind that gave you immense pleasure in the moment even if you were filled with regret later. Like pounding an opposing player you hate—enjoyable at the time though you have to sit your ass in the sin bin after.

Now all he could think of was the pillowy softness of her body. How supple her lips had felt moving against his. How she gave it her all while he was trying desperately to rein it in. How sweet she tasted, unlike anyone or anything he could recall.

Consider his diet, *all the fucking diets*, blown.

Offering to hold her when she needed it was absolute shit-levels of stupidity. As if he could separate that from her taste and touch and scent. But in that moment he'd seen Kennedy's need, the emotion she tried to cover with her independent streak.

Her most precious possession, indeed.

This morning he'd gone for a run, taking Bucky with him, and now he would share breakfast with Kennedy and they would discuss what had happened and how to ensure it didn't happen again.

The first thing he heard was Kennedy's laugh. She rarely used it around him but she did when she was on the phone, talking to her grandmother or one of her clients.

Next came a deep rumble. Someone else was here.

"No! I don't believe you!" That was Kennedy, her tone animated. "Oh, Bucky's home. Hey, boy. Did you enjoy your walk?"

"Hey, fella." Bastian. Of course.

Bucky came rushing back and hid behind Reid's legs, something Reid shouldn't enjoy because he wanted Bucky to be at ease with new people. But he didn't completely hate if his dog wasn't immediately at ease with his brother.

In the living room, Reid found his brother doing what his brother always did: ingratiating himself, just one of his many talents along with hogging the last pizza slice and whining to Mom when Reid was mean to him.

"Reid!" Bastian beamed at him, as if genuinely glad to see him. He probably was. His brother didn't have an inauthentic bone in his body.

"What are you doing here?"

"I brought over groceries. On my fucking day off, too, asshole."

So maybe he had sounded ungrateful, but it was a surprise to see him here, so comfortable with Kennedy.

Reid snuck a look at her. She was rubbing Bucky down, letting him know he was cared for. She had a tactile way about her, probably because she was in tune with her body. The yoga thing.

Don't spare a thought for her yoga-tuned body.

"I didn't expect you. Maybe text next time."

Bastian turned to Kennedy with a look of *this guy*. She smiled like they were in cahoots, Bastian's new best friend.

"I need to wash my hands." Reid headed to the bathroom and shut the door, aiming for calm.

He and his brother were so different, night and day. Anyone would think that Bastian, the biological son of Henri Durand, the ball-busting enforcer of the NHL would be the asshole, but not so. Bastian was sunshine, not like his father at all. Reid was more like Henri—uncompromising, gruff, rude. It was weird that he was so similar to the old man when they didn't even share a strand of DNA.

He had never thought so until his mother pointed it out. *He might not have given you his genes but you are Henri Durand's son to the marrow.*

Reid had hated hearing that. Hated knowing he had absorbed so much of Henri's personality that now he was just as much a dick as him. The natural-born son had inherited their mother's charm along with his father's hockey talent. Reid was left with the rage and the will to prove himself.

A tricky legacy.

Reid hated himself for his jealousy of Bastian's ease with

people as well as his talent on the ice. It was absurd and unmanly.

Henri had created the cauldron of tension but he didn't mind pointing out that Reid was stupid to be envious. It was another way to maintain the competition between brothers. Reid knew exactly what his father was doing, yet even that self-awareness couldn't veer him away from his tunnel vision.

You just need to work harder, Reid. Put in the hours.

Now Kennedy was laughing and giving his brother sly looks. He had left the apartment for thirty minutes and Bastian was already ahead. Again.

"You're better than this," he said to his reflection, hating the taste of the lie on his tongue. Because he wasn't better. He was petty and small-minded.

He opened the bathroom door. Kennedy stood there, arms crossed, eyebrows drawn together.

"What's wrong with you?"

He blinked. "What's wrong with me?"

"Your brother came over to say hi, brought you groceries, and you're all 'doom and gloom, I need to wash my hands.'"

He held his hands up. "I did need to wash them. It's a cess pool out there!"

She laughed and squeezed his forearm. "I know, I know. I'm sorry. I just thought you were mad at me."

"Why would—I'm not mad at you."

"Because of yesterday afternoon. You headed out to your game right after so we didn't get a chance to discuss it." She placed a hand on his chest, leaned in, and whispered, "That kiss."

He would do anything—fucking anything—to kiss her again. But he would only be doing it to one-up Bast. Probably.

So he said the first, most stupid thing he could think of. "It was a mistake."

Her eyes remained bright and oddly amused. "Of course it was! But it was good, Reid. Really good. Just in case you were worried I didn't enjoy it."

What the—? "I wasn't worried at all. I could tell you did."

"As did you." She grinned. So infuriating. It felt like he was falling into some sort of trap here. Falling into something.

"We've established the kiss was enjoyed by both parties, but I've already said it can't happen again." He wouldn't mention the offer to hold her—not unless she brought it up. And somehow he knew she wouldn't. Kennedy had let down her walls in that second and now the bricks were being rebuilt before his eyes between her ready agreement with him that it was mistake and her blasé discussion as if it was all a grand joke.

He should be happy she was being such a cool girl about it.

"Right, you did say." She tilted her head. "So you and your brother don't get along?"

"We get along fine. We were supposed to play each other this week but he's injured." Though not enough that he couldn't just show up out of the blue. "Instead, he's here to mess with me. Typical mind games."

"Ah, got it. Well, don't worry, Bucky and I are on your side, roomie."

Roomie. Every time she said it, he felt warm. Unworthy.

He followed her out, his eyes inevitably drawn to her perky ass covered in yoga pants. On days like this he wouldn't mind if she wore some of her grandmother's tat, anything that might cover up those sweet cheeks he wanted to grip and hold and ...

"There he is! Kennedy invited me for breakfast." Bastian grinned.

"So kind of Kennedy," Reid said, and she rolled her eyes and stuck out her tongue.

"I'd make pancakes but Reid won't eat the carbs."

"Who cares about Reid? Bring 'em on!" Bast stood and stretched. "I can always do a little extra time on the treadmill later."

"Thought you were injured," Reid said archly.

Bast turned glum, and Reid regretted his poke. "Yeah, I am. Bad enough not to play but I can still get my exercise." He winked at Kennedy, who giggled. Jesus.

"Pancakes it is!" She moved toward the fridge. "Reid can eat the fruit you brought. Not even any melon in that fruit salad—well done, Durand the younger! Sit at the kitchen counter and talk to me while I cook. I get lonely in the kitchen."

"Can I help?" Bastian offered.

"No need. Make yourself a coffee in the Keurig and then prepare to be wowed by my chocolate chip beauties."

Reid pushed his brother toward one of the island stools. "I'll make your coffee. There's not enough room in the kitchen."

It was a lie but he didn't want Bastian anywhere near Kennedy. While she started whipping up an eggy batter, he made the coffee. No need to ask his brother what he liked. He would get what was given to him.

"So I want to hear all about growing up in the wilds of Quebec." Kennedy smiled at Bastian. "Was it a farm?"

"Why would you think it's a farm? What has Reid been telling you?"

"Not much. I've been trying to guess but he said you

guys had a rink so I assumed it was a farm. Or some place with tons of space."

"Not a farm," Bastian said. "But it was in a wooded area just outside of Grenville. Dad and a couple of his buddies chopped down trees and cleared a space to build a rink. It was so cool. I was three and Reid was five when we started." Bast shook his head, a fond smile touching his lips. He always got this way when their childhood came up. Nostalgic. Forgetful. "He was better than me for a while. Then I caught up but he must have improved over the summer. Getting plenty of shift time these last couple of games, bro!"

"You are?" Kennedy nudged him. "You never said that."

"Do you even know what that means?"

She quirked those luscious lips he'd explored with abandon yesterday. "It sounds like somebody likes you enough to let you play this sport you love for the big bucks. Am I right?"

"A-plus," Bast said. "So, Kennedy, tell us all about you. You're a world traveler, I hear."

"I've traveled. I will travel again."

"Favorite place?"

She gave it a moment's thought. "Halong Bay, Vietnam. Or Cinque Terre, Italy. Or maybe Santorini, Greece. Ask me again next week and I might change my mind."

"Afoot and lighthearted, take to the open road," Reid murmured.

"Healthy, free, the world before you," Kennedy finished, looking more than a little surprised. "That's one of my favorite poems."

Reid's as well. Walt Whitman had always spoken to him, especially those lines, even though he'd never gone anywhere or done much of anything. He finished the verse in his head. *The long brown path before you, leading wherever you choose.*

For a moment, he imagined she was doing the same before she shifted her gaze to take in Bast. "I'm guessing you guys travel a lot, too. In the off-season."

"Saint Reid here heads back to Canada to coach a youth group in the summers," his brother said. "I take some time for myself at a place I have on Vancouver Island. But we're going to be taking a big trip soon. Heading to Beijing in February for Team Canada."

"The Olympics? Both of you? Wow!" She shot a look a chiding look at Reid. Back to their dynamic of him, the closed-off curmudgeon and her, the free-spirited wanderer. He was actually an alternate for Team Canada, so it wasn't as big a deal as she thought.

"Giving back to the kids. Skating for your country. Well, I hope you get a chance to let off some steam, see the sights. Makes me wonder ..."

"Wonder what?" Reid asked.

"After the season is over and you're a free agent, so to speak ..."

His heart thundered in his chest. Was she suggesting they might take a trip together after the season? This talk of travel and favorite places had him yearning for something ... more. It would be amazing to see new lands with Kennedy.

She studied him through the veil of her lashes. "So how many people do you bang?"

He almost spit out his coffee. After he'd swallowed, he was still speechless.

She patted his arm. "If you're not partaking during the season, I'd imagine that's the first thing you'd do. I'm just curious if it's a one-week fling with one person or do you spread the Reid around."

Reid could feel his brother's hot stare as he put two and two together and came up with bang-a-thon.

"*Not partaking*. What the fuck am I hearing?"

"Oh, dear," Kennedy covered her mouth. "Was that a secret?"

Bast was shaking his head, his dumb mouth agape. "Are you kidding? You don't fuck anyone ... all season?"

"It helps me focus."

Except since Kennedy had come to stay, focus was a thing of the past.

Kennedy squeezed his bicep. "I'm sorry. I thought it was common knowledge, like your diet or your exercise regimen. Reid Durand, Hockey Monk!"

Bast looked shocked. It was nice that Reid still had the capacity to surprise him.

"So bro, answer the question."

"What question?"

Bast exchanged a look with Kennedy. "How many people do you bang in the post-season?"

"A couple. I don't want anyone to think it's ..."

"Special," Kennedy finished.

He nodded. "It's biological. A release. But sometimes the first time is over quickly ..."

"How disappointing ..." Kennedy pointed at him. "For the first person who encounters a post-season Reid Durand on the prowl!"

"Oh, shut up," he said, unable to stop the laugh building in his throat. This woman was trouble. "No one is shortchanged. It's just not always as satisfying as I hope. After a few months without sex, you tend to build things up and then that first time might be a letdown. So I usually try again."

"And again?" Bast said, then added a *bow-*

chicka-chick-bow.

Reid shook his head, trying to hide his smile. Sex, or discussions of it, didn't make him uncomfortable. He was just surprised that Kennedy was so forward about it. Admirably so.

Reid had grown up with a father who insisted that nothing should get in the way of his ambition to be the best, including women. For Henri, sex was a biological function rather than an opportunity for intimacy. Until you proved yourself, connection wasn't an option. It only led to weakness. Work first, play later.

Henri had married Reid's mom on the downside of his career when he realized he needed to do more to extend his legacy. Creating a family was one way to do that. Reid had often wondered why he'd chosen a woman who already had a toddler, the result of a one-night stand. Perhaps he wanted to be sure she could produce a child. Not a charitable viewpoint, but Reid understood his stepfather's psyche better than most. The man wouldn't want to risk an infertile wife.

His parents had divorced when Bast went to college, which meant his mother had held on through years of Henri being gruff, brusque, and emotionally constipated. She was happily remarried to a chef who adored her while his father was on his third wife. Conclusion: men like Henri didn't make women happy.

Men like Reid, either.

"You know Henri's gonna freak about this," Bast said, reading Reid's mind.

"Not if you don't tell him." Reid held his brother's gaze until he shook his head and addressed his roommate.

"So what about you, Kennedy?" Bast asked. "Have you left broken hearts in all these places you've visited?"

"Oh yeah. That's me," she said with a laugh he might

have considered strained if he examined it closely. “Love ’em and leave ’em Kennedy.”

Reid wondered, especially when her eyes turned a little sad. “That was too personal. Bast is very sorry.” He glared at his brother who merely shrugged.

“Not at all! After all I’ve done poking at you? Turnabout’s fair play, boys. Okay, pancakes are up and Reid, you will eat at least one!”

He ate five—because it was one more than Bast.

18

Kennedy couldn't tell if Reid liked his brother. There was definitely love there, but it was mixed up with a ton of other emotions she tried to label throughout breakfast.

Bastian was Reid's opposite: lightness, charm, a chatterbox, and easy with his smiles. They shared the same mother and even though Bastian (*call me Bast, Kennedy!*) referred to Henri Durand as "our dad," Kennedy sensed her roomie's unease with the dynamics. With both Bastian and his stepfather.

About ten minutes after the last pancake slid down Bastian's gullet, he left with a slap on the back for his brother, a (double) cheek-kiss for Kennedy, and a friendly rub of Bucky. Quite the glad-hander.

As Reid started on the dishes—and he just jumped right in without prompting, what a good roommate—she got straight to the point. "So are you close with your brother? I couldn't really tell."

"We are. It's complicated."

She would do anything to have even the chance of a complicated relationship with her family. Sometimes the pain in missing her parents was almost unbearable. "In what way?"

"Henri would prefer we didn't get along. He's always wanted us to be competitive. He thought it would make us stronger players, but Bast doesn't need that kind of push. He's already too good."

"And you? Are you good?"

"I'm a grinder. I work hard to be good. Henri used to think that toughening us up, putting us in contention for his approval, would push us to greatness. He's a stick-not-a-carrot kind of coach."

"But as a father, doesn't he want you to get along?"

Reid's cynical smile broke her heart a little. "If we get along too well, it means we might not strive to better each other. Henri is a coach first, a father second."

"Not digging Henri much."

His expression was mildly amused. No doubt he'd heard this criticism before. "He just has high standards. It's okay, I want to be the best. I've always trusted him to be tough on me for the right reasons."

"Sounds like you're tougher on yourself than your stepfather is. I'm sorry about my blabbing, by the way. I really thought your brother knew."

"It's not something I talk about. And Bastian wouldn't understand. Most pro athletes are fucking anything on two legs."

That's what she thought, so Reid's approach fascinated her. He really shouldn't be so hard on himself.

When he could be hard on her. Zing!

"Maybe you shouldn't expect such perfection all the time."

Plates stowed in the dishwasher, he flipped and leaned against the counter with his arms folded. The move made his guns bulge even more indecently. She had touched one bicep earlier, in a roommate-friendly kind of way.

Big mistake. Huge.

"Isn't yoga all about achieving some sort of perfect state?"

"Not quite. It's more about fostering harmony in mind and body. One of the reasons I love it is that it helps me to eliminate all those negative thoughts, even if it's just for an hour. For that hour, I only wallow in peace instead of self-pity." And then for the other hours in the day she found more ways to keep the negativity at bay. A busy little bee had no time for navel-gazing.

"You should try it." It had to be better than the strategy he was employing now.

Thoughts chased each other across his face for a second. Rivers ran deep with this man, and she loved watching him think. "Peace is ... I don't think I've ever known it. And I don't think it's attainable on a yoga mat."

"Don't knock it until you've tried it. It has to be better than shredding the skin off your dick on a daily basis."

He gave an eye roll but then two seconds later, the oddest thing happened: Reid's climb-aboard-me shoulders started to shake.

"Oh my God, Reid!" She grasped his arm. The bicep was calling and this was the perfect excuse. "Are you actually laughing at something I said? Let me capture this moment." She closed her eyes, and though ostensibly she was joking, she found herself snapping a mental image and storing it away.

"It wasn't even that funny," he muttered.

"Is this one of those can't cry for laughing situations?"

"Sure it is, Coffee Shop Girl."

"Really? Two can play at that game, Hot Jerk."

"You said that in the lake! I thought I was hearing things." He cocked his head, which was so damn sexy. "You think I'm hot?"

"It's a modifying word, a what do you call it? Adjective!" She squeezed his arm, not wanting to let go of all that heat and because, yes, the man was smokin'. "Meaning that it modifies, and in this case, emphasizes the primary word in the compound phrase which is jerk. Did you hear that part?"

"Just heard hot." He bent down, bringing him close enough to kiss again.

Could she push him? *Should she?* "I don't mind admitting it. In fact, I think you're *really* hot and when we kissed yesterday, you knew that. Anyway, it doesn't matter. I'll continue to think you're hot, you'll continue to be mildly attracted to me, and you'll also continue be a self-denying-can't-have-sex-gotta-jerk-off-in-my-room-now idiot."

His eyes went wide. "Mildly attracted to you?"

"That's the part you zeroed in on?"

He stared at her, then after a long, heated beat, straightened and said ... nothing. Which was hot in itself and made her rush to fill the pause.

"We're healthy, reasonably attractive adults who aren't yet friends so we can't use that as an excuse. But you've got your standards and I don't want to mess with your game prep."

"Yet, you throw it out there. The notion that if I wasn't so hard on myself, we'd be going at it like bunnies."

Not having hang-ups about sex often meant she was more honest about it than people expected. She wasn't a nymphomaniac, but she had needs.

She'd seen Reid looking at her. She'd felt his lips, his tongue, his attraction wrapped in a hot, hard package. He had kissed her with both tenderness and abandon, and then threw out some Walt Whitman as if it was nothing.

Walt. Whitman.

In any other situation, with any other guy, this would be a done deal.

Now it was out there—the *knowing* about how he kissed and tasted and felt. The bullet had been released from the barrel and was hovering midair in slo-mo, waiting to be either slapped from existence like a Wonder Woman move, dodged a la Keanu in the Matrix, or embedded deep into her sensitive, receptive flesh.

She knew which option she'd rather have.

The bullet was waiting. Her body was ready.

"I admire your restraint," she said with a whole lot of fucking restraint.

"It hasn't occurred to you I might not be all that into you."

"Not in the slightest."

He laughed, a deep boom of a sound that shocked both her and Bucky, who ran around in a tight circle and started barking.

Reid pointed at him. "Quiet, you."

Bucky stopped immediately. He was definitely improving in his relations with humans.

Reid squatted and petted his friend, getting a face lick in return. Looking up, he snagged Kennedy with another shocker of a grin. Someone else was also improving in his relations with humans.

She could be in big ass trouble here.

"It must be great to go through life with such confidence," he said. "I'm envious."

"I'm not confident about everything. Neither am I blind.

It's okay that you can't act on this but there's no need to pretend there's nothing happening here, oui?"

"Oui?"

"What do I have to do make you speak hot, dirty French to me, roomie?"

As he drew up from his crouch, his gaze seemed to coast up her body, incinerating her skin inch by inch. He inclined his head so his eyes were close to hers. All that deep, sink-into-sex blue.

"D'accord, vous gagnez."

Her breath caught. "What does that mean?"

"It means, you win. When the season ends, I'll break my fast with you."

Oh, wow. Break my fast. That was a thigh-clenching statement if ever she'd heard one. The thought of being on the receiving end of Reid's first time in forever ...

Except that would be months away and she wasn't a slow burn kind of girl. Hit it fast, early and maybe often, then move on. That was her MO. She wouldn't be waiting around for Reid Durand to grace her with the favor of his penis.

"As attractive as that offer is, I don't think it'll work. One, it's unlikely I'll be here and two, even if I was, it'd be too weird."

"Why?"

"Because we'll either be friends or enemies by then and I never sleep with either, or I'll probably have slept with someone you know in the meantime, so it would be awkward for you and this other person. I could never do that to you."

His brow darkened. "What other person?"

"Maybe someone on the team or—"

"My brother?" A thunderous expression set his mouth hard.

It hadn't occurred to her, but it had obviously occurred to him. *Tres interessant.*

"Now you mention it, he is pretty cute. Cut-rate Durand but if I can't have the prime beef, I'll go for the next best thing." *Evil, Kennedy Clark, so evil.* "And then, you and me? Off zee table, miss-your."

She patted his arm with all the condescension one could put into it and took a little final enjoyment of that hard bicep. "But like I said, probably won't happen. I've got to go to work. See you later!"

19

REID'S PHONE BUZZED.

RIGHT WING MASSHOLE

You busy?

He couldn't help the expletive.

"What's wrong?" Kennedy pressed pause on the serial killer documentary they were watching on Netflix. Well, Kennedy was watching it. Reid was employing his excellent peripheral vision skills, drinking in her pink-varnished toes and slim ankles and forcing his brain to take it no further.

He had tried being rude.

He had tried being distant.

He had tried kissing her hot, sweet mouth.

Now he was going with the age-old let's-pretend-this-is-normal strategy. So far, it was working.

Just kidding. It was so not working. Two weeks of Kennedy in his space and he was a wreck. Bast had been sending texts every ten minutes asking after his dick, usually followed by gifs of eggplant explosions. Someone had gone to the trouble of creating that shit. Now this fresh hell.

"Foreman is texting me." Reid had been in Chicago for three months. Had practiced and played with Foreman. Had roomed with him for away games. Had been on the receiving end of his fist. This was the first time the man had sent him a text.

"You mean Mia's Foreman?"

Mia's Foreman. That sounded about right. He texted back:

Probably.

The phone rang. Fuck. The asshole had done the sneaky check-in with that text and now Reid had no choice but to answer. He hit the accept call button though acceptance was far from his mind.

"Yeah?"

"Some of the guys are coming over in thirty minutes or so. Thought I'd extend an invite."

"Why?"

Foreman muttered something unintelligible, seemed to confer with someone else—a female someone else—then, "Because I'm a nice guy."

"I've already eaten."

"Good because I'm not offering food. Though Kershaw and Jorgenson usually order pizza because they're fucking garbage cans."

At Reid's snort, Foreman pounced. "Have I amused the unamusable Reid Durand?"

"Don't get carried away." He caught Kennedy's eye. She had paused the cheerleader-cannibal manual, and was now leaning on her palm, smiling like one of her favorite serial killers.

"I would but my dog sitter is busy tonight." Kennedy had something on, *another* side gig at a community college with an art class.

"Bring the dog," Foreman said. "I'd like to see him again. I miss my own."

Boxed in and no way out. "Thirty minutes, you said?"

"Yup. I'll text the address." Then he hung up before Reid could. Fuck-*er*.

Kennedy fluttered her eyelashes. "You got a play date with your buddies?"

"It wasn't clear what exactly would be happening, but yeah, I have a play date."

"Aw! And you're bringing Bucky." Bucky was currently cowering at the side of the sofa because he was scared of the Netflix *ta-dum* sound, though it had reverberated through the apartment thirty minutes ago. What a dummy.

Kennedy leaned down and petted him, revealing a whisper of lace of her underwear.

Jesus. Maybe anywhere but here would be a good place to be.

"You should bring the raspberry brownies. I made two batches and I'm going to bring the other one to Edie."

Another thing that bugged him—the constant baking.

"The guys won't thank you."

"I don't need thanks." She studied him closely. "So tell me your strategy."

"My strategy?"

"You don't seem to be too friendly with your teammates."

"I'm new."

"But you're not making an effort either. Mia says you're a dick, but a dick with purpose. So what's the strategy?"

What the hell was a dick with purpose? "It's easier to keep my distance."

"Really? In a team sport?"

"I'm in competition with most of the NHL, even the people on my own team. Take Foreman. He and I are both on the right-wing, so for each game, Coach has to choose one of us to play the first line or demote us to the next line. He's been switching us off, but every minute I'm out there I have to prove that he made the right call. That his faith in me is justified. Only now I might be playing a different position."

"Oh, yeah?"

"Coach thinks I might work better as a center. On the same line as Foreman and Petrov. Mia's brother."

"Ooh, the hot Russian. I've seen photos of him. All those tattoos. So playing together ... you might complement them in some way. Be stronger together than apart." Her grin was what was known as the shit-eating variety. She probably thought that was an epically profound thing to say.

"We're not required to all get along, kumbaya and all that hippie shit."

"Ha, I bet someone brings out a guitar tonight!"

Mon Dieu, he hoped not. "It's just playing cards or video games. Not a big deal."

She grinned and leaned in, planting a soft kiss on his cheek. "I've got to get ready for work myself. Have fun and don't forget the brownies!"

He didn't watch her perfect sweetheart-shaped ass leave the room. He wasn't that much of a masochist.

~

"CAPTAIN CANUCK!"

Theo Kershaw stood at the open door to Foreman's apartment, his gleaming eyes on the tray of brownies. Reid had also brought a six-pack. He might not drink during the season but it would be churlish not to bring beer to a gathering.

Kershaw took the brownies. "Nice. Good to see you—hey, and the team mascot, too!" He reached down and rubbed Bucky's head. "I was worried you were going to keep up this asshole act all season."

"Asshole act?"

The defenseman grinned. "No one is that bad-tempered all the time. Unless you're not getting laid. I went through a spell of that after I knocked up my girl and we were dancing around the sex thing and I was pretty hacked off for about six weeks until she realized she couldn't resist me. Pregnant women are exceptionally horny, did you know that?"

He did now.

Kershaw talked a lot in the locker room, on the plane out, at the team lunches and dinners, on the plane back, on the bench, just ... a lot. So Reid wasn't really surprised to be confronted with the Michigan Motormouth in rare form on a night in with the boys.

"So is that the case then?" Kershaw threw out over his shoulder as he walked ahead. "You're not getting laid?"

"It's not responsible for my mood, but yeah, I don't fuck anyone during the season."

The entire room went quiet.

He had uttered that gem right as he walked into Foreman's living room, filling a convenient lull in the conversation.

"Durand," Foreman said from a position in an armchair near the fireplace. "Nice entrance."

Bond, Jorgenson, Hunt, Burnett, and Kaminski made up the rest of the party. Bucky scurried into the center of the room.

"He's kind of shy," Reid said about his dog, who proceeded to make a liar of him as he happily sniffed each of the players' legs in turn. "Usually."

"You serious?" Theo asked, still hung up on Reid's announcement. "You don't have sex during the season? At all?"

"I find it helps me to focus more." If he had a penny for every time he said that …

"On your balls of blue," Jorgenson said, which made everyone laugh.

Foreman stood and moved toward them, taking the beer from Reid's hands. "This your contribution?"

"Sure, for the crew. I'd like some water."

"You don't drink either?" Kershaw was acting like an alien had crash-landed in the middle of Foreman's living room.

Foreman placed a hand on Reid's shoulder and gave a gentle push. "Come on into the kitchen."

With a quick glance to check that Bucky was okay, Reid followed Foreman, who grabbed a glass, filled it from a Brita pitcher in the fridge, and handed it off.

"How pissed are you that you're here?"

"I'm not pissed. I needed to get out of the house anyway."

Cue the Masshole smirk. "How's the roommate situation?"

"Fine. It's—" *Kumbay-fucking-nope.* "It's good to have someone there for Bucky."

"But for you, maybe not. With your no-sex-during-the-season rule."

"It's not that big of a deal."

Foreman put Reid's six-pack into the fridge and withdrew a bottle of a different beer. "Seems sort of masochistic. Cute girl running around your apartment."

"Can only make me stronger." Reid found himself smiling for the first time since this whole business had started. He was being ludicrous, acting as if the challenge of Kennedy in his living space was welcome. Would only benefit his regimen. Who was he kidding? Living with Kennedy was torture and he had only himself to blame.

"Heard your brother's on IR, so the clash of the century will be postponed until next time."

"Yeah, my father canceled his trip." Shit, he hadn't meant to say that. That was exactly the kind of thing Foreman would use.

"Oh yeah?"

"He likes to see us push each other." Like a Roman emperor viewing the gladiators. It wasn't as much fun with only one of them against strangers. "He doesn't travel much anymore. It has to be worth his while."

Foreman sipped from his beer, remained silent. But he looked like he wanted to weigh in so Reid elected to do something he would normally not do: ask a question.

"Have you met Henri?"

"He did a brief coaching stint at the Royals." The Royals was based in Montreal, Foreman's previous outfit before he joined the Rebels. "Not a great one for positive encouragement, to be honest."

"He likes things a certain way so coaching within the regulations of the league was never going to work for him."

"Means he can devote all his time to you and your brother." Foreman took another drag of his beer. "What does he think of you trying things out at center?"

Reid hadn't told him. It had only been a week since Coach Calhoun suggested it and they were still playing around with the idea in practice. Reid had felt good out there, like he had a renewed sense of purpose that didn't have anything to do with what Henri wanted.

When he didn't comment, Foreman gave a slight eyebrow raise to indicate he understood. Mr. Sensitivity.

"More pressure on you now that you're in the same city as Durand Junior, I imagine."

"Not because of Henri."

"Oh, yeah, who needs a taskmaster like that when you've got yourself wielding the whip?"

"Something wrong with pushing myself hard?"

Foreman shook his head. "Nah, as long as you don't overdo it. You have enough to contend with. Not sure adding an attractive woman you can't bang to the mix is a good strategy."

"She's not *that* attractive."

"Fuck yeah, she is." Theo walked in, put the brownies down on the counter, and started yanking open drawers. "We're talking about Kennedy, I assume?"

"No," Reid said at the same time Cal said, "Yes."

Kershaw removed a steak knife from a block and eyed Reid. "So how does that work?"

"How does what work?"

"Are you turning the thermostat down?"

Reid exchanged a puzzled glance with Foreman, who elected to take another sip of his beer and leave Reid to ponder the hard questions.

"What the fuck are you talking about, Kershaw?"

"The best way to ensure you don't have a half-dressed woman running around your living area, tempting you into a sexual frenzy, is to turn the thermostat down a couple of degrees, keep the place chilly, and then she has to layer up. Simple!" He snapped his fingers.

Foreman gestured toward Kershaw with his beer bottle and spoke to Reid. "There's a certain method to that madness."

Jorgenson came in. "What have I missed? Wait, there are brownies?"

"We're talking about Kennedy," Theo said as he handed a square of Kennedy's brownie to Erik. No plate or anything. Heathens. "Specifically about how to keep Reid out of her panties."

"Oh, good. That means you and she are not ..." Erik trailed off as he stuffed his face with a big slab of brownie. Some of the crumbs fell to the floor, making Reid itchy.

"Sounds like she's a free agent, Jorgenson," Tate Kaminski said, the latest entrant to this annoying conversation, "so go for it."

Erik nodded while he chewed. "That's what I thought. I texted her this week to ask her about getting a goat."

"A goat?" Reid spluttered. Better that than do what he really wanted: punch Jorgenson in the throat. As for Kaminski with his free agent observation? Number two on Reid's throat-punching list.

"I figure she'd have some advice about animals. Women really dig baby goats—it's big on social media—so I'm wondering if that would be better than a dog. Then I could get Kennedy in to look after it."

"She's taken," Reid bit out. When Cal gave him a weird look, he added, "She has a full-time job with *my* dog."

"She already texted back that she wasn't sure a goat was a good idea because you can't keep them in an apartment.

But she said she'd meet me for coffee to talk about it. She wants to go to her old place of work with a hot hockey player to show them she's doing just fine after they fired her."

"Good work, Jorgenson." Kaminski offered the high-five, and Reid came *this* close to intercepting it. *Not good work, Jorgenson. Bad work.*

That conversation with Kennedy a few days ago came to mind: he'd offered to, well, fuck her when the season was over and she said it probably wouldn't work. Because she might have already slept with someone he knew. Like Bast. Or a Rebels teammate.

And why wasn't she asking Reid to hit the coffee shop for her show-and-tell? He went there every day!

"Still doesn't solve Durand's problem," Theo said. "He has a hot woman in his apartment exactly at the time he doesn't need a hot woman in his apartment."

"I do need her." Before he could get pissed at Foreman for another knowing look, he added, "*for my dog*. What I don't need is to make my apartment into fucking Antarctica just so she can overdress and keep me from going into a blue ball toxic shock whenever she walks around the place she's living in. We've already discussed it."

"So it *is* a problem!" Kershaw pointed dramatically and searched the faces of the rest of the crew for consensus.

Jesus. There was a reason he didn't do this buddy-buddy shit. All the conversations devolved into this nonsense. Yet at the same time, there was something comforting about knowing these guys understood what he was facing.

"It's ... sort of a problem. But I'm working on making it not a problem."

"Twice a day in the shower," Tate chimed in.

Theo nodded. "Hell, when I was keeping little Theo on the down low after I knocked up Ellie it was more like three."

"Three times a day? And now? You'd better not be doing it at work, Kershaw," Cal said. "I don't need that kind of imagery when I come out of practice."

"Now I'm going to wonder what Theo's up to if he takes too long in the hotel bathroom," Erik said.

"Moisturizing." Theo raised his eyebrows comically. "That's what I'm doing."

"How are you working on it not being a problem?" Cal asked Reid.

"Not three times a day in the shower." Which everyone found hilarious.

Erik wiped his mouth. "These brownies are fucking amazing."

"My roommate made them."

Kaminski chuckled. "She bakes as well? Durand, you are fucked."

Burnett put his head around the door of the kitchen. "Hey, ya kickers, quit the jerk-off talk and come watch me beat Bond into submission in Battlefront 2."

"Heh, beat Bond into submission," Theo said. "Good one, Alamo. Add that to the collection."

"Jerkin' the gherkin," Kaminski said.

"Cruising for an oozing," Theo offered.

"Five knuckle shuffle." Kaminski again.

Reid caught Foreman's eye, and it was all either of them could do not to laugh.

"Painting the ceiling," Jorgenson said as they headed into the living room, to which Theo went as wide-eyed as a child confronted with a giant ice cream cone.

“Fish! Something you need to tell me about your super powerful joystick?”

Foreman grinned. “Aren’t you glad you stopped by, Durand?”

“Thrilled.”

He was only half-lying.

20

KENNEDY TOOK a break from researching tattoo parlors for Edie—she would automatically find all of them wanting—and checked the flights to Bangkok for New Year's Day. She had the money, she knew she wanted to be on the road soon, and Edie was very clear that Kennedy should not be putting her life on hold for an old lady.

The last few years had kept her busy. If she couldn't find work teaching yoga, it was relatively easy to pick up jobs for cash under the table, usually in the ex-pat communities of Europe and Asia. As lifestyles went, it wasn't for everyone. She kept a bank account in the US, her passport up to date, but otherwise no roots, no reason to stay still. Her next gig would be a six-month stint teaching English, extendible for a year, as soon as the work visa was granted.

Edie wanted to see her settled—with someone special—but it didn't have to be near her. If Kennedy was going to stay put anywhere, it would be here because Edie was her touchstone. But Chicago was expensive and staying put for longer than a few months required she do more tending to her life. Get health insurance and a place to live and a Netflix subscription. Adulting.

Someone knocked at the door.

Bucky jumped to his feet and ran to it, his tail wagging. Usually that meant one thing: Daddy was home. But he couldn't be. He would be gone for at least another day on an away game trip to New York.

She shut the laptop and headed to the door. Bastian stood there with a Whole Food's bag under his arm.

"Hi ho, stranger! Figured I'd better knock seeing as you're living here now." He walked by her, put the bag on the kitchen counter, and leaned against it, so proud of his magic trick.

"Reid's not here."

"I know that." He grinned. "I'm here to see you. The groceries are my toll."

"To see me? Why?"

"You seem like a cool person and I like cool people."

She took a glance inside the shopping bag. "Fancy gelato? That's not for your brother. He'd have a fit if he saw that in his freezer."

"He won't see it if it's all gone by the time he gets home."

"You *are* a devil in disguise—those are Reid's words, not mine—but I'll allow it." She headed to the cupboard and brought out a couple of bowls.

"So how's living with Brother Reid going?"

"Not bad."

Bastian eyed her as she unlidded the tub of gelato. Salted caramel, some fancy brand.

"It's weird that he'd put himself through this. The temptation." He waved his hands dramatically.

"Don't worry. He's doing just fine resisting me."

"And how are *you* doing?"

Laughing, she grabbed a couple of spoons and handed one off. "Your brother is hot and moody which is an irresistible combination to my inner teen. Not so attractive to the adult me."

Bastian raised the Durand eyebrow and added a smile, probably because she was obviously lying her well-toned ass off. She saw what Reid might be like if he went easier on himself.

"Sure he's moody, but he seems to be less so since you and Bucky moved in. It's nice to have him around, too."

"So this is the first time you've lived in the same city in how long?"

"Since Reid went to college. I was sixteen when he left. I thought about going to the same school but Dad figured it made more sense to keep our trajectories separate. That way we wouldn't be compared as much until we both got drafted."

"I don't know much about hockey but Reid said you're incredibly talented. One of the best."

Bastian preened a little. "It's always come easier for me. But Reid's no slouch. He spent a couple of years in the AHL, which is like minors hockey and really had to prove himself to move up. He works harder than anyone in the league."

"I know. Turning into a dull boy." Though that wasn't true. No matter how much he refused to rise to her teasing, Reid could never be accused of dullness. "Your dad wanted to raise a couple of champions. He sounds tough."

"Yeah, he was pretty hard on Reid. I mean, he was tough on both of us but Reid got the worst of it."

She hated to pry but this seemed important. "Like violent?"

"No, nothing like that. Listen, I'm just telling you this so you can be kind to him."

Her mouth dropped open. "I'm not—hey, do you think I'm unkind?"

"No, not at all. I'm not explaining well. Reid's more sensitive than he gets credit for. He internalizes a lot." A brief flash of something crossed his face, a memory that might be painful. "You're here, so he's obviously surrounding himself with good people and good doggos. Or one good person, one good dog. And that might make him realize that he doesn't have to be such a loner."

"What about you? You're here for him." Oh, now she got it. "Is this why you bring over food he doesn't want, so he'll be kinder to himself? He thinks you're playing mind games."

Bast's face went soft. "I know. But that's not it at all. I just want him to realize that it's okay to stray outside the lines and eat a fucking bowl of ice cream."

Acts of service to demonstrate fraternal love. As sweet as the ice cream on her spoon. "You could tell him that."

"Nah, he'll think it's some reverse psychology thing. We're not really an 'I love you, bro' type of family. Listen, I'm always here for him, but in order to get through the season, to stay sharp and competitive, Reid has to maintain a certain distance from me. I get that. He can't really go from buddy up with me to my competition on the ice. He has to go method and just be a jerk all the time."

She understood. Maybe. But it was still strange to treat his brother like the enemy even off the battlefield. This had an *Avengers: Civil War* vibe to it.

"Hmm," she hummed, taking a bite of the ice cream. It was smooth and silky on her tongue. "Is there a reason you're telling me all this other than warning me to be kind?"

Which she was! The nerve.

"Reid would never admit he needed anything, but there might come a point where it's all a bit too much."

"What exactly are you saying here?"

His lips twitched around his spoon.

"You think I should seduce him?"

"There's a thought."

Maybe Reid was right and Bast had ulterior motives that were game-related. But she considered herself a good judge of character. She actually bought his explanation that he was trying to sneakily coax his brother into adding self-care to his regimen.

Even if that involved giving her a gentle shove into his brother's bed.

"You know, this is none of your business." So what if it was pretty much all she could think about since she'd woken up in Reid's arms in Reid's bed with Reid's ...

Hot flash!

He offered the least casual shrug she'd ever witnessed. "I know. I just worry about him. I want him to be happy."

"And you think sex will make Reid happy. Have you met your brother?"

He laughed. "Yeah, you're probably right. Whatever was I thinking?"

REID WALKED out of the apartment building to find a ranting woman engaged in a heated conversation with a car. He stood at the doorway, taking it in.

"I just need you to last for six freakin' weeks! All you have to do is take me from Point A to B. Just do your job."

Predictably, the car didn't respond. She kicked the tire, and he was glad to say she knew how to do that in a way that didn't hurt her, with the side of her foot so she didn't damage her toe.

Reid looked down at Bucky, who watched with great interest.

"Let's try this again, shall we?" she said cautiously like she was talking to a small child before a spurt of spirit overtook the proceedings. "When I turn that key, you had better cooperate!"

She clambered back into the driver's seat, shut the door, and put on her seatbelt. After a moment where she seemed to be offering up a prayer, she turned the key in the ignition. There was a sad sputter followed by a muffled scream.

He walked over and knocked on the window. She rolled it down, her mouth in a sexy sulk.

"Trouble?"

"My car won't start."

"I gathered. Well, we gathered." He dropped his gaze to Bucky. "Sorry you had to see that, fella."

He had hoped to make her smile, but no go. This woman was not in a smiling mood. Today must be Roommate Freaky Friday.

"I'll give you a ride."

Her face looked like the morning sun as it snuck up over the horizon. "Oh, would you? That would be so awesome."

Two minutes later they were in his car, headed to the seniors' home where her grandmother lived.

"These heated seats are something else." She ran her fingers over the dash and the hand-stitched leather armrest in a way that had him jealous of the car.

He hauled his gaze back to the road. "You do this yoga class for free?"

"Sure. It's really for Edie because I'm trying to ensure she gets some exercise after her stroke. But it seemed silly not to offer it to everyone."

"And she's not your grandmother?"

"She's as good as. Married to my grandfather, who passed away several years ago."

For all Kennedy's openness on a variety of topics, her past was still a closed book. Normally he wouldn't pry. He preferred not to delve too deeply into people's private affairs as it encouraged confidences and an intimacy he wasn't ready to reciprocate. But Kennedy fascinated him. Had done so from the start.

Where were her parents? Why did she seem so alone? What was the deal with that watercolor on her nightstand? "What about the rest of your family?"

Her face crumpled. "Oh, Edie's all the family I need." The book slammed shut.

He sought more neutral territory. "How long have you been traveling?"

"Since I was nineteen. I went to college but I couldn't settle or connect with it as an experience. The students seemed weirdly sheltered, living in this bubble, and I just wanted to get moving. Get out there. So I did. Picked up my yoga certification along the way so I'd have some sort of trade." She rolled her eyes. "Edie doesn't approve of my country-hopping lifestyle, so knowing I could get a job teaching something soothes her some. That's why I got my teaching English as a second language certification, too. It's always good to have options."

The journey lasted for another minute. Too short, though Reid wondered why he thought that given she had barely imparted any information at all. They pulled up outside a pleasant-looking building.

"Do you need a ride home?"

"I wouldn't say no. I'll be a couple of hours, though. Actually it would—never mind."

"Dis-moi."

She gave a little shiver though the car was quite warm. "Could I bring Bucky? The residents love when I bring dogs to visit and it would be good socialization for him, too. But I'm sure you have tons to do today on your day off."

Laundry, house-cleaning, gym time, jerking off to fantasies of his hot roommate ... "We could come in for a short visit."

"Awesome!" She smiled and his heart flipped uncomfortably. Bucky took it better. He hopped out of the car the moment Reid opened the door.

She took his leash from Reid and their hands brushed. Reid ignored the static charge. He didn't believe in static charges. "I've got him. Could you grab my yoga mat and blocks? That would be really helpful."

"Sure." So he was the yoga boy now. Cute.

The moment they went inside, people crowded around Kennedy and Bucky. At first he was worried that Bucky would be frightened but the brave fella took it in his stride. These last couple of weeks he had definitely become easier around people, such an improvement from that first day.

A mix of staff and residents made a fuss, and Reid wanted to think it was the dog, but it wasn't.

It was Kennedy. She brought sunshine into their lives.

About a minute in, someone screamed, "Reeeeeeeeeeeeed Duraaaaaaaaaaand" with an upswing on the last syllable like it was building to a cymbals crash.

Everyone, who up until now had been cooing over Kennedy and Bucky, turned and stared as if he'd made that horrendous sound. The crowd parted and a mini-Moses with gray hair and sparkling green eyes appeared in the center of the group. She looked him up and down, and declared, "I can't believe Ryan Reynolds beat you out for Sexiest Canadian Alive. It was rigged!"

Mon Dieu. He shot a beseeching glance at Kennedy, who made the introductions. "Reid, meet Edie. Edie, Reid owns Bucky."

Bucky was currently humping his leg, proving that he pretty much owned Reid.

"Are you joining us for yoga?" the screecher—Edie—asked.

"Just here for a visit."

"I need a word with you." She put her arm through Reid's and he waited for her to give him some of the usual fan-to-player spiel.

That last drive to the net would have gone in if you did X, Y, or Z.

Let me tell you about my nephew who has an amazing slap shot.

Bet your dad is proud of you! Henri Durand, just imagine!

Everyone had an opinion, thought they could see inside his head. He prepared to be hit up for tickets or asked about Theo Kershaw (the grannies loved Kershaw), so he wasn't quite ready for what came next.

"Are you dating my granddaughter?"

"Edie!" Kennedy shook her head.

"It's a simple question."

"I'm his dog sitter," Kennedy protested, and mouthed "sorry" at him.

"Kennedy would never date someone like me. She has more sense."

Edie was having none of it. "Why not? You're very handsome."

"Thanks, but Kennedy and I are just ... roommates." Hot kisses and offers for post-season oblivion notwithstanding.

"When has that ever stopped anyone? In fact, it should be easier with you both in the same house."

"Edie!" Kennedy had gone red, which was strange because she came across as incapable of embarrassment. "Could you stop it? The guy's also my boss."

Though it hadn't felt like he was the boss, when he woke up with his arms wrapped around her, his dick a rod of iron nudging her ass and seeking a way in. It felt like she was in charge and he was along for the ride.

Edie was already on another subject. "You'd do better on the same line as that Cal Foreman."

Sometimes he had to explain hockey to people. "We play the same position. When's he's on, I'm off and vice versa."

She gave a low growl, but it wasn't because she didn't understand. She was trying to tell him something. "You should be playing center."

Huh, Edie was pretty sharp—or had an in with Coach Calhoun. "You know your hockey."

"You bet your steel buns I do. So what's wrong with my granddaughter?"

"Edie!" Kennedy yelped.

Nothing was wrong with her. So she tempted, teased, and drove him crazy. But other than that, she was perfect.

"Reid, what are you doing for Thanksgiving? I know they do it differently in Canada. You should come to us!" Edie squeezed Kennedy's arm. "Right, honey?"

Another apologetic look from Kennedy. "I'm sure he has plans."

Thanksgiving was next week. "I actually do—have plans, that is—but thank you anyway."

"Well, you're welcome, anytime, Reid. I know you're new to the city so you probably don't know many people."

"Except his brother and the entire team." Kennedy sent another apologetic look his way.

"But his brother has been here for years and probably

has his own life. And Reid's like you, hasn't settled yet. Sometimes it takes a while to find your place in this world." Edie divided a look between both of them when she said that. "Sometimes it takes a while to find the right people."

Later that afternoon in downtown Chicago ...

BAST OPENED the door of his apartment and grinned. Reid wanted to smash his face in. He had another full fridge and a report that Bast and Kennedy had an ice-cream date.

"Hey, you brought your buddy!"

Bucky was still a touch leery of strange men, especially ones who had the nerve to cozy up to a brother's roommate. Ever careful, he molded his scarred body to Reid's leg.

"Didn't bring Kennedy, then?"

"No." Not waiting for an invitation, Reid walked in. "She's working."

"Aren't you paying her enough?"

Ignoring Bast's question, Reid sat on his sofa and got Bucky settled at his feet.

His brother sighed. "I got that water you like. The flavor-free kind."

"Très drôle." Reid liked his brother's apartment, which looked lived in after his six years in the city. Art on the walls, books on the shelves, even a case for his trophies. The Championship ring, which his brother had won three years ago with the Hawks, twinkled on a shelf.

Reid wandered over and picked it up, something he always did when he stopped by, like it could transfer some of its shine to him. Bast had told him he could put it on, but

Reid would never do that. Bring a slew of bad luck on his head? He set it down again, his envy pitiful.

"Dad should have made the trip anyway," Bast said, though Reid hadn't said a word. It was annoying to be known so well.

"We both know why he didn't."

Bast frowned. He never liked the reminder that Henri viewed his sons differently. "He expects a lot. Of both of us."

Perhaps. Yet Reid felt the weight heavily on *his* shoulders. "Coach wants to put me in as center."

Bast's eyes lit up. "You've always wanted to play that position."

Had he? There had been a time when he thought it would suit him better, but the doubts had seeped under his skin and into his blood. He went for the glory position of winger because it would score more points with Henri. Scoring points was what his life consisted of: with his father, his brother, his teammates, the league.

"I might suck at it."

"You won't. You're incapable of sucking at anything, Reid." He leaned forward, elbows on his knees. "Remember when we used to go to that rink at the community center in Grenville and that big piece of shit, Teddy Something—"

"Gunderson."

"Teddy 'Tree Trunk' Gunderson challenged you play tender for a puck challenge and you didn't even have pads?"

His body was bruised but his spirit was unbroken. "The first of many reasons to despise him."

"And then you beat the shit out him in the parking lot. Defending me."

"He shot that puck at your head."

"Yeah, after he shot twenty of them at yours in goal. And half of them didn't miss."

When Henri heard that Gunderson had made the mistake of directing a dangerous puck at Bast he scolded Reid for coming to his brother's defense.

You're not his keeper, Reid. Let him defend himself.

No matter how much Henri tried to drive a wedge between them, Reid never took the bait. At least not anymore. They were competitors on the ice but brothers everywhere else.

It had taken a while to get here. Bast had been in awe of Reid when they were little and Reid had taken that hero worship and thrown it back in his face. Not just verbally, either. He had not been a good brother to Bast and now he wanted to be. Edie's comments about Reid not knowing many people in the city had resonated—Reid had Bast and he needed to nurture this while he had the chance.

Only now Bast was getting close to Kennedy and Reid didn't enjoy this new influx of negative feeling. He had a hard enough time escaping his guilt at not being better at his job of big bro.

"You could play goalie for the Rebels and you would be amazing at it," his brother said, his tone gentle. "Whatever you put your mind to."

"Are you seeing Kennedy?" The words had left Reid's mouth before he could stop them.

Bast didn't even look surprised at the sharp change in conversation. "I've *seen* her. I stopped by yours yesterday, but she had to leave for one of her gigs. Busy, busy girl." He let the beat hang for long enough for Reid to get really pissed. "Bro, I don't think I've ever seen you like this. You're, like, glowing!"

"No, I'm not."

"You are! This is so fuckin' cute. Reid's got a crush."

Damn, he had, from the second he walked into that coffee shop.

Then said yes to his crush living with him.

While he was on a sex fast.

Stupid, stupid Reid.

"She likes you," Reid muttered, not knowing if it was true, but needing to say something to leech this tightness from his chest.

"Sure, as a friend. She's gorgeous, I grant you, but I wouldn't do that to you. I might have before you came over and spilled your guts—"

"How exactly did I spill my guts?"

"Reid. You. Here. With your cute-as-fuck dog. Asking me if I'm seeing Kennedy. That is like a full-scale admission of your infatuation with this girl."

Reid offered up his darkest scowl.

His brother merely laughed and pointed. "Now I *know* you're crazy about her."

"I'm not. I'm ..." He reached for Bucky and rubbed behind his ears. "She's not the kind of person who sticks. I have to figure out a plan for Bucky."

Bast considered that for a second. "You know I'm glad you're here in Chicago. Maybe you're not but I think this is a good place for you. The Rebels is a good fit for you, center is a good position, and Kennedy likes you. Trust what your gut's telling you."

"She's attracted to me and I'm attracted to her. It's just a physical thing, nothing more. And she won't be around for long anyway."

His brother snorted. "So go for it! Lock her down. Plant your fucking flag, bro, before someone else does."

Could he do that, knowing it would throw his regimen off course, but worse—and he couldn't believe he was even thinking this—that it was only short-term? He already liked her. A lot. He liked how easy it felt around her. She might be the key to unlocking some part of him he didn't know existed.

The not-Henri part.

To taste that potential—for himself, for them—and have it ripped away was a risk he couldn't afford to take.

21

KENNEDY REREAD the email from the school she had contracted with for her work visa in Thailand. They still hadn't received the documentation from the consulate and now, heading into the busy holiday season, her plans might be delayed.

She could still head back by New Year on a tourist visa and see more of the country, but her placement in the school would be pushed back to the next semester. Luckily she was saving money because of the free room and board and the additional dog-walking clients, as well as some personal errand gigs. She could afford to bum around Asia for a few months except ...

She was starting to like the current situation.

With Bucky.

With Reid.

So used to being on the move, she had forgotten the pleasures of sitting still for a moment—and not just with yoga. Sharing a meal with someone whose company you enjoyed, watching TV and looking over to see if he got that joke, leaving Post-its and texts for each other about the most mundane things … the comfort in it was tempting.

Too tempting.

It would be so easy to get attached. The root of all suffering, right?

And they hadn't even banged yet!

She heard the TV come on, which meant Reid must have returned from one of his twenty thrice-daily trips to the gym. She headed out, needing to talk to him anyway, determined not to be swayed by his thick thighs and awesome pecs and blue-on-blue eyes.

"Reid, could I have a word?"

"Sure." He gave her his full attention from his spot on the sofa.

"My car is outside in the residents' parking. And it … works."

His look was *so fucking what?* Also known as Reid Scowl No. 5.

"Did you take my car to the mechanic and pay to get it fixed?"

"Oui."

She had planned to pay for a tow-truck this morning. It would bite into a chunk of her savings but she needed that car to get around for the next few weeks. When she found it in a different spot outside and turned the key in the ignition, it started up just fine.

"What do I owe you?"

"Nothing. I gave game tickets to the guy."

Oh. If he didn't pay money, she couldn't get huffy about it. "Thanks for doing that. It was really kind."

His cheeks flushed. "You need the car. You're a busy woman."

"It was still a nice thing to do."

He nodded curtly, a sign that the gratitude fest needed to end now. That should have been enough, but something inside her chest couldn't let it go. Something inside her chest was rearing up in response.

Reid fixed her car. The car she had lived in for three—no, four—days. The car she needed to get to the jobs that paid for her crappy boxes of mac and cheese. The car she needed to see Edie.

"What's wrong?" That deep voice sounded so close, and then she realized it was. Or he was. He had eaten the gap between sofa and woman and was now regarding her with a hybrid of concern and horror.

"I—" She sniffed, but it was too late. The tears had already burst the dam around her heart. "I'm sorr—" Her words were muffled by a wall of steel: Reid's amazing chest. His arms caged her in the best way possible. All in. No hesitation.

"What did I do wrong, Kennedy?" The words were a hot puff of breath against her scalp.

"Nothing," she sniffed. *Everything.* "It's just been a rough couple of weeks. I hadn't realized how much I depend on that car and your kindness took me by surprise."

"Unexpected from the cranky roommate, huh?" He drew back, still holding on, but his eyes watched her closely. The words were light, the gaze anything but.

"Just kindness in general, not the source."

"You know I said you only had to ask me to hold you. Comfort you. I'm not the best with speeches but I can listen and give out hugs."

She wrapped her arms around him tightly and felt him relax into her in return. "You're good at this roommate business."

They held each other for a few minutes, and it never got

awkward. Unless you counted the bolt of lust that slammed through her and was now boomeranging around for another pass.

Enough. She would have to see if someone else might be willing to give her a good clearing of the pipes. Maybe Bryan, one of her dog-walking clients, who was always asking her to stop for a drink after she dropped Smoky the Yorkshire terrier off. Recently-divorced, a bit older, very fit ...

Bucky nuzzled her leg. "Someone wants attention," she said.

"I'd better take him out for a spin. Did you want to come?"

Yes, please!

But he actually meant for a walk. The bracing November air would probably be effective in calming her down, but she needed to be alone. Fifteen minutes with Reid and Bucky out of the house would be enough for her to take care of business.

At her hesitation, he spoke up. "Sorry, it's your night off and I'm asking you to work."

"Oh, no, not at all."

"You relax. We'll be back soon." He smiled, a move that sent a pulse to a spot that did not need blood flow right now. Within sixty seconds he and Bucky were out the door—and Kennedy was headed to her room for some much needed relief with her battery-operated friend.

About six minutes in, she was close, so close, so—

"Kennedy!"

They were back already? Frustrated, she pulled her yoga pants up, hid her tool (ha!) in the nightstand, and put her head out the door.

A surprising sight greeted her—two very dirty boys. The left side of Reid's sweatpants and Henley was caked in mud.

Bucky was even worse. He looked like he'd fought a dirty puddle and the puddle won.

"What happened?"

Reid looked down at Bucky who looked up at Reid, and it was so damn cute she wanted to hug them both. "This guy decided he wanted to jump in some wet leaves, which turned out to be muddy wet leaves. When I tried to grab his leash, I lost my balance." He held up mud-streaked hands.

"Reid Durand, Ice-Dancing Superstar, losing his balance?"

"It was slippery and I wasn't reckoning on this scoundrel going rogue. I think he saw a rat." He gave her an up-down look that seemed to see everything. "What were you doing?"

"Just getting ready to ... uh, take a shower."

As she spoke Reid reached behind his back and pulled his Henley over his head in that one-hand move guys must have embedded in their DNA.

Kennedy's body had been humming before, but now graduated to a full-scale *vroom-vroom*.

Those muscles could *not* be real.

She had seen him in shirts, sweaty and not, but this was the first time she'd encountered naked, hard-blocked flesh. Add to that thick, corded muscle on those delicious, hairy forearms.

"I'll have to run a bath. Could you help me out?"

A bath. Her skin tightened at the notion of soapy, sudsy water trickling down her body ... or Reid's body. Yes, Reid's muscle-packed, perfectly-sculpted, lickable body.

"Help you?" She felt a touch dizzy.

"With the bath? Only, I don't know if regular soap is okay for dogs." He frowned at her. "For Bucky?"

Right. Bucky. "Sure! The bath! I bought some special shampoo for him earlier. There are oils in his coat that we don't want to strip." She headed to the bathroom, anxious for a task to occupy her dirty, dirty mind.

"Is he going to be difficult, I wonder?" Reid sounded a little pleased at the prospect. Like he had an image of how a dog should behave and mischief was preferred.

"He might be," she called out from the bathroom. "Dogs don't usually like it. But if they roll around in mud like this scamp did, they have to accept the consequences."

True to his billing, Bucky was indeed difficult. He didn't want to be a good boy and just get into the warm, soapy water. Kennedy sat at the side of the tub testing the temperature with drifting fingertips while Reid loomed over her with big hands on trim hips. There was something rather appealing about looking up at him like this, and not just because he was shirtless and the view was top-notch. Something in the nature of being a supplicant, she supposed, especially when Reid pointed at the hot tub.

"In, Bucky. You stink." He said it so gently that he may as well have been telling the puppy that he loved him. Of course, every word Reid spoke to Bucky was love.

"Maybe lift him?"

Reid scooped him up, but he squirmed and yelped as soon as he got closer to the water.

"Perhaps he's flashing back to his trauma in the lake."

Reid's concern was palpable. Kennedy loved how his whole demeanor changed around Bucky.

Later she would insist to the court of sex opinion that she wanted to help Bucky overcome any fears he might have about being deposited in a large body of water.

"He might feel better if one of us was in there with him."

Reid's brow wrinkled. "Really?"

"Yeah, it might put him at ease."

At which point all Kennedy's dreams came true and

Reid Durand dropped his sweat pants. She didn't even have to ask!

Not the underwear, though, but hell, wasn't that a sight to behold. And remember, she was seated on the bathroom floor with the perfect view of this Adonis's log-cracking thighs and quarter-bouncing buns. All of which was just the undercard to the main event: a perfectly-crafted ridge that bulged against the silky black fabric of his boxer briefs.

While he was distracted picking up Bucky, she took the opportunity to memorize for later. Because there would be a later, a time where she would be dreaming about this man's body and that cock filling and stretching her good.

Reid stepped over the lip of the bathtub into the water and with absolutely perfect balance, sat down while holding the puppy safely until they were both submerged—Reid to his waist and Bucky to his shoulders. Reid held him firm, setting him carefully down until his paws touched the tub's floor.

"Nice job!" Kennedy grabbed some of the shampoo, anxious to give her hands something to do. She knew what they'd be doing later under the cover of her bedsheets, but for now she'd try to be the good dog nanny. "Is it too hot in there?" *Because it's a sex sauna out here.*

"No, the water's fine. You should join us."

She squinted at Reid, trying to ascertain if that amounted to flirting. Reid wasn't the flirting type, or if he was, he had yet to grace her with his banter gifts. There was an appealing quirk to his mouth.

"Watch it, Reid. If I didn't know better, I'd think you were inviting me to get hot and wet with you."

No response to that, except that she had only turned herself on even more. *Top of the class, Kennedy!*

Reid's hands moved with assurance over the puppy's

body and in the process, his thumb brushed across her palm and wowza, that was quite the zing. Pushing thoughts of talented thumbs deep, she focused on the job at hand: getting Bucky clean while trying to avoid staring at Reid's chest. The pectoral muscles appeared to be chiseled from marble. No wonder he only ate the best foods and worked so hard—look at the results.

Yet all she could think was what a crime that he wasn't sharing that body with someone.

Screw someone. With *her*.

"So what are you doing for Thanksgiving?" When he hesitated, she said, "Not being nosey. I'll be headed over to see Edie at Larkvale so I wanted to know if you needed me to look after Bucky."

"Actually, I can take him. One of my teammates, Levi Hunt, volunteers at Uptown Mission, a homeless shelter on the North side of Chicago. He asked some of the guys if they wanted to help out."

Not what she expected at all. "That's amazing. Why didn't you mention it before?"

"To be honest, I thought you'd try to muscle your way in. You're always helping out and volunteering for stuff. They have an animal shelter attached to it because some of the homeless have pet companions. I'll bring Bucky along to give you a break."

"I don't need a break."

"Yes, you do. You've been working every day nonstop for as long as I've known you. You hardly ever relax and when you do, you're still on the clock because you're looking after this guy."

"But it's not even work." She peered down at Bucky, who appeared to be finally enjoying himself. "You're no trouble at all, Buck. Don't listen to the mean man."

Reid smiled, and so did she, and the combination of all the things—that smile, a half-naked Reid in the hot tub, the man fixing her car, and now that same man spending Thanksgiving with the homeless—made her teary again.

"Kennedy," he whispered.

"It's okay, just some soap in my eye." She wiped away the moisture with the back of her hand.

"About earlier, when you got upset about me fixing your car," he said. "Was there more to that than just unexpected kindness?"

"Just a bit of bad news about my visa for Thailand. It might be delayed. Some paperwork mix-up." She raised her eyes from Bucky to find Reid staring at her with nuclear bomb-level intensity. "But don't worry, I won't impose on you for any longer than a few more weeks."

"You can stay as long as you want. This is your home."

Was he trying to make her dissolve into a tearful puddle? Earlier she'd been thinking of those creature comforts she was starting to enjoy, and *home* was as good as any word to describe it. But it couldn't be replaced. She had lost it ten years ago in a fiery blaze that destroyed everything she loved.

"Good to know, but I promised Edie I'd stick around Chicago through the holidays and then I'll be off traveling again, visa or no visa. By that time, Bucky should be a bit more settled but you'll have to figure out a plan for overnights. I can look into finding someone, assuming you're keeping him."

Reid had that same expression he wore the first day she'd come by for her "interview," when she accused him of not being good enough to be a dog daddy. He had looked wounded, just like now.

"I'm keeping him." The way he said it sent a shiver

corkscrewing down her spine—or maybe it was the dampness after being splashed by sudsy water.

She had slipped off her cardigan so it wouldn't get wet, which meant the cami and bra combo was winning the day. Reid was staring at her, his eyes roving over her damp breasts. He didn't even try to hide his interest and she found herself loving the way his greedy gaze drank in her body.

"I think he's done. We don't want him to prune." She scooped Bucky up and out, and rubbed him dry with a towel. "We could give him a run with the hairdry—oh, and there he goes." Bucky ran out of the room, probably anxious to get back to his bed or the sofa.

Maybe the sexual tension was too thick for *him*.

While she was drying Bucky, Reid had emerged from the water like a male Venus, dripping with semi-sudsy water. He stepped onto the mat and Lord help her, she would remember with embarrassment what she did next for as long as she lived.

With the towel in her hands she swiped it over his chest, a proxy for the hands she didn't dare use. She wanted more of those muscles, that heat, this man. Touching him properly—towel-free—would only happen at his invitation. She'd be RSVP'ing the hell out of that if she got it.

A dip of her gaze to the space between them told her all she needed to know. That erection was ... wow.

"Might be best if I handle that myself." He took the towel from her, as if this was a normal interaction. None of this was normal! "I'm going to take a shower."

Kennedy dismissed.

Backing up, she kept her eyes on his face because to look anywhere else would turn her into a crazy, sex-starved nympho. Only *his* eyes were burning suns of Reid-level intensity that told her exactly what would be happening as soon as the shower spray hit those pectorals.

She didn't even bother with headphones back in her room. When Reid Durand came, he probably made a sound no louder than a church mouse.

22

Downtown Riverbrook was dressed and ready for the holidays now that Thanksgiving was a memory and Christmas was just three weeks away. This had always been her mom's favorite time of year, and Kennedy couldn't help but remember Libby Clark's infectious joy as she trimmed, cooked, and yuletided her way through the season. Without her—without them both—it was hard to imagine ever enjoying the holidays again. There was a reason she avoided visits to the US.

Tonight, though, Kennedy would give it a shot and try to enjoy it at a surface level. This bar was certainly festive with garlands draped over the mirrors, the staff crowned with Santa hats, and "Fairytale of New York" blasting from the speakers. Kennedy might have to buy some of those hats for her doggie clients. Bucky would look adorable in one!

Apparently the Empty Net was the regular hangout of Rebels and their fans. Why would a famous person go to a place with the expectation of being left alone by fans, unless you didn't want that at all? Unless you wanted to be seen and fawned over.

Sports ball people, the strangest people of all.

Tonight was Rebels-free as far as Kennedy could tell, but some of those present were Rebels-adjacent. Mia and Sadie were dating a couple of them, Kennedy was rooming with one of them, and Tara was—Kennedy wasn't sure what Tara's deal was but she definitely harbored ambitions in the Rebels' direction.

First, the woman was shocked to her "strong-as-shit core" that Kennedy had somehow managed to sneak her feet "under the Reid Durand king-sized bed."

"But she had to jump into a freezing lake and save a dog to do it," Mia pointed out, not unreasonably.

"She saw an opportunity and went for it." On the back of a hilarious, faux-weepy "Way to go, Paula" rendition from *An Officer and a Gentleman*, Tara clinked her wine glass against Kennedy's, still sitting on the table because she wasn't officially acknowledging that as a valid toast. Also, twelve bucks for a glass of Pinot Grigio? She would be sticking to the one and nursing it to the bitter end.

"Believe me, I'm not looking for a shot at Reid. He's wide open, so have at it."

"But you're living with him!"

"As roommates. Not even friends." Though that felt like a lie given that he'd gone out of his way to get her car fixed and had held her when she needed it. And then there was the Great Hot Tub Incident. On that last one, she suspected Reid was getting revenge for spotting her baking in her underwear. Well, joke was on him!

"It's a purely business arrangement. I look after the dog and go about my day. That's it. If anything, I have more of a relationship with Bastian."

Tara grasped her arm and dug her talons in deep. "His brother? How did you swing that?"

"He's stopped by a couple of times and we've become friendly."

Tara looked like she was about to pass out.

"Now you've done it," Sadie said with a throaty laugh. Mia had introduced her as a fashion designer shacked up with Rebels player Gunnar Bond. The dress she wore, one of her own fabulous designs, certainly put Kennedy's old-lady wardrobe to shame.

"I don't get it," Kennedy said. "Sure, they're hot and fit and have great bodies—okay, I get it. But the personalities on some of them leave a lot of be desired. So moody. So grumpy."

"That's hot, too!" Tara wailed.

"Listen, I know most of these guys," Mia said. "Hockey players, on the whole, are dicks. Sure, if you can find a good one, gold star." Insert smug grin from the woman here. "But we're talking about wading through deep oceans of dick to get there and not in a good way. Speaking of dick-wading, there's Casey." She waved at someone at the bar, who waved back and walked over.

The new arrival had long dark, curly hair, bright blue eyes, and an easy smile. Kennedy instantly took to her.

"If anyone has opinions on the players, it's Casey Higgins," Mia said with authority. "She sees them every day as they pass through the inner sanctum."

"Uh-oh," Casey said. "What have I walked in on?"

Mia turned to the table behind her and asked if she could borrow one of their chairs, then stood and placed it for Casey. "Sit and tell us all the Rebels gossip. I might have family and a boyfriend in the Rebels weeds but none of them will spill to me because of the vault. Casey, meet my pals Kennedy and Tara. And you know Sadie. Casey is Harper the boss lady's assistant. She has all the dirt."

My pals. That felt nicer than it should have.

Casey blinked. "Which I am sworn to keep close to my chest. I only popped in here for a bottle of wine because the liquor store on the corner is closed for inventory and Tina has the kind I like." She held up a bottle of red with a picture of a fox on it.

"And now you're going to sit with us and have a drink. Unless you have a hot man to go home to."

Casey slumped in her seat. "No hot man, just this lovely bottle of wine, which is all I need. I'll stay for one drink, but don't make me say anything I shouldn't."

"Two drinks it is, then," Mia said as she got the attention of the server.

By the time Kennedy was on her second glass of wine—Mia had ordered a bottle, the sly vixen—it was clear that Casey was not the problem. Kennedy had always been a lightweight. Now she was the embodiment of loose lips sink ships. As in relationships.

"But no sex? At all?" Mia gawped at Kennedy. "For a whole season?"

"That's what he said. Something about focus. All part of his training regimen."

"Cal tried that for a few weeks after ..." She glanced Tara's way. "I think he wanted to punish himself because he and Tara had that weird breakup."

"You mean when he forced me to dump him at Levi Hunt's wedding? The rascal." Tara seemed very amused by this, which was good because otherwise, Awkwardsville. If Kennedy had the story right, after the Cal-Tara breakup, Mia had asked her brother's best friend to train her for a shot at the Olympics—and a shot at another man. Sounded complicated, but probably no more so than Kennedy's own living situation.

"Too right he should take a hit in the sex department," Tara was saying. "Of course that didn't last long as soon as you started wowing him with your moves on and off the ice. So how do we get Reid over his hang-ups and onto the Kennedy train?"

Kennedy held up a hand. "That's not the goal here. Of course I'm attracted to him." The memory of him emerging from that hot tub was burned into her retinas and playing on a loop. "But this isn't just a case of hot, horny roomies with no choice but to consummate their lust. There are brains involved."

"Hearts, too," Casey said wisely.

"Yes—no! Not hearts. Not souls. Nothing in the chest area." She waved at her breasts, then realized that this didn't help the point she was trying to make given that her breasts, or more specifically, her nipples turned into bullets in Reid's presence.

Nipples were always the first to know.

She came at it from another tack. "It's not like whatever that dude said when asked why he wanted to climb Mount Everest?" When all she received was a collection of unfocused stares—everyone was on their third glass by now—she said, "Because it's there. That's what the guy said."

Mia squinted. "So you're saying that proximity alone shouldn't be enough to dictate how your genitals are used or not used in this situation."

"Precisely! If you were to ask me 'why do you want to ravish Reid Durand?' the answer shouldn't be 'because he's there!' That's ridiculous. It should be because there's a connection, an attraction, a buzz whenever we're in a room together."

"And is there?" Casey eyed Kennedy over her glass. "A

connection, an attraction, a buzz?" She emphasized buzz to the point Kennedy looked around for a nearby hive.

"Yes! But it's probably only because he's put it out there. Like a challenge. Behold, look at my muscles and hot scowl and cute dog. Do not touch!" Did she sound frustrated or was that the wine talking? "It's just that I'll be gone soon and this feels like a missed opportunity."

"For boning," Sadie said.

More than that. She felt a pull toward Reid unlike any guy she'd ever met. Maybe if they gave in to their attraction, she could treat him like any of her other on-the-road conquests. Place him firmly in her rear view instead of wondering *what if*.

"I can't believe you're only here for a few more weeks," Mia said, her smile fond but sad. "A lot of clients and their humans are going to miss you."

"And I'll miss them. The dog-walking thing was only supposed to get me by for my few months here. I didn't expect it to take off." Or that she would enjoy it so much. She'd also started adding more personal errands for clients to her to-do list. "One of the players—Tate Kaminski—even asked me to help him with his grocery shopping. Apparently apps aren't good enough. He needs someone he trusts to feel up the mangoes."

"He's recently divorced, right?" Tara asked as if she didn't know the exact details of the settlement.

"Watch out," Mia said. "Tara would *love* to give Tate a shot at feeling up her mangoes."

"Mangoes? These babies are in the cantaloupe range!" Tara plumped her excellent rack, drawing appreciative cheers from the table. She pointed at Kennedy. "But seriously, that personal assistant lark can be good money. Ask Sadie."

"You do that?"

"Used to for Allegra McKenzie of Punani Power fame," Sadie said. "I do *not* miss that job but I did enjoy the free dildos. Before that I did concierge services for several clients. It was kind of fun, actually. Bigger in LA but definitely taking off here, especially if you have a needy and wealthy client base."

"Hmm, like a team of multi-millionaire athletes," Mia said with a wink at Kennedy.

Concierge services? That was a real thing? She had tried a number of jobs, and as much as she enjoyed yoga and teaching, there was something about her current gig that spoke to her. She liked the busyness of it and the notion she was truly getting shit done, even if it was other people's shit. It didn't hurt that she felt so comfortable under Reid's roof.

In his arms, the lure of the open road faded.

"She's already got one player on the hook," Tara said. "Now she could have her pick of them."

"Well, I'm living with one of them and he's not interested in what I have to offer."

Tara leaned in. "You two are *so* going to do it."

"Tara! That is not the moral of the story. He's hot. I'm hot. But these are not good enough reasons to be getting down and dirty."

"I understand what you're saying," Casey said. "Though I'm a little worried about whether all this self-denial is good for the team."

"She's right," Mia said, waving her empty glass. "*What about the children?* And by children, I mean, the players. These guys have killer libidos and urges up the wazoo. They need an outlet and the ice, while an excellent mistress, can also be cruel. No Rebel should be relying on the game to get his jollies!"

"Jollies," Kennedy said with a tipsy giggle. That was a fun word, especially because it *so* did not apply to Reid.

"Harper wouldn't like it," Casey said. "She's very much in favor of the guys taking a healthy stance to sex."

"Do not tell Harper what you have learned here!" Mia pointed at her. "You're in the circle and you better not break the sacred trust we've placed in you while we discuss how Kennedy can get inside Reid's hockey pants."

"But, I don't—"

"Reid's hockey pants? What have we missed?"

They looked up to find Erik Jorgenson, the Rebels goalie with a big grin on his face. Beside him was Theo Kershaw, one of the defensemen. Insta-famous, Kennedy had heard, as well as hockey-famous.

Mia's eyes gleamed with mischief. "Just joking about Reid's roommate situation."

Theo shook his head sadly. "You mean how he's keeping little D under wraps?"

"Oh, you guys heard about that? Hold on—does Cal know?" She threw a semi-annoyed look around the group. "What did I tell you? The damn team vault!"

Erik laughed. "Durand let it slip the other night by accident, the weirdo. Not that he should be automatically jumping on you, Kennedy. We gave him some strategies on how to resist you."

Reid had sought advice from his teammates on how to *not* give her the satisfaction she was starting to see as her God-given right? This man's training regimen was going to be the death of her.

"Thanks, I appreciate it," she murmured morosely, which drew a laugh from everyone but Casey who was too busy throwing eye-daggers at Erik.

Erik seemed oblivious to Casey's stank-eyed stare. "Ladies, can we get you a drink?"

Tara opened her mouth to no doubt say yes, when Casey stood suddenly and grabbed her unopened bottle of wine.

"I have to go. Uh, thanks for—" She waved at the table and added, "I need to leave."

Erik took a step back to give her room. "Something I said, Casey?"

Her eyes flashed with emotion then dimmed quickly, almost practiced in its control. "No, not at all. I—I need to get home, that's all." Before anyone could dig deeper, she was out the door leaving a gust of wind and wide-eyed confusion in her wake.

"Hell, with moves like that, we should have her on the team," Theo said. "Fess up, Fish, what did you do to piss her off?"

Erik appeared as baffled as the rest of them. "I've no idea. Maybe she really just had to leave."

Theo rubbed his hands together. "Well, that awkwardness aside, how about another round? And then we can gossip about the people we know and who they're banging." He pointed at Kennedy. "Or going to an awful lot of trouble *not* to bang."

23

Reid's phone rang with a call from Henri. Usually he would pick up, but tonight, Coach was planning to put him in at center. If he talked to his father now, he'd have to tell him about the position switch and suffer an earful.

Almost immediately after the voice mail notification, a call came in from Bastian.

"You okay?" his brother asked.

"Fine."

It was BS, but then so much of his life these days was. No such thing as *fine* anymore. Kennedy was at the sink, rinsing something and moving fluidly in a way that was far too attractive for Reid's kitchen or peace of mind or sanity of dick.

Everything turned him on. Kitchen counter stools. The toaster. That fork, just lying there.

A couple of nights ago he had just about lost his mind when she touched him, toweling him off after he'd given her a nice show of cute dog-bathing and wet muscles. Only moments earlier she had mentioned her visa problem and how it wouldn't stop her from leaving.

You can stay as long as you like. This is your home.

He couldn't believe he had said that, or maybe he couldn't believe that she had dismissed the offer so readily. Not even a hint that she might regret leaving Reid and Bucky behind. Her heart was set on a place far away from here. From them.

This shouldn't have surprised him. He wasn't boyfriend material, hadn't dated much, and had a hard time making connections. A woman like Kennedy with friends all over the world wasn't going to change her plans for a man with ice in his veins.

"You're trending on Twitter."

He refocused on Bast who was yammering on about something. "What?"

"The no sex thing. Someone spilled."

He hung up and started checking the bird app. Sure enough there was some tabloid rag discussing the inside track they had on Reid's preparation for his game.

"No sex, said one of our insiders. Reid Durand is one of the most focused players in the NHL and he's determined that not indulging his vices during the season is the best way for him to prepare. We haven't seen it pay any dividends on the ice yet, but maybe Reid knows something we don't. Will the Rebels reward that kind of dedication with a multi-year contract? Only time will tell."

The rest was the usual commentary from fans, non-fans, and the perennial know-nothing know-it-alls. Maybe the source was Foreman, trying to throw him off his game.

On cue, a text came in from the man himself.

That wasn't me.

"What's wrong?" Kennedy was leaning on the counter.

"You look like you're—oh no, are you getting another headache?" She reached out to his jaw and cupped it, as if that had ever helped anyone with a headache. It helped with something, though.

He shifted on the stool, glad he was behind the counter.

"Someone told the press about my no sex rule."

She dropped her hand. "It wasn't me!"

"I never thought it was."

"Oh, okay, then." She looked stricken. "I thought you were accusing me."

"I'm pretty sure it was some big mouth on the team. Though Foreman has already reached out to deny."

"What are they saying?"

He passed his phone with the news article to her and watched as she scrolled.

"You've made a list of the greatest sportsmen to keep it in their pants during the season, though I find it hard to believe Tom Brady is on here. I'd be all over Giselle if I lived with her."

He snorted. Maybe this wasn't so bad. He would just have to "no comment" any questions at the next press bloodbath.

"My father won't like it."

"Sounds like your father doesn't like anything. Oh, wait a second." She scrolled some more. "Listen to this: *Reid Durand has a female roommate, a situation, which while challenging, he uses to prove his mettle.*"

"That's not on there."

"There's more: *Durand now spends so much time with his right hand that the circumference of his right bicep is three millimeters thicker than his left.* Fascinating. And in metric measurements, too. Must be a Canadian source."

"It does not say that." He went to retrieve the phone but

she deftly dipped away from him, so he rounded the counter and bore down on her. She held the phone behind her back which forced him to cage her in, his forearms on either side of her curvy, fuckable body.

"Maybe I'll sell *my* story to the tabloids. Flexible dog-nanny slash roommate tells all! Reid Durand and his never-cold-enough showers!"

Okay, that was funny. "Give it back."

"Or what?" She set her chin, her ruby-pink lips in a tempting pout. In outright challenge. The air churned thick with sudden—or not so sudden—sexual tension.

"You want to push a man this close to the brink?"

"Maybe." She splayed the hand not holding his phone on his chest, right over his thumping heart. Her heat, her nearness, her scent ... he was about to lose all semblance of control. *Just step away.*

Or move closer.

He could resist her. He'd already held her in his bed, hugged her when she cried, kissed her until he almost exploded. This should be child's play, yet his hips had their own momentum. His cock was a heat-seeking missile, and there was no missing its intent.

Destination Kennedy.

SHE WASN'T sure how they got here.

You little liar. You know exactly the route you took.

One minute she was joking around with fake news, the next she had two hundred pounds of magnificent male all up in her space. The heartbeat of incitement in between had been all her doing.

"You're playing a dangerous game, roomie," he muttered.

More like a growl, and she felt it deep in her core. Her mouth dried to dust, about the only part of her that could claim to be parched.

"Am I?"

The constant charge in the air for the last week since the make-out session was a powder keg ready to blow. This moment felt different, though. Like the burning fuse had almost reached its end, explosion was imminent, and not even MacGyver could save them. His breathing had picked up, evident in the lift of that magnificent chest, unfairly covered by a plain gray tee. His pupils were wider, flared with dangerous intent.

Whip fast, he grasped one wrist firmly. It didn't hurt. Reid didn't have it in him to hurt anyone but himself. Surprised, she dropped his phone on the counter, and now got the full effect. Reid Durand, a tower of energy ready to uncoil. Muscled back to the counter, she relished the edge as an anchor.

She had nothing else to keep her moored.

Provoking him was a mistake, though her body didn't agree. Her body thought it was the best possible result if the fizz and bubble through her veins was any indication. Body, heart, soul, mind—amazing how these intimate parts of her could all have differing opinions on the same situation.

She didn't have time to analyze further before Reid grasped her other wrist and brought both of them down by her sides.

With anyone else she would have demanded to be released. With Reid, she was fascinated. What would he do next? What the hell was going on inside that brain of his?

He watched her closely from above, his eyes flickering, a torrent of choices examined and abandoned. This must be how he played hockey. Making split second decisions to go this way and that, assess each play, shoot his shot.

"This is harder than you thought it would be, isn't it?" he murmured.

She nodded, swallowed. "It's been a while for me."

"How long?"

"A couple of months."

He scoffed. "Talk to me when you're four months out from your last fuck."

She licked her lips. His eyes blazed with a flash of threatening heat.

"So what are we going to do about it?" That was about as blatant an invitation as she could make it. If he said "nothing," she would be disappointed but at least she'd know where they stood. Again.

"I realize it's difficult for you, Kennedy. I'm here with my excellent body and my adorable dog, so you're bound to be susceptible. Any woman would be."

Hold the phone. Was he implying she was the one dying for release here, and not him?

"And I realize it's difficult for you, Reid. Four months celibate and maybe another five—"

"Six."

"Six to go. I'm here with my yoga-flexible body and my great rack and my in-your-face cheer, so you're bound to be a little desperate. Any man would be."

He laughed, a deep sound from the gut that revealed hidden lines around his eyes and something shocking about herself.

She was falling for this grumpy, serious, surprising man.

It shouldn't be possible. This was merely forbidden fruit, a yearning for what he wouldn't surrender. She refused to become tangled in a man as complicated as Reid Durand.

He still held her wrists but now he let them go, slipping his hands to her waist which he squeezed as he pulled her closer.

There it is.

His cock was as hard as the ice he would skate on tonight and nothing had ever felt so right against her belly. His hands coasted to her hips, his thumbs pressing into the crease of her thighs, then V'ing down lower. And all this time, those piercing eyes stayed on her face. The rare Reid laugh was no more; now he was back to that gravity which had its own delicious pull.

"No funny business," he murmured as his mouth drew near. His lips brushed hers. A teasing tickle.

But she would not be satisfied with that. No funny business indeed! Realizing that her hands were finally free, she gripped his biceps for leverage and pressed her lips to his. His mouth slanted, parted, fitted, seeking the perfect angle.

He moaned and it was glorious.

"Kennedy, tell me what you need."

"Everything." *Too much. Too greedy.* But she would not take it back.

She hooked her leg around his hip—he was tall but she was flexible—and gave him a recess in which to settle. One hand stretched up to palm his neck. His hand, that large, long-fingered, artist's hand gripped her ass, pulling her up and flush until they were slotted like the final two pieces in a too-complex-for-this-moment puzzle.

He remained still. So still she almost wondered if this was all he wanted. A moment's peace in the cradle of her body. A home for them both.

Then it started.

A slow, dirty rock of his hips against her core.

Oh God.

The hardest part of him found the softest part of her and set about destroying her for anyone else. Because they were playing by some weird rulebook that said *this* wasn't breaking Reid's vow of celibacy, they found their erotic, wet kicks with his mouth devouring hers, his tongue licking inside her in a way that promised unbelievable oral talents. Yet she didn't feel like she was missing out. This was as intimate an experience as she'd ever had.

His lips moved to her jaw, a nip of her ear, a suck of her neck. He whispered her name, which she'd never thought sounded all that special. On Reid's lips it was poetry.

Lifting her body against his, he ground his cock into the notch of damp heat between her legs. Their mouths clashed in a smash of need and want, so much so that explosion seemed to be the only possible conclusion. Dry humping her against a kitchen counter probably wasn't the plan but this was where they'd ended up.

There was a strange, restrained beauty in it.

The pleasure rising in her blood had already exceeded foreplay levels. This was close to peaking. Close to coming.

"Reid," she whispered as the pleasure started to wind its way from where his lips and hands and eyes touched her. His erection dragged along the seam of her yoga pants, each pass ratcheting up the tension. Substituting his hand in a lusty drag between her legs, he applied his fingers to the holiest of work, massaging and pressing just right.

She shook her head, barely able to fathom how good it felt. His breaths were pants against her lips, and *oh god oh god oh god,* she was flying, breaking, falling.

She was a shaky, shuddering mess.

He held her gaze, his stare brutal and uncompromising. A step back, and she knew, she just *knew* he was going to pull that monk shit.

"Reid, don't."

His eyes searched her face, as if committing it to memory for some lonely time with his hand later.

"I should—" He thumbed over his shoulder. "Head to morning skate."

Damn.

~

Ten hours later ...

"So, Reid, Coach put you at center tonight. How do you think that went?"

Reid stared death into the reporter for a good ten seconds before answering. "How do you *think* it went?"

The scribbler—Jim Krugman from the Trib—remained unfazed. "There's been some talk about your unusual training regimen. Its" ... *checks notes* ... "restrictiveness. Have you considered if you should be doing something different?"

"Such as heading to a bar and picking up someone to suck my—"

"I think that's all the questions we have for Reid tonight!" The Rebels PR woman whisked him away before he could say something that got the team or Reid fined.

Or throw a punch that got him prosecuted.

24

THE FRONT DOOR opened and Bucky ran to it.

A handsome but defeated hockey player stepped inside. Still dressed in his game day suit, Reid immediately fell to his knees to greet his canine friend. Kennedy leaned by the hallway wall and watched the reunion.

Reid kept his gaze on Bucky. "Was he okay tonight?"

"Uh-huh. I think he even recognized you on TV. Sorry about the game."

The Rebels had lost 4-2 at home to the Montreal Royals. Reid had been playing at a different position than usual—though Kennedy didn't know enough about the game to be able to say if that was a good or bad thing. He didn't seem to get much on-ice time.

Now she was wondering if the Kitchen Sex Diaries this morning had thrown him off his groove. It had certainly thrown her off hers. All day, she'd been out of step, stumbling around in a lust-induced haze. Missing a street turn here, blanking out on conversations there.

Reid still hadn't looked at her. Oh, God, he must be furious. "Has he been out?"

"Yeah, I took him out about half an hour ago."

He stood and slipped off his jacket.

Let it fall.

This was not the typical neat-freak Reid. His gaze met hers and ... oh.

Her body went on high alert. Something about the way his eyes burned into her got her blood pumping to all points south.

She took a chance. "Did what happened this morning affect your play?"

"Yes."

He moved forward, pulling at his tie. Tore it off. Dropped it. Started on the buttons of his shirt.

"I'm sorry," she repeated.

Still he came, Terminator Reid. "Are you?"

That she got an amazing orgasm? Not really. That he had chosen to continue with this ridiculous self-denial? Yes, she was sorry about that. Suffering this much for your art—or sport—should not be allowed.

He halted inches away, his shirt open, that chest of glory on display, and she couldn't help herself.

She reached out to touch him.

He shuddered under her fingertips and she went a little weak. To have this impact on him ...

"Please," she whispered.

Lightning fast, his mouth met hers in a clash of fire and need, only for him to break off to utter, "Say you want this." His voice sounded wretched, torn from somewhere deep.

"I want this." The kiss resumed, ratcheting up in heat and intensity.

I want this. I want this. I want this.

She had never wanted anything so much in her life.

With a strength that shouldn't have surprised her, he scooped her off the ground. Her legs naturally settled on his hips as she found another angle of pleasure, her mouth against his, her core already pulsing with need against his hard-on.

He walked this new Reid-Kennedy combo back to his bedroom and pushed the door open. The landing on the bed was soft, which was good, because what was coming would likely be hard.

"Lift your arms." Dazed and lust-struck, she did as she was told. He peeled off her tee and spent a moment gazing at her breasts, still cupped by her bra. "Beautiful."

He placed a big hand flat in the center of her chest, his eyes burning midnight suns. "Tell me this is okay."

"Yes. It's more than okay. Please just do it."

"Do what?"

"Touch me, Reid!"

He chuckled, the sound dark and chocolatey and rare, an epic turn-on. Carefully and far too slowly, he peeled her yoga pants down over her hips.

Then past her ass, taking her panties with them.

Then clean off so she was exposed to his hot, thunderstorm gaze.

Lying over her body, he inhaled at her neck, licked it, nuzzled some more, then sucked on her ear. Riotous sensations moved through her with a shocking speed. Yet it was also happening too slowly, perhaps a hangover from the build-up of weeks for them to get here. She needed this now.

He still wore his clothes though his bare chest was accessible. She took advantage, moving her hands over all that unexplored territory.

"Naked. Need to see you naked."

He knelt up and pulled at his shirt, so much slower than the situation called for.

"*Reeeid ...*"

His lips curved in a half-smile. She was starting to live for those brief flashes, so different from his usual gravity.

A flutter of doubt assailed her, as she remembered that look when he first got home. The crushing pain of defeat after a bad game. She needed to know there was more to this than Kennedy as consolation prize. "Are you here because you lost?"

"I'm here because you've won."

"But nothing's changed. If anything, what happened this morning and tonight proves that sex does indeed throw you off your game. My orgasm made you lose!"

He scowled. "That's the dumbest thing I've ever heard."

"Uh, this is your crackpot theory. I'm only the messenger."

"Kennedy, neither you nor your orgasm made me lose. I just had a bad night." He cupped her jaw and gave her the Reid sex stare. "I want this. I've wanted you forever. I'll never not want you. D'accord?"

"D'accord," she whispered. *Okay.* Only Reid could make casual sex sound like the end of the world.

Because it's not casual ...

She shouldn't go there. Better instead to go here ... She went to unbutton his pants.

Zipper scrape, pants down, cock freed.

Oh my.

She squirmed on the bed, trying to enjoy the hot slickness between her thighs but knowing it would be better when it coated all of that Reid girth. The man was packing.

Hurry, hurry.

Standing, he removed the rest and now he was back, a

condom on the nightstand, his beautiful body stretched out over her.

They spent a moment drinking each other in. She was short and curvy, he was tall and built. The admiration on both sides was clear. Even the scar tissue on her torso, the brand of the worst night of her life, couldn't detract from the moment. Sealed in a special bubble, it was too important to let the bad memories in.

His hand moved over her body, down, down, his middle finger parting the cleft between her thighs to the soft, wet flesh within. The tingle of the hair on his arms added another layer of thrilling sensation.

"Look how wet and pink you are," he murmured, his voice filled with awe.

She looked.

She was.

And she had never been so aroused in her life.

THIS WAS NOT how Reid imagined his evening going. Play like shit. Lose a game. Suffer through the rollicking his father had dealt him on the phone call after.

"What the fuck was that? You're not strong enough for that position," Henri had said on the message when Reid didn't answer the call. "That's not your lane at all. You need to stick to what you're good at. That dump in the lake has made you soft."

Sure, Dad. Thanks for your input.

All he'd wanted was to come home to Bucky and Kennedy. Home to where no one cared about his plus-minus. Or his shooting percentage. Or that he was Henri Durand's stepson.

The moment he stepped across the threshold and saw his puppy happy to see him and his roommate—his gorgeous fucking roommate—standing there, waiting, he knew.

She would be leaving in a few weeks.

She had no reason to stay, but maybe he needed to *give* her a reason. *Lock her down*, like Bast said. If he didn't make a move now, then when? After she fell apart in his arms this morning, surrendering to him in the sweetest possible way, he had known this night could end in only one way.

Inside Kennedy.

All this pent-up need should have found an outlet on the ice, but tonight he couldn't connect with the puck, his teammates, or his game plan. Everything was closed off, except the rush of feeling in his veins when it came to Kennedy. This woman had blasted into his life and made him question everything.

His mind was a mess but his body knew the score. It needed the tight sheath of her body. It needed the comfort of a place to land. It needed this woman.

He had told her he was here because she won, but that wasn't the truth. Or the whole truth. Though he left the Rebels arena a loser, with Kennedy he felt like a champion.

His thumbs lingered on her inner thighs, coasted up, nudging her legs apart to give him access.

She was primed, her pussy wet with need. His mouth watered. His cock, too.

He touched his lips to hers. After the hunger of before, this was surprisingly sweet. Kissing Kennedy was different. Revelatory. Just like the last time when he'd had a headache, it had soothed and comforted. Or at least, in this moment, he tried to take that from the melding of their lips.

He was on fire for her.

He cupped her sweetheart-shaped ass, dragging her thigh over his hips so he could grind into her softness.

Keeping the thrusts slow, circular, he let his mouth pick up the slack and plunder. No more comfort, no more gentle nuzzling, the kiss took on a life of its own. He squeezed her ass, dragging a moan from her as he kneaded the supple flesh.

Leaning back, he cupped one perfect tit—somehow her bra had vanished along the way—sucking on a peaked nipple and almost coming on the spot. Maybe his restrictive diet made her taste better than anything or anyone that had come before. Sweet and necessary to his physical and mental well-being.

Still he ground against her, relishing skin-on-skin. It was torture, but what else was new? This was the default setting with Kennedy.

"You ready, ma belle?"

"Y-yes!"

She sounded frustrated. *Welcome to my world.* His hands shook while he rolled the condom on, and she reached out, doing the Kennedy thing, settling him while completely unraveling him.

"This might be over too quick," he warned as he nudged at her entrance, like a first tentative kiss. He was trying so fucking hard to slow down. Make it good for her. Make it perfect.

But Coffee Shop Girl wasn't in waiting mood. Her heel dug into his ass and her sweet pussy sucked him in. Mon Dieu, the feel of her was heaven and hell in one delicious plunge.

"More," she whispered. "Don't stop."

He held her still, absorbing her heat, every shudder and shimmy of her body. As he rocked into her, she squeezed her inner walls, hugging his cock so tight he knew he would not last.

His thrusts became faster, deeper, more rhythmic, finding spots that made her moan. *There*, she sounded like a kitten. *There*, her moan was deep and sultry. *There*, she begged for it harder. Each one revealed something new about her body and all the ways he could pleasure her.

Would pleasure her.

Because no way in hell would this be the only time. He had many filthy plans for Kennedy Clark.

Tonight, the plan was to make her come, then make her come again.

Just as he thought it couldn't get any sweeter, she cupped his face and drew him toward her lips, swallowing his moan of pleasure-pain. His hand pressed between their bodies, finding her clit because damn, it needed to happen soon. She arched off the bed, her nails digging into his biceps.

That's right, bebe. Mark me, score me, make me yours.

Through her orgasm, she worked his cock, imprinting her pussy on it and guaranteeing it would be no good for anyone else.

Fine with him.

One final thrust took her over, triggering an explosive release from him that wiped out all the shit that had happened tonight. And maybe more.

Maybe everything.

25

REID HAD GONE to sleep with excellent plans for his day off.

Wake up.

Give Kennedy an orgasm.

Coffee.

Another orgasm (both of them this time).

Walk his dog.

Make breakfast (he had a craving for a Denver omelet, maybe with ... cheese?).

Cuddle both dog and woman for the rest of the day.

He had even considered skipping the gym.

It started well. He'd awakened to a furnace of soft, curvaceous heat sprawled across his body. With several weeks to make up, he woke her with a kiss between her legs, his new favorite place. She was halfway to paradise before her eyes opened and screaming to the heavens before the sun was up. So far, so good.

"Hi." She snuggled into him after a brief, orgasm-fueled nap. (The nap was not on the schedule but he was willing to be flexible on this one issue. The Kennedy effect.)

"Morning." He kissed her softly. "You sleep okay?"

"No, terribly. Someone woke me up at the crack of dawn. So annoying."

"You should complain to the landlord."

She leaned up on her elbow, her silver eyes laughing. Had he done that? He wanted to think so.

"Complaint lodged! This girl needs her sleep."

"Understood. You have what you want, now I'm no longer of use."

She coasted her hand over his chest. "I wouldn't say that. I can think of plenty of uses for you."

"Dis-moi."

Her body gave a little shiver and he leaned over to kiss the tattoo cuffing her upper arm. A Thai peace symbol, she had said.

"What does that mean?" she asked.

"It means 'tell me.' Tell me about all the ways I can be of service."

She considered it for a moment. "Other than the obvious orgasm provision, I'm thinking coffee-making, hot-tub preparation, smoothie-blending—but without the kale, please, because *ugh*—and foot rub-giving. Got any of that on your resume?"

"Tout ça et plus."

"Which means?"

"All that and more." He pulled her close, his hand smoothing over the scars on the side of her body. She had them on her leg as well and an urge to know more, to know everything, rose up in him swift and sharp.

"What happened here?"

She didn't shut him down like before, possibly because pillow talk lent itself to a naked vulnerability. "A house fire when I was fifteen. My parents died and that's when I went to live with Edie."

He gently skimmed the hurt with his fingertips. "I'm so sorry, ma belle."

"Thank you. I won't deny it had a huge effect on me. Losing your parents is hard under any circumstances but as a teen, it really crushes you. I went through therapy, took some time for self-care. I'm not really a suffer-in-silence kind of person."

Like him. Was that what she meant?

Not always about you, dummy.

Given her loss, her independent nature was completely understandable. Admirable, even. But she didn't need to do it solo. She had teased him about his self-denial and about going easier on himself. Yet here was Kennedy pulling the lone-wolf act for which Reid was famous.

Words weren't his strong point but he had other ways.

"I told you once I would hold you whenever you needed it. You don't even have to ask."

With shining eyes, she nodded and let him take charge of the cuddle.

"All those things I said I could do," he said against her temple. "Coffee, hot tubs, smoothies, foot rubs?"

"And orgasms," she whispered.

"And orgasms. Those things are just the beginning." He whispered a few more skills on his resume, ones that were hers for the taking. "Mon corps pour vous garder au chaud. Mes bras pour vous garder en sécurité. Mon cœur pour te garder ancré."

My body to keep you warm.

My arms to keep you safe.

My heart to keep you anchored.

That same heart thudded wildly, recognizing the importance of this moment. He was falling for a woman who had said she couldn't stay, but maybe he could convince her.

Maybe he could bone up on the resume needed to keep a woman like Kennedy in his life.

"What does that mean?"

"Just some nonsense."

Bucky bounded into the bedroom and jumped on the bed.

"Bucky!" Kennedy said with a laugh that broke the tension. "You shouldn't do that. You're a terrible advertisement for my services."

"He needs to go out." Reid kissed Kennedy's forehead. "I'll take him and get the coffee started.

"COME ON, BOY, DO YOUR THING."

Bucky sniffed a patch of tree bark and decided it wasn't worthy of his efforts. So fickle.

Reid's phone rang and he steeled himself for a call from Henri. Surprised, he saw it was Coach Calhoun. Shit. He hadn't said much after Reid's performance last night, but obviously he preferred to do his bawl-outs in private, which was better than the Henri way, Reid supposed.

He answered. "Coach."

"Durand. So how are you this morning?"

"Disappointed." He was, about the game, but he couldn't claim disappointment about anything that had occurred in the aftermath. With Kennedy, hockey's importance—his reason for being on this earth, he had thought—diminished, a conclusion that shocked him and would never pass his lips. "I'm sorry about last night."

His body tensed, waiting for the harsh critique he deserved.

"So you didn't play to your potential. That happens. Not everyone can be on at every minute."

"But you put your faith in me and I let you down—"

"Reid, listen to me. I'm a hard-ass, but hell, no one is harder on you than you are on yourself. It was your first shot at center in prime time. Did you think it would click just like that? Foreman and Petrov have history and are in tune with each other. But you're the linchpin on that line. You've got to get in sync with both of them. It'll just take practice, which I know you're not afraid of."

No, he wasn't. His heart should have felt heavy but it didn't. It felt fucking hopeful.

He wanted a multi-year contract with a team. With *this* team. With a coach who saw his potential and not everything he did wrong.

"I don't mind working hard."

Coach chuckled. "That's what I want to hear. Enjoy your day off and be ready to grind at practice tomorrow."

"Will do. Thanks, Coach."

He didn't have time to enjoy this novel feeling of contentment because a text had come in from Kennedy while he was on the call.

So you're not going to like this ...

He read the rest and cursed loud enough to make Bucky finally pee *and* take a nice, healthy dump.

REID WAS fine with the sound of his own dog barking. After all, Bucky's voice was almost melodic and usually meant he was happy about his latest treat. Reid was less sure about other dogs especially in an enclosed space while people knocked back Mimosas, Bloody Marys, and eggs Benedict.

Foreman looked about as pleased as Reid to be spending his Sunday at Fido's on Main, Riverbrook's very own dog-friendly restaurant with a heated indoor patio. Apparently this was the latest thing. Man and canine, brunching together at last.

"They have this amazing bread pudding," Mia said. "We could get one for the table or maybe a half-one for me. I could probably eat the whole thing."

Foreman's eyes softened. "Wouldn't want to deny you your bread pudding rights, gorgeous girl. We'll get a large one for the rest of us and you can have a bowl all for yourself."

"Best. Boyfriend. Ever."

Foreman grinned, then caught Reid's eye and dropped the act. "You still pissed about last night, Durand?"

"Yeah," Kennedy said, her wicked smile stretching wide, her eyes sparkling like shining quarters. "Are you?"

He pressed his thigh against hers, hoping to discourage her from being too mischievous. He certainly didn't want his business known by all and sundry. Apparently Kennedy and Mia had set this brunch up a few days ago, but the way the two of them were grinning like Cheshire cats, he had to wonder if there were some shenanigans afoot.

Reid wasn't one to waste an opportunity. As he was here breathing the same sugar-on-French-toast-scented air as Foreman, he may as well get the man's opinion. "So last night didn't go so well."

Oh, that confused the *hell* out of the Masshole.

Foreman eyed him with suspicion, then after a beat said, "I feel like it was coming together in practice, so I guess it's just performance anxiety." He winced and turned to Mia. "What? Why did ya kick me?"

"Because you're being mean to Reid. He needs positive encouragement."

"I really don't."

Foreman waved a hand. "See? No one needs the soft soap here. We're all adults and Durand played like a donkey."

Reid snorted his appreciation for Foreman's candid assessment. "Thanks, Foreskin."

Cal muttered a curse under his breath.

Kennedy sent a baffled look Mia's way. "I don't understand sports people."

"This is standard intra-team smack talking," Mia said cheerfully. "You'll figure it out."

The server stopped by to take their orders, including from a special dog menu for Bucky and Gordie Howe, who were both lying on the floor, checking each other out.

"So how's the roommate thing going, guys?" Mia asked, in one of those oh-so-innocent tones that no one bought for a second.

"I'll let Kennedy answer that." Reid ran a hand under the table over her thigh and squeezed because even though he was in favor of keeping his private life private, he couldn't resist touching her.

She turned to him, that gorgeous smile already lighting up her face. "He's a neat freak."

"She's never met a dish she couldn't dirty."

"While I'm cooking awesome meals for you, ingrate!"

Reid let his hand wander inside thigh and inch north ... "Her coffee is undrinkable, her curry is inedible, she hogs my shower because the guest one isn't good enough for her

…" He shrugged. "Bucky likes her. That's something, I suppose."

She leaned into his shoulder, and just that simple press sent him into the stratosphere of joy.

"As you can see, living with a roommate hasn't softened him up in the slightest."

"Oh, I dunno." Foreman took a sip of his OJ. "He seems a changed man. Pity it doesn't translate to the ice. So Kennedy, I hear you're leaving the country in a couple of weeks."

Reid shot a sharp look at Foreman, whose lips twitched.

"Right, I'm usually in Asia during the winter and I have a job lined up teaching English in Thailand in January. Just waiting for my visa to come through. This is the longest I've stayed in the US for years."

Reid's heart started an unsteady thump. Kennedy had made no secret of her plans, but talking about it pissed him off. Foreman had clearly deduced this.

"Just as your dog-walking business was taking off," Foreman continued with a flicked glance at Reid. "Seems a shame."

"Calling it a business is a stretch." Kennedy picked up a torn Splenda packet and turned down the corners. "But it's definitely helped to pad the travel funds."

"Well, Gordie Howe is going to miss you. Bucky, too." Mia sent a look of abject pity at Reid. Just great. Then to Kennedy, "You should come to a game. Be Reid's good luck charm!"

"Watch him at work?" She turned to him. "You'd hate that, wouldn't you?"

Nope. "Might not be so terrible."

She didn't say anything, just held his gaze. *So it was a terrible idea …*

"You don't have to if you don't want to."

"I'd love to! I might not know much about hockey but I bet it's even better in the stadium."

Foreman opened his mouth to correct her, and Reid kicked him under the table. He wasn't sure which he enjoyed more: Foreman's yelp of pain or Kennedy's enthusiasm about seeing him play at the "stadium." Call it even.

"I get four tickets per game and I don't usually give them out."

"Why doesn't that surprise me?" More wisdom from the lips of the Masshole.

"Ooh, if that's the case, could I bring Edie and her gentleman friend? I think she'd love it."

"Of course. Only ..."

She was on it in a flash. "I know you don't want to leave Bucky alone but we could ask Sandy to watch him for the evening." At his questioning look, she added, "Your neighbor in 3B? She has this gorgeous Mastiff, a gentle giant. She'd be happy to help out."

A stranger? A neighbor-stranger, though he couldn't place her. Probably because he hadn't made any effort with his neighbors. Of course Kennedy would know her.

She gripped his hand under the table and squeezed. "Listen, just think about it. I'd love it if you can get tickets for Edie even if I can't go. She'd go nuts for that."

"We'll figure it out."

With Kennedy, it seemed he was saying that more and more these days, in complete opposition to his usual inflexibility. She smiled at him, and yep, he was lost in that sun. For someone who didn't enjoy the light, he sure as hell was drinking in all the Vitamin D he could these days.

Don't get used to it. After all, she had a one-way ticket out of here in a few weeks, as Foreman had been so quick to remind him.

Foreman sniffed. "Look at you two, problem-solving like good little roommates."

Annoyed, Reid broke his gaze with Kennedy and redirected it at someone far less deserving. The Masshole smirk was in full flight.

The bread pudding arrived, which was about the only reason Reid didn't kick Foreman again.

~

"ASK QUESTIONS IF YOU HAVE THEM."

She grinned. "You're going to regret that offer."

They had just returned from a walk around the park with Bucky. Reid had given her a scarf and too-big beanie because he was worried she'd catch a cold and pass it onto him, which would interfere with his play—at least that was his story. His spare pair of gloves were too big so he insisted on keeping her hand in a warm cocoon in his pocket.

Brunch with Mia and Cal had been good for Reid. He wasn't a natural mixer, so Kennedy was all in favor of pushing him into "playdates" and modeling healthy relationships. Post-brunch they had spent the afternoon modeling a few new sex positions, and now she was cuddled up with him on the sofa, about to watch a game she knew nothing about. The Hawks, the other Chicago-based team, were playing the Boston Cougars in Beantown.

The TV was on mute during the pre-game because Reid said the commentators were "know-nothing idiots." A grid of headshots appeared on the screen.

"Hey, it's Bastian! I thought he was injured."

"Hard to keep him down."

Something occurred to her. "So how come your father didn't come down to see you play, even if Bast couldn't?"

"My father's fine with watching me on TV. He's a purist. Bast is so talented that watching him live is a thing of beauty."

"And you're not talented?"

"I'm a grinder. Effort's not as pleasurable to watch."

He really believed that, or someone had convinced him. Kennedy was *not* a fan of this Henri character.

The game started, and for the next thirty minutes, Reid patiently explained how it worked.

"So tell me more about this position switch you're trying. What does the center do?"

"Everything. It's the toughest position on the ice. Needs good offensive and defensive capabilities. Should be a steadier player rather than a flashy one. That player has to be the bulwark of the team, directing traffic, controlling the center of the ice. The team that controls center ice controls the game."

"Would've thought your control freak tendencies would make you well-suited to that."

She turned away on the last word, but now felt his stare.

"My control freak tendencies?"

"Reid. Come on." She met his gaze head on. "Are you going to pretend you're not a teensy bit controlling? It's hot but it's also kind of freaky."

"You think it's hot?"

She smiled at his smirky eyebrow. "Yes, Reid, I do."

She usually had no problems discussing sex, and as long as she was teasing someone and keeping it light, then it was perfectly fine. But this had the potential to get personal. To get into the weeds of who Reid was at his core.

"I like things a certain way. I know it comes off as rigid, but as you once advised me, I'm trying to lighten the fuck up." He rubbed a hand over Bucky's back. "We're not all brave world travelers."

On any other day she would have let that comment slide, but after that conversation about her travels at brunch, she wondered if there was a little shade in there. Even if Reid was interested in more than just a hot, hormonal fling, she sure as hell wasn't going to change her MO for a guy she hardly knew—not even if he was amazing in the sack.

Or needed an on-site dog nanny for a long-term gig.

Or made her feel warm and fuzzy because every smile he sent her way was so hard-won.

Instead she focused on the first thing he'd said. That he had taken something she once said to heart sent her own heart into overdrive.

"Beware of wisdom from women serving coffee. Not much better than bartenders."

He nuzzled her nose and dropped a kiss on it. "Sure, Coffee Shop Girl. You were right, though. I can't become a different person overnight but incremental changes here and there, I can work with that."

Pride suffused her chest. On her travels she often ran into people who claimed to be on a path of self-discovery or were fixing themselves one mile on the road at a time. It just went to show that you didn't have to leave home to make those changes. Here was Reid, a man who recognized his limitations, and who was willing to do the work to be kinder to himself.

A few minutes before the end of the period, his body language changed when his brother came on the ice. He angled forward, his fists balled, his entire being focused the next play. As much as she liked Bastian, she didn't want him to score—not if it ruined Reid's night.

She wasn't quite prepared for Reid's reaction when

Bastian plugged the puck into the back of the net within seconds of coming on the ice. Her roommate shot upright, as if he'd forgotten he wasn't alone, and yelled, "Yes!"

Bucky barked and Reid sat beside him quickly, running a hand over him to soothe him.

"You're glad he scored? Aren't they the competition?" *And isn't your brother your biggest rival?*

"Of course I'm glad. I'm always happy for him when he does well."

"And with that goal, Bastian Durand shoots to the top of the conference scoring table. Pity his brother didn't play so well last night! Bet that'll be awkward at the next family dinner."

"Wow, they really like playing up this rivalry, don't they?"

"Rivalries are the lifeblood of sports. But Bast and I aren't really in the same league. I recognize that and it's okay."

Her heart did a weird flip. She'd expected a begrudging acceptance of Bastian's talents, not this sheer joy in his brother's good fortune. That should not have turned her on more. It really shouldn't have.

Though she now realized that by "turned on," she meant something else. Something far riskier to cool, no-attachment, rolling stone Kennedy Clark.

26

REID JUMPED the boards and headed out to the center for the faceoff. Kevin Maclin, the Philly captain lifted his chin and grinned—or as much as you could with a mouth guard in.

"Well, well, well, if it isn't pretty boy Durand in a new position. Your coach gettin' desperate, huh?"

"Not as desperate as that redhead you used to screw in college. What was she called again?"

"Keep her name out of your mouth."

"Right, you married her." Reid's chuckle was dark. "Merde, she definitely took pity on you."

"Asshole."

But he was the asshole with the puck. Sometimes people forgot the heights of dickishness he was prepared to scale in service to the game. Reid had already flicked the puck to Foreman before Maclin's insult had died on his lips. He shouldered his way past the big Philly man, determined to be out of his range should the puck come flying back.

Which it did.

If Reid squinted, he might be able to make out a pocket of light through the Philly tender's leg pads. He could take the shot ... or take advantage of Petrov who was already in position on the left. Back to the Rebels captain who struck, clean and true.

The horn went off, the crowd went fucking nuts, and Reid felt better about that goal than if he'd scored it himself. Petrov skated over, his gloved hand raised, and Reid high-fived him.

It would be rude not to. While he might be a dick to others on the team, he had a lot of respect for the big Russian.

"Good work, Duracell. Keep it up."

Duracell. He hadn't lasted long enough anywhere to acquire a nickname. Reid nodded and headed back to the center.

An hour later, he'd accumulated eighteen minutes and thirty-two seconds of ice time, two assists, and was uncomfortably accepting the praise of his teammates in the locker room after a 5-1 win.

"Jesus, you must hate this," Foreman said with a grin as he pulled his jersey off.

"It's not my favorite thing." He shot a sharp look at Foreman, who was having a hard time not laughing. Or not a hard time at all. "Unlike you who needs constant ego massaging, I prefer to play my game and not make a fuss about it."

Kershaw clapped Reid on the back. "Fuckin' awesome, Duracell. Drinks are on you."

Now wait a minute. "I play great *and* I have to buy the drinks?"

Gunnar called out, "As you don't indulge during the season, this'll be a cheap*er* round for you."

"Doesn't indulge in anything!" Jorgenson's comment drew plenty of laughter. Well, the joke was on them because for the last few nights he had indulged. He'd indulged all night long.

Someone smarter than him might argue he'd unlocked some sort of magic as soon as he accepted his fate: sex with Kennedy was inevitable, and he had no intention of fighting the thrill in his veins at the very thought of her. But it was more.

Bastian was right: Reid was crushing hard on this woman.

"Yeah, Durand, buy your buddies a drink."

Reid snapped his head back because that was not the voice of one of his asshole teammates.

Kennedy stood at the entrance to the locker room in all her glory—if you could describe that old lady parka glorious. On Kennedy, undoubtedly. She brought a shine to everything.

She stood back a few feet, her silver-gray eyes dancing and taking it all in. Then she caught his gaze again and smiled, a bright grin that ripped something apart in his chest.

He should not be this glad to see her. But all he could think about was Sunday, once they got that dumb brunch out of the way. They had spent all afternoon in bed, then cooked together, walked Bucky in the park, watched a hockey game, and ... well, an early night was *always* good for his regimen.

Couple stuff. The kind of connection he would never usually seek and couldn't have imagined he would crave.

Tonight he played well but the victory happened before he touched skate to ice.

He stood and walked toward her, gratified when she met him a few steps in. So she was leaving in a few weeks, but he intended to make it harder for her. Failing that, he would enjoy this time they had left together.

You're here, he told her with his eyes, before he gathered her in his arms and claimed her with his mouth.

You're mine, he told her with this kiss. The wolf whistles of the crew couldn't compete with the thunder in his veins and the rabbit-kick thumps of Kennedy's heart beating against his chest.

He didn't want to let her go, not now that he had found her. Neither did he want to share her. On opening his eyes, he found her with a glassy look and kiss-stung lips. Absolutely perfect.

"Where's your grandmother?"

"Nice to see you, too." She laughed, sounding nervous, and her eyes asked if he had really done that. "She's getting her gentleman friend to buy her a hockey shirt."

"I can get her merchandise."

"Oh, let him do it. There's some contest for his affections at Larkvale, so if she can bamboozle her way into his good graces this way, we shouldn't question it. Good game, by the way."

"Merci."

She gave a little shiver. His girl liked the French. "And before you ask, I texted Sandy about Bucky and he's fine."

Sandy was the neighbor down the hall, who Reid didn't know existed until this past Sunday.

"That's good. We probably should get home and—"

"Oh no, you don't, Duracell." Cade Burnett butted in. "You're buying the first round, whether you drink it or not. And I need to talk to your lady here."

Your lady. He was about to deny it but it would be a barefaced lie. Besides, Cade had already turned on a big, toothy grin for Kennedy. "Howdy, Ma'am, we haven't met officially. Cade Burnett at your service."

Reid glared at his teammate. "For fuck's sake, you're not *that* Texan."

"Quiet, please, we're conducting business here," Cade said without any heat. "I heard you're the woman to talk to about getting a puppy. My guy's at home with our little one and—"

"A new baby?" Kennedy was all smiles. "Aww!"

"Aww is right. A gorgeous little gal called Rosie and my hot husband is taking on the lion's share of the childrearing duties. But I think he could do with some canine company and a little bird told me you're the woman with the connections at the shelter."

"I volunteer there, so I'd be happy to help you find a new companion. What did you have in mind?"

"Something friendly, doesn't have to be pure breed or anything fancy, just good around babies."

Someone else pushed his way in. Jorgenson, the big lummox. "Kennedy, thanks so much for picking up my dry cleaning. Did you get my payment?"

"I did, Erik, thanks! And the woman at the counter said she was really sorry about that stain on the shirt sleeve. She tried but it wouldn't budge."

Puppy matching? Dry cleaning? Reid glared at Jorgenson who was his usual oblivious Swedish self.

"It's okay, I can cover it up with a jacket. So my parents are coming into town next week and I need some ideas for stuff for them to do. I thought about Second City but they don't really get all the political humor."

"Shoot me the dates and I'll work around your playing schedule. Maybe a show at the Magic Lounge? Everyone loves card tricks."

Erik turned to Reid. "Isn't she amazing? And if you're free for dinner, Ken—"

"She's not free for dinner," Reid choked out. Did the man not see Reid's arm wrapped around this woman? "Every waking minute is spent minding Bucky or walking other people's dogs or visiting her grandmother, so stop trying to monopolize her time. All of you."

Kennedy patted Reid's chest. "I can accept or decline my own dinner invitations, thank you." She turned to Erik. "Let's chat when Grumpy Pants here isn't giving us the evil eye. And Cade, send me the specs for your puppy and I'll see who's looking for a forever home the next time I'm at the shelter."

"You are a queen among women, Kennedy." Cade picked up her hand and kissed it, making her giggle. The guy was gay but Reid couldn't help his scowl. Hands off, Burnett!

Kennedy was now busy ogling—and that was definitely the correct term—his teammates. Most of them were in various stages of undress, not caring that they had female visitors. Mia was also here, canoodling with Foreman.

"Maybe you should wait outside," he said.

"What? It's just naked hockey butt." She peered up at him, all mischief. "I'm a world traveler. I've seen plenty of butts before, y'know."

"Not the asses of the guys I work with. It looks like I have to go out with them for a while." He'd rather she was with him than not, even if these other shitheads were present and flirting. "Come with me."

"I would but I really should get Edie and her man back to the asylum before they send out the search dogs."

"I should go say hello to her."

"Would you? She'd love that!"

"I need to get changed but I can meet you outside in a few minutes. Near the west entrance."

She smiled, and his heart went boom. This crush was the worst.

Ten minutes later he approached Kennedy's group, wearing a baseball cap and a hoodie to keep under the radar. Since he started playing so well, fans were more forward, but his subterfuge went to shit as soon as Edie saw him.

"Reid Durand! You were amazing."

He felt a smile tugging his lips. "Thanks, Edie. I hope the seats were good."

"Are you kidding? They were the best. And George got me a jersey!"

"I can't wait to see it on you," George said, his gaze adoring. "And then off you."

Huh, George was really going for it. Reid caught Kennedy's eye; she was clearly trying her best to keep it together.

"I picked up a few extra from the merchandise people." He handed a bag over to Edie. "You can keep it or give it to some of your friends and enemies at Larkvale."

"Oh, that's wonderful. And you should come and play bingo!"

Kennedy chuckled. "Not sure that's a true quid pro quo, Edie. Reid gives you free merch and you make him play bingo?"

"No, it's fine. I'd be honored to join you for bingo one day." He raised an eyebrow at Kennedy who responded with a look of touché.

Only now they couldn't stop looking at each other. Really looking. Kennedy's color rose, staining her cheeks, and he realized he must be giving her that intense, scorcher of a look that let her know everything he was thinking. How was he so good at hiding his emotion on the ice but turned to a movie reel of feeling around this woman?

"We—uh, we should call that Uber," Kennedy said quietly. "Get you two back. Reid has team stuff to do."

"No, I'll drop you off," he said, an offer that was declined then argued over then finally accepted as he ushered them back through the center and out a different entrance to the players' lot.

"You don't have to do this," Kennedy said. "I know you need to get to that after-game celebration."

"Plenty of time for that. They'll be there 'til the bar closes."

But she stayed quiet on the car ride to Larkvale. Perhaps he had been too intense, too forward in stamping her "property of Reid Durand" in front of his teammates, and it caught up with her a little late. Edie and George kept the conversation going, and Reid responded to their questions and comments about the game as comprehensively as he could. They pulled up outside the home and Kennedy undid her seatbelt.

"You're going in?"

"I just want to get her settled—"

Edie cut in. "No need! I have an escort here."

Reid helped them both exit the car—this took some time and several exclamations about how high the car was off the ground and how dangerous the ice that didn't exist was—but eventually the back seat was empty.

The tension, however, was thicker than ever.

"Looks like they're okay," Reid said when he got back in the car, trying to put her at ease, or bring them back to the roommates-with-benefits they were before the kiss in the locker room.

"Yeah, they don't need us."

"So you can come out to the bar after all? Everyone should be at the Empty Net by now."

She lifted her gaze to his, licked her lips. And then in a heartbeat, their mouths met and every fucking reason for not being this close *all the time* went out the window.

She tasted of fire and victory, of wild midnight wishes. Of all his hopes and dreams for the future.

But mostly she tasted like his.

"I thought, maybe, I got it wrong back there in the locker room," he murmured against her lips. "Came on too strong."

She looked conflicted, but after a beat, she said, "No, not at all. I—I loved it. Still want to go to the Empty Net?"

In her eyes he read her need and it matched his own. "No." He kissed her again, savoring her taste because it would be at least ten minutes of driving during which he'd have to keep his eyes on the road.

Her hand moved to his leg, squeezing his thigh. "Maybe I can—"

"Non." He placed her hand back on her side of the car. "Keep that weapon to yourself. I won't last if I let you have your way. I want to make it good for you, better for you than before."

"Not sure how that's possible, but I'm all for you trying." She squirmed in her seat. "Just drive."

27

"Penny for 'em."

Kennedy looked up to find Edie studying her closely above the straw of her raspberry razzmatazz smoothie.

"Oh, nothing."

Edie snorted. "You're thinking about Reid. Maybe that great shot he made in the final period of last night's game."

"Sure. That's what's on my mind. Hockey."

Edie was half-right. The last week had been a whirlwind with Reid and Kennedy passing like ships in the kitchen. He had spent a couple of days away at a game in Nashville, then had to turn around and play a home game last night. She was a busy woman herself, though she'd stopped taking on more dog clients. As much as she adored the work, it didn't seem fair to them if she was leaving in a few weeks.

Leaving. It was all happening so quickly.

She loved seeing the happy, smiling faces of her doggie clients. She loved contributing to the mental well-being of their humans. She loved having this chance to connect with Edie. And she loved the comfort she felt in Reid's arms.

Possibly a little too much.

That passionate claiming—because she couldn't think of any other way to describe it—in the Rebels locker room a few nights ago had taken her off guard. She had told Reid she loved it, and that was true. Who wouldn't want to be the focus of a man of such intensity? Yet she couldn't help thinking about the Mount Everest question.

Why did you climb that mountain?

Because it's there.

He was her boss, her landlord, and now her roomie-with-*uh*mazing-benefits. She had pretty much driven him to distraction during an intense period of his career. Not that she was irresistible, but she certainly pushed some sex-shaped buttons. They were connected by their love of a dog and a shared roof.

Why did Reid bang Kennedy?

Because she was there.

Was there more to it than scorching looks and hot sex? She wasn't sure she should examine it, not when her plans were moving along. She had received an email from the Thai school where she would be teaching. Her visa had come through and her documentation was in order. The only thing to hold her here was Edie and her developing feelings for a certain surly Canadian and his dog.

"Edie, do you ever wish I was here more? In the States?"

"Of course I do. I love when you visit me here and I love our chats. Sure, I know you have a life that's separate from me."

"But ..."

"Aren't you tired, honey? Don't you ever think of slowing down?"

Slowing down gave her time to think, a commodity she would rather have less of than more. Who wanted to be stuck in her head with all those memories? Better to act, move, live in the moment.

That had been her mantra for so long she wondered if they were only words on a page instead of affirmations in her heart.

Edie's phone vibrated and she picked it up, squinting.

"Oh, good, Reid's here."

Kennedy started. "Reid? My Reid?"

"Yes, *your* Reid." Elder smirk, which were the most annoying smirks of all. "He's in reception. Go down and meet him, will you?"

Reid was here? "He's texting you? Since when?"

"Just a few days. I send him gossip about the players so he can confirm or deny. He's very indiscreet."

What the hell was happening here? She shouldn't be this excited, but her heart was in charge and zooming ahead of her body toward Reception.

Reid waved through the glass doors at seeing her, his lips turned up in a rare smile. Bucky sat at his feet but jumped forward upon seeing her.

"You're here!"

"Yeah, Edie asked me over to play bingo."

Of course she did, the wily minx. Kennedy turned to Janice at Reception, who was waiting to jump in with her rules and regs hat on.

"He can't bring the dog into the dining room."

"Oh, I know that! How about we put him in Edie's room? Just for an hour or so." She leaned on the counter. "He's completely housetrained and as gentle as a lamb. And we already registered his shots record with the front desk a few weeks ago."

She slid a glance at Reid. If ever there was a time for him to act like a hottie hockey hunk, it was now.

Her guy stepped up to the face-off circle. "Janice, I promise we will both be good boys." That barely-there French lilt was slightly more pronounced.

Janice responded with a giddy giggle. "Well, you don't have to be *too* good. Just your dog."

Reid winked at her and Janice looked like she was about to collapse in an orgasmic puddle. She waved them on through.

"Where the hell have you been hiding Reid the Flirt?"

"The charm emerges only when necessary."

It was so good to see him. She had left him an empty husk post-sex this morning but that was then. That was the physical connection they shared and this—*this* was something entirely different.

They arrived at the entrance to Edie's room and stepped inside. "He should be okay here while we hang out." She unhooked Bucky's leash and hung it on a hook inside the door. Before she could say *bingo*, her back met the door and she was covered by a hard-bodied hockey god.

"Hi," he murmured before capturing her mouth with his.

She moaned, loving the taste and feel and weight of him. The gravity that was Reid.

"Is this weird?" he asked after he let her up for air.

"Necking in the bedroom of a senior living facility? No, not at all."

He rubbed his nose against hers. "I don't want to interfere with your special time with Edie."

"No, it's fine. I'm glad you're here."

She loved that he was making such an effort with someone she cared about—it said a lot about the man. She was used to making casual friendships on her travels, and this had the potential to be anything but. She felt safe, grounded, and desired with him.

Two of those three things terrified her and neither of them involved lust.

He pivoted, taking in the room. "Now, Bucky, be a good boy and no climbing on Edie's furniture."

Bucky lay down on the rug and went perfectly still. He'd come such a long way.

Reid picked up a photo of Edie and Papa John. "Is this your grandfather?"

"Yeah, he was a Chicago firefighter, but he died before it happened." She found him watching her closely. "Before the fire."

"Holidays must be tough for you, ma belle." He put the frame down. "When's the last time you spent one in the US?"

"Six years. It's not hard to find some ex-pat deep-frying a turkey on a beach somewhere. I haven't gone without."

His look was searching, grave. "What were they like?"

She blinked. "My parents?"

He took her hand and sat her down on Edie's bed. "Just curious to know about the people who made this beautiful girl before me."

Oh, wasn't that lovely. She took a breath and waited for the pain to wash over her. Sometimes it snuck up on her with the scent of gardenias, her mother's perfume. Sometimes it was a short, sharp shock with a glimpse of a dead politician on TV and her father's voice ringing clear as a bell in her head. *That guy's a crook!*

For now, the ache stayed at bay.

"Mom—Libby—was a high school teacher. History. She loved to garden and paint—I inherited none of her talent."

"The watercolor by your bed. That's hers."

"Yes, it is. When I saw that Calla lily in the pot, I couldn't believe it. It's the same flower. Did you buy that?"

"At the garden center the night before you stayed over the first time." He looked diffident. "To make the place more welcoming."

It had worked. Her mother's favorite flower, the subject of the one thing Kennedy had saved from the flames, was waiting for her in Reid's guest room like a sign from the universe.

"She was also a good cook."

"You got that from her."

"I did!" She laughed, remembering those days at her mom's side in the kitchen. "My Dad, or Benjamin—and he preferred the full name, no Ben or Benny—was a poli sci professor at IU. Indiana University in South Bend. He was a big fan of seventies TV, donuts, and embarrassing me in front of my friends. John F. Kennedy was his hero."

"Hence the name."

"Yep. When I was mad at him for something, I'd yell that JFK was a mafia-loving philanderer who almost caused World War Three with the Bay of Pigs invasion. How dare he name me after that loser?"

She'd completely forgotten that and the memory was like a whiskey dram of warming nostalgia to her heart.

"A little more intellectual than the usual teen rebellion."

"Yeah, it was. The dinner table was never dull. A history teacher and political science professor with a kid named Kennedy. We had a dog, too—Peanut, because Jimmy Carter was a peanut farmer before he was president. Dad thought Carter was ineffective but a good palate cleanser after the Nixon-Ford debacle. His words. Peanut was always wedging himself under the sofa. Such a dummy."

"So, you've been a dog person forever." His hand stroked the inside of her palm, such a comfort.

"I have." Of course, if Peanut had made it out, her dad wouldn't have gone back in to find him. All because Kennedy had made a fuss about her best friend. Why had she done that? Crying about her dog so much that her father had tried to soothe his daughter by playing the hero.

She looked down at Bucky with his missing eye and his multiple scars and cursed the person who had abandoned him, or worse, so that he ended up in the lake. Reid might have had it under control in those frigid waters, but the last time she let someone else do the saving, her world stopped spinning. Her father had died inside the house looking for Peanut under the sofa. Her mother, later at the hospital, from her injuries and smoke inhalation.

These days Kennedy did the rescuing—puppies, players, and herself.

"It seems like another part of my life, so long ago, yet sharp enough to still feel it deeply."

Still stroking her hand, still holding her gaze. Just giving her the space to let it out.

She sniffed, wiped a stray tear. "Luckily I had Edie to help get me through. I was hell to live with those first few months. She was a real trouper."

"She thinks that about you."

"Yeah, we're quite the mutual admiration society. I've really missed her. She doesn't have anyone. Not really." Neither did Kennedy, but that was largely her fault. Arm's length was the safest distance. "Edie said I was always welcome. She loves me like I'm a blood relative, though I'm not."

"She loves you because you're Kennedy. It might have started out that way but you're not defined by your relationship to her husband. Edie cares about *you*, not her husband's granddaughter."

"I love her, too."

He kissed the top of her head. "Of course you do. I know you're an open person about some things—your sexual demands, your James Garner obsession, your criticisms of me—but with other things, personal things, it doesn't come so easy. I'm honored when you let me in a little."

A little could so easily give way to a lot. To everything.

"I'm glad you're here," she whispered, repeating the words she'd said earlier, only now they were imbued with a heartwarming magic.

"Me, too, though, I'm a little worried."

"What about?"

He leaned in close and whispered, "I've never played bingo."

She laughed, loving this playful side of Reid. "Oh, they're going to eat you alive."

28

REID WASN'T big on relaxing. Long, restful baths were not his thing. A couple of guys swore by cold water immersion (Kazminski did it during the second intermission, which everyone thought was nuts). Reid was not about to jump on that train.

But no one had told him that a hot, sudsy, candlelit bath with a woman you were obsessed with might be almost as good as sliding into her tight, fuck-me body.

"This was a great idea," Kennedy murmured, reading his mind. She covered his much bigger hand—currently cupping one gorgeous tit possessively—with her small one.

"Just what I was thinking." His lips trailed along her temple over damp curls and soft skin. The last few days had been busy, but whenever he and Kennedy crossed paths it inevitably led to his bed, the shower, or here. (There had been one enterprising moment against the kitchen counter.) The cage door was open—off its hinges, in fact—and they couldn't get enough of each other.

Talking about her parents had loosened Kennedy up.

She might think Reid reserved but she was as tightly-wound as him when it came to sharing what was in her heart. Not that she was treating him like a therapist, but something had unlocked between them.

Unlocked his game, too. The Rebels were on a mini-streak of three straight wins and were third in the conference. Reid wanted to think his play was helping. Something was happening, that click-into-place that Coach has said needed to happen. Reid was becoming integral to the front line. It felt good to be needed.

"So, big game soon," she said. "Bastian's excited."

The gruff sound in his throat let her know exactly how much he cared about Bast's excitement. The two had become friendly with texting and sharing memes and all that nonsense.

"You know he's trying to needle me through you."

"Because I'm not worthy of being his friend independently of Reid Durand, Superstar?"

"That's not what I meant. You two are pretty alike—cheerful little chipmunks with evil streaks. I can see exactly why you get along."

"He actually wants you to be happy."

Deep down, Reid knew that to be true. Bast was decent to the last drop, the kind of guy you would want in your corner or on your team. But the real issue wasn't whether Bast wanted Reid to be happy—it was whether he *should* want that. After all, Reid had been a bullying dick to him for much of their childhood, all caught up in craving Henri's approval. He couldn't get it the natural way, with talent or blood, so he took it out on Bast.

Yet here was his baby brother being nice to him, thrilled to be in the same city, enjoying their crosstown rivalry. He might not mean to do it, but Bast's friendship with Kennedy added another layer of self-doubt. Sure, Reid made her feel good physically but his brother filled a different need. A woman like Kennedy naturally gravitated to someone with a sunnier disposition. Like Bast. Like anyone else, probably.

Kennedy might not be looking for a soulmate, but if she was, it wouldn't be a moody grouch like Reid.

"Your dad's coming to visit. How do you feel about that?"

"Well, Dr. Clark, I'm not sure. How am I supposed to feel?"

She kissed him mid-laugh, and he let himself steal a smidge of her joy. "I'm just interested. He sounds … difficult."

"That's one word to describe him. It's part of what made him such a great player. When I was little, I used to watch his old games, trying to figure out how I could play like him. He was an enforcer—"

"What's that?"

"The guy who checks aggressively, starts fights, responds to dirty plays. That kind of player isn't used as much anymore. Dad saw the writing on the wall so when Bast and I were growing up, he focused our training on speed and goal-scoring. Enforcers are considered one-dimensional and don't always get a lot of respect. Henri Durand is all about respect."

She took his hand and placed her pruned fingers against his. "He must be so proud to have both of you playing at this level."

"He is. He wants us to fulfill our potential so when we don't play as well as we should, it hurts him."

She was quiet for a moment. "But it's not like you purposely play bad to disappoint him, is it? No one *plans* to be a disappointment, so he should really cut you some slack."

"He just expects us to try our best. But our best is a product of many things: talent, training, effort, will. Bast's success has always been easier for him to root for."

She turned in the water, her eyes flashing with ... huh, anger. He could have told her she needn't be angry for him but his heart had already skipped several beats in anticipation of her defense of him. Was this what it was like to have someone in your corner?

"What does your mother think of all this?"

"Mom isn't a huge hockey fan. She doesn't like to see her sons in competition, especially the kind of competition encouraged by Henri. They divorced as soon as Bast went to college and she's much happier without him."

"Sounds like your mom has Ornery's number."

"Ornery. Cute." He kissed her, trying to smooth away that righteous anger—but not too much. He liked the lingering taste of it. "Don't worry, I won't be too hard on your favorite Durand when we meet in the hexagon."

"So one of you could get hurt?"

He shrugged. "*One* of us could, oui."

"Reid!"

"*Reid!*" He mimicked her, then kissed her gaping mouth. "Don't worry, a few stitches. Maximum."

She withdrew, her brow lined. Shit. That was insensitive of him given how much she had lost.

"Kennedy, it's part of the game. We're both tough, and people rarely get hurt. I promise." He was touched that she cared, though more likely she was worried about Bastian's pretty face.

And then because he was sick of thinking about his brother, he moved his hand below the water and worked what skills he had—the giving of pleasure.

"STAIRWAY TO HEAVEN. SIXTY-SEVEN!"

All eyes down for the game of the century: bingo at Larkvale, played twice weekly by the residents. Reid and Bucky had stopped by with tickets as a bribe for Janice, so his dog could sit at his feet while Reid was shafted by elderly grifters.

"Life begins at forty!"

"Oh, I have that one." Edie blobbed a circle over the number with her special pink marker. "You have that one, too."

Reid crossed off the number, 40, on his card. He'd been worried that the bingo caller—a woman with a very loud voice, necessary because half the residents were hard of hearing—might bother Bucky, but the pup was taking it in his stride. He lay at Reid's feet, perfectly content.

"It could be a ghost," Edie said.

Reid thought about that for a second. "I don't believe in ghosts."

Edie gave him some serious side eye. "That's a very limited viewpoint."

"I'm a very limited person."

For the fifteen minutes prior to bingo, Reid had listened to Edie's theories on who was stealing her chocolate bars. He wouldn't put it past the staff to get light-fingered but it seemed more likely to be another resident. Instead Edie was offering the ghost option.

"What would a ghost want with a Milky Way?"

"To be mischievous. That's what they are, or some of them are. Like leprechauns."

"You believe in leprechauns as well?"

"Who knows their Abba? It's dancing queen. Only seventeen!"

"Leprechauns are not mythical creatures," Edie muttered, her eyes never leaving her card. "They're documented."

"But there are none here. Unless it's a ghost of one." Ghost leprechaun? Now *that* gave him chills.

"I know there are spirits. I see them."

"Who do you see?"

Maybe it was her husband, Kennedy's grandfather, or perhaps residents of this place long gone. Edie assessed him for worthiness, decided he didn't pass, and returned to her card.

"Man alive. Number five!"

He marked that one off. "Let's assume for a moment that the thief is part of this earthly plane and hasn't yet passed to the other side ..."

"That's why they're ghosts. Because they're stuck in the in-between."

Munching on candy? "Okay. Assume they're alive and well and capable of enjoying chocolate—" At her raised eyebrow, he added, "as only real, live, flesh-on-their-bones, non-spirits can." He suspected she was being difficult on purpose but she was old and had a right to be. When he reached that age, he planned to terrorize the staff of whichever home he ended up in.

"All the threes. Thirty-three!"

"So if we make that assumption, then what are we looking at? Who has access to your room? Do you really think the staff would risk their job for a Three Musketeers?"

"That leaves one of this lot." She gave a shifty glance right, then left. "Kennedy thinks I'm making up crimes so I can strike solving a mystery off my bucket list."

He had heard all about the famed bucket list. "Whatever works, Miss Marple."

"You laugh, but I'll figure it out."

"Of course you will. What else do you have to do around here?"

She sighed, so resigned. "Passes the time until the end."

"Good to have a hobby during your final days."

She burst out laughing. "Why are you such an asshole during those press conferences? That's not you at all."

"Knock at the door. Number four!"

He marked that one, giving him three out of five on one row. "That's exactly me. I'm just unusually polite to *you* out of respect for your age."

She snorted. "You're nothing of the sort. You just put on a front with the press. And other players. And the world." She patted his hand. "But here with the elderly and with my Kennedy, you can be yourself."

"Because inside this pro-athlete lives a cranky octogenarian who wishes he could spend his days eating Jell-o, playing bingo, and taking naps. I've found my lane."

"No wonder she likes you."

He perked up like Bucky when he heard the jangle of the leash. "You think so?"

"You made her day when you turned up here for bingo last week."

He hadn't dared hope. "You'd like if she spent more time here, I think. Stuck around for a bit."

"I don't want to hold her back but I wouldn't object to a regular delivery of smoothies. And you two suit each other."

He would never say he had a type when it came to women. Yet Kennedy defied type. She was so full of life and made him want more than was probably good for him. "Kennedy suits everybody. And she doesn't want anything more than a fling. She's made it clear."

"Kennedy doesn't know what she wants. She's been

doing the same thing for so long she thinks it's all there is. Stuck in a rut of traveling, moving, working, every waking moment spent on thinking about others—*their* errands, *their* dogs—so she doesn't think too hard about herself. She's relaxed around you."

"Down on your knees. Forty-three!"

That sounded filthy. Someone actually took the trouble to come up with these rhymes.

"I don't know about that." He decided to take a leap. "Do you think she might stay in Chicago?"

Edie looked up. "Are you giving her good orgasms?"

That he didn't redden or freeze up was a testament to the fact he and Edie existed on the same wavelength. "You think that might be the key?"

That made Edie chuckle. "If you're good enough. I just want her to have something for herself. Some little spark of pleasure." She grinned. "Or a big spurt of pleasure!"

"I'm taking care of her," he said quietly. Not just orgasms. He wanted to look after her yet she was the one looking after him. His home, his dog, his life.

She eyed him, considered her next words. "You're gonna have to fight for her, Reid."

His heart thundered like a galloping horse. Fighting was the one thing he was good at. To be better, to get into the AHL and out again, for the first line, to prove he was worth his spot on the Rebels.

But would it be enough to make Kennedy happy? He wasn't sunny or cheerful. He didn't have any special skills. He worked hard on the ice. That was it. Hardly enough to win a woman like Kennedy who was a force of energy.

"Bullseye. Five-oh. Fifty!"

"Bingo!" Which was followed by loud groans of disappointment. A woman near the back raised her hand to claim victory.

"Rats." Edie put the used card to the back of her pile. "I'm going to need your help with something. You up for an adventure?"

29

KENNEDY CHECKED her to-do list and struck through what she'd already accomplished so far.

Collect Cooper at 10:10, Sylvester at 10:20, Dylan at 10:30.

Pick up Erik Jorgenson's dry-cleaning and Ann Sather cinnamon rolls.

Collect a case of wine for Dante Moretti, Cade Burnett's husband, at the Wine Goddess store.

December was a real boon to the dog-walking, and now, personal assistant business. No new clients, just taking care of the current ones. Everyone was so busy for the holidays, and Kennedy was the perfect Gal Friday to both players and WAGs. Harper Chase, the Rebels owner and CEO, had even asked her to provide a pet-match for her trio of daughters.

She'd been so busy that she had missed one of her visits to Edie at Larkvale. Usually she went over every day, but this morning, when she stopped by, she learned that maybe she didn't need to visit so often after all.

She had a rival for Edie's affections.

Now she was back at the apartment for a quick bite to eat before jumping into her afternoon to-dos. A volunteer stint at the animal shelter and phone calls to make for Tate Kazminiski, who needed help setting up fun events for his kids while they were in town. (Divorce was tough and the man was kind of clueless, bless his heart.) Kennedy was thinking that Whirlyball might be the best option—who wouldn't love bumper car basketball?

Kennedy put her bag on the hallway table and walked into the living room.

Or what had once been the living room. In the two hours since she'd been here, a new world had been terraformed made up of cushions, pillows, comforters, and sheets.

"Hello?"

She stepped closer to what looked like it might be the entrance. Sofa cushions shored up a tunnel, over which was draped a sheet. Another sheet had clothes pins holding it in place—he must have bought those. She pulled back the sheet and what she saw made her heart hitch.

Man and best friend.

Reid lay in a nest of cushions, a flashlight upturned to give an eerie spot on the blanketed roof, his e-reader reflecting a glow on his handsome face. By his side, Bucky was lying with his head tucked into Reid's side. The perfect spot to be.

Reid smiled at her. "You're home."

Well, didn't that catch somewhere in her chest. It had been a long time since she felt like she belonged somewhere.

Don't get carried away. It's a blanket fort.

"Are you receiving visitors?"

Reid turned to Bucky. "What do you think? Can Kennedy come in?" Whatever Reid saw on the puppy's face was enough to give her the nod. "We are."

She crawled inside, pulling the sheet door down behind

her and closing the rest of the world off. Reid shifted slightly so there was a sliver of space beside him on the other side from Bucky.

"So what's going on?"

"Since I recycled the TV box, I noticed he likes to sit in the hearth or the laundry cupboard. I figured he probably just craves warm, cave-like spaces."

Bucky lifted his head, aware they were talking about him.

"And you thought you'd like to try it, too?"

"Sometimes it's nice to get away without packing a suitcase."

"It sure is." As she leaned back, Reid rearranged some pillows to support her head. "Thanks."

"Don't mention it. How's your morning gone?"

"Good. I walked Gunnar Bond's dog, Cooper for the first time as well as a couple of my regulars. And Harper Chase asked me to stop by and talk about doing a yoga class for the WAGs. Like a brunch n' stretch. We're calling it Downward Dog and Daiquiris. We're going to do it between Christmas and New Year." Before she left for good. She rushed on, not wanting to dwell on it. "I checked in with Edie. Turns out she's been busy."

"Yeah?" His breath was warm against her temple.

She lifted her head. "I can't believe you took her ice-skating without me!"

"She said you've been putting her off because you're, in her words, 'a coward.' And it was just a quick circuit of the Rebels practice rink."

"A Foreman-Durand sandwich is how she described it, then "the three-way of her dreams" in the next breath. Please tell me someone filmed it."

He extracted his phone from his pocket and after a few

seconds, played the video of Edie being squired around the Rebels rink in the safe hands of Cal and Reid. A crowd cheered off-camera and Kennedy's heart squeezed at the happy memory Reid had created.

If it was happy, then why did she feel teary?

"Ma belle, what's wrong? Are you mad at me for not clearing it with you first?"

"No. Maybe. Edie's a grown woman and it's probably better I'm not involved. This bucket list business freaks me out. That's what people do when they think they're going to go soon." She rubbed her eyes and faced him. "You've probably figured out by now that I don't have a lot of people."

"It's hard to make connections if you move around so much."

"So I have only myself to blame?"

He admonished her with a look that said they were better than that. "That's not what I meant. I know a little about it. This is the fourth city I've lived in for the last five years, but that's largely down to me. I'm a dick."

She burst out laughing. "But you're a dick with talent. With a talented dick."

He doffed an imaginary cap, which made her laugh again. God, she loved how droll he was.

"My talent—on the ice—isn't enough to keep me on any team. Which means I really should try harder to be nice to my teammates, to the management, to the press, to the fans. A team might be more likely to keep me around if I was easier to get along with but I'm usually suspicious of people. Of what they want from me."

More lessons from Henri, no doubt. "People just want to connect with you, Reid. It's not rocket science."

He squeezed her hand against his chest. "So connect with me."

She brushed her mouth against his. "How's that?"

"You can do much better."

She applied more pressure, her lips curving into a smile. "Bon?"

He closed his eyes and slanted his lips over hers. "Tres bon," he whispered. They kissed for a while, another perfect moment in the blanketed dark, crafting cozy healing with a kiss.

Her eyes felt wet. "God, I'm ridiculous."

"You're many things, but ridiculous isn't one of them. You endured a heartbreaking tragedy. And today, you were reminded of that loss when you thought Edie might be hurt. I'm sorry."

"No, don't you dare apologize!"

"Do you know how rare this is? Take the win, Coffee Shop Girl."

That made her laugh. And then it made her kiss. Perhaps saying sorry was the perfect seduction.

"I'm sorry," he whispered, kissing her eyelids, then her nose. "So sorry." He whispered his lips over her cheekbone, down to her jaw, then a brush at the corner of her mouth. "Sorrier than I could ever be."

He was commiserating with her over so much more than not running Edie ice-skating jaunt by her first, and she adored him for it. Her lips found his and applied a sweet, sultry pressure. The tightness in her chest eased slightly in this precious space with Reid, who was so solid, serious, and generous.

"Thank you for spending time with her. It's sweet of you."

"It's not sweet. I'm determined to become a bingo champion."

Reid playing bingo with the oldsters was adorable. "Always the competitor."

"And when you're gone, I'll continue to visit her. If that's okay with you."

When you're gone. She didn't have time to process the words—the pain of them—because he was still talking.

"Unless ... you've thought about staying longer. It seems a shame to disappoint all your doggie clients, old and new. And maybe this yoga thing with the WAGs could turn into something. People need you."

In the half-dark, she watched his eyes fixed on hers. What was he asking? That she stay with him as his roommate, employee, or something else? It would be so easy to nudge her way into this life that didn't really belong to her. Enjoy the comfort he offered. The peace inside these sheet walls.

But Reid could be on a different team next year, or he could get tired of her, and she would have involved herself for nothing.

The hardest things in her life had already happened to her—or so she had thought. Wrapped in the safety of Reid's arms, she worried that relaxing her guard would put her in danger of feeling so deep all over again. Attachment is the root of all suffering. *Right?*

"I like my life. I like making my own way, being my own boss, deciding my own destiny."

"You don't have to travel halfway around the world to do any of that. All that could be achieved right here, except you'd have a network of people to rely on. A team on your side. A home, employment, security. Where were you living before here?"

She started at the abrupt query. "Before?"

"I saw your suitcase in your trunk that day at the beach. Where were you staying before here?"

"My car."

Shocked blue eyes met hers. "Ken."

"I'd been living at Edie's place but her son sold it and they changed the locks. Every roommate lead had dried up but I was ever hopeful—and look, it worked out. I've stayed in worse places."

"Than your car?"

She'd slept in sketchy hostels, in dark doorways, on foreign beaches. She knew what it was like to be alone, but she always made sure it was her choice. It was safer that way.

"I always manage, Reid."

"By putting yourself in danger? Does Edie know about this?"

"No, and she won't."

"Ken—"

She planted a kiss on his lips because as much as she loved listening to Reid, she didn't want anything to ruin their final days together. In his arms, in this blanket fort, in this temporary life, she felt safe but Walt Whitman knew the score.

However sheltered the port,

However calm the waters,

You shall not anchor there.

The road was calling, and no matter how wonderful this felt in the moment, her heart might not survive a lengthier stay.

30

REID PARKED the car about a block from the restaurant and checked his watch. Ten minutes early.

The occupant of the passenger seat wore a sexy red dress she'd borrowed from someone. Tara, she said. Reid would have bought her a dress if she needed it, but knowing Kennedy she wouldn't take a gift.

Reid didn't think he'd ever get tired of how the material bunched up, giving him a flash of strong, well-toned, oh-so-sexy leg. He reached over and ran a hand under the hem.

"We're going to be late."

"Non."

She raised an eyebrow. Of course Reid would never be late, that eyebrow arch said.

"I'm sorry in advance if he's rude. He's kind of abrupt."

"I'm a whizz at abrupt." Her gorgeous grin instantly relaxed him.

His phone vibrated with a text from Bast.

We're here! Where the hell are you, bro?

One-upped him by getting here early. "Let's go."

"Reid." She took his hand and returned it to where it had lain under her skirt, only now she moved it up, up, up until it reached—fuck.

"Ken."

"I forgot to do laundry." She moved his hand until he finally realized the gift she was giving him.

"You're wet. So fucking wet."

She curled a hand around his jaw and brushed her lips over this. "Just remember that this is waiting for you when you get home." *Home.* His hand positively trembled at the use of the word. It wasn't fair, though, because she would be gone soon.

Could you call a place home if the heart of it was ripped out?

"I might need it sooner." He ran a finger through her, turning it so the callus could have the best impact.

"Just let me know. You need a quickie in the restroom and I'll be there," she whispered against his lips, her eyes shutting on the pleasure he was dealing.

His phone buzzed again and she smiled. "Let's do this."

SMITH & Jones was one of those fancy restaurants where the servings were so small that Reid knew he wouldn't be breaking any of his diet rules tonight. Bast knew the sister-in-law of the chef, a former Marine, so they had a great table in a private alcove.

"Reid, baby!" Nadine, Henri's third wife, jumped up on seeing him and drew him into a tight hug. "You look so good." Nadine was pretty great and deserved a medal for her efforts in the face of his father's crankiness.

"Nadine, don't mollycoddle him." *Yep, there it is.*

"I haven't seen him for months. He couldn't even come home for Thanksgiving."

"I had a game."

She rubbed his jaw. "Your brother made it. And I can still miss you, can't I? Your father's in a bad mood. He had an argument with the Uber driver."

Sounded about right. "Dad." He put out his hand because that was how they always greeted each other. His father shook it wordlessly.

"This is Kennedy. My—"

"Roommate!" Nadine kissed Kennedy on both cheeks. "Bast's been telling us all about you."

The ever-informative Bast sat at the table and raised a beer in Reid's direction. Big mouth.

Roommate was as adequate a description as any. She wasn't his girlfriend, though he was about 99.99 percent sure he would jump at the chance to call her that if he thought it would work.

He wanted her to stay in Chicago with him and Bucky. It was as simple as that.

"Welcome to Chicago!" Kennedy took it upon herself to shake Henri's hand, surprising him with her forthrightness. "How's your hotel? Do you have a good view of the city or the river?"

Nadine slid Reid a shrewd look, the one that mothers—and stepmothers—everywhere had graduated with honors in.

"It's lovely. We can see the Wrigley Building and part of Michigan Avenue. Very pretty at night. Now sit, sit! Let's get some drinks in to celebrate being together with our boys—and Kennedy."

Bast stood to hug Kennedy but first he gestured at his outfit. "French blue, Kennedy. What do you think?"

"Matches your eyes, handsome."

As Bast wrapped Kennedy in a tight embrace, he grinned at Reid over her shoulder. "Kennedy chose my shirt."

"Just like Mom used to," Reid said.

Nadine gestured to them all to sit. "Kennedy, I hear you're looking after Reid's dog?"

"I am. But he and Reid get plenty of quality time together as well. They're such a cute duo."

Henri scowled. "This is the mutt you risked your career to rescue? You kept it?" He took another look at Kennedy, as if only now realizing her part in all this. Perhaps he recognized her from the video. His father rarely dwelled on details that didn't feed his narrative.

Kennedy went on the charm offensive. Reid could have told her that was *never* going to work.

"Mr. Durand, don't worry, I was there. In fact, he really jumped in for me because I was such a dummy thinking I could save this little guy. He was so brave! And Bucky's so happy." She grinned her dazzling smile and turned smoothly to the server, who had just arrived. "I would *love* a glass of Pinot Grigio."

"Make that two!" Nadine seemed happy to have a woman in the mix. These dinners were usually dull for her. "Or maybe we should get a bottle. What do you think, Kennedy?"

"I'm game if you are, Nadine."

~

Henri Durand was a handsome man, a weathered silver fox with plenty of scars from the ice battlefield to give his face character. Kennedy could see shades of Bastian in there, but that broodiness he was giving off was all Reid.

"How much longer are you in town?" Kennedy asked.

"Just a couple of days," Nadine said. "We leave after the game. I'd like to have time to shop but you know ..." She waved in explanation at her husband.

"Oh, that's a shame you can't stay longer. Next time, we could do something fun together."

Next time? The only way "next time" was happening was if Kennedy slowed her roll and stayed put. Yet saying it didn't feel wrong on her lips.

Not at all.

"I hear you used to play hockey, Mr. Durand, and that you coached the boys to greatness. You must be so proud of them."

He muttered, "They've done well." It obviously killed him to admit it, which made her want to needle him even more.

"I'll say! Both of them at this level. That's amazing. Learned from the best."

He assessed her, unsure what to make of her relentless cheer. "So what do you do?"

"Oh, this and that. Yoga by trade, but I also look after dogs for a number of clients. That's why I'm here so Reid can be assured Bucky is being cared for while he travels."

"You're living with Reid for the dog? Then why are you *here*?"

"Even dog sitters need to eat," Reid said dryly.

"True, and this dog sitter loves to eat! As for living in, Reid was determined to keep Bucky and kenneling him while he's away wasn't feasible. That's where I come in."

She wasn't sure why she wanted to poke at this man, maybe because his reputation as an asshole preceded him. Hard to believe he had fathered sunny Bastian. Genetics, so strange.

Henri merely stared at her, evidently mystified. Fine, she didn't need to win him over. After a little small talk about the meals they each had their eye on and the restaurant scene in Montreal versus Chicago, Nadine prompted Kennedy for information.

"A dog walker *and* a yoga instructor. That sounds interesting!"

Nadine was definitely the peacemaker, kind of like Bastian, though a little less peace-making and little more bomb-throwing might be better for this lot. "Sure, I love it. Do you do yoga, Nadine?"

"Me? Oh, no. I'm not sporty."

Bastian laughed. "Nadine, yoga requires no sporting aptitude whatsoever. You're essentially lying down the entire time."

Kennedy gave him a playful punch. "Hey! I'll have you know that yoga requires exceptional core strength."

"I'm trying to not scare her off. I think she'd have a blast at yoga." He grinned at Nadine. "Honestly."

"Speaking of trying, I've been needling Reid to join my class but he's worried about looking silly."

Reid sipped his water. "That's not what I'm worried about. I just don't want to show *you* up in front of your students."

"My students would love you joining in." She shot a smile at Nadine, and included Henri in it, too, though he didn't deserve it, the grump. "I do a yoga class at the senior home where my gran lives and Reid is quite the hit there.

The ladies love him, especially when he hangs and plays bingo."

That woke Henri from his sunshine-inflicted stupor. "You've got time to play bingo, Reid? Not from where I'm standing."

Reid tensed beside her, and for what? Not spending every single second doing his job? Not even that, *practicing* to do his job.

Reid was the hardest working person Kennedy knew. A beast when it came to preparation, and it showed. Since she'd moved in, he had played at least ten times and had scored in more than half the games. If anyone deserved a little R&R, it was this guy.

"He's having a great season," Kennedy said. "Not that I know much about it but my sources tell me he's doing well." She slid a smile Reid's way.

He held her gaze for a moment, just long enough to tease a secret grin from him. Meaning that he didn't smile at all but she felt it in her soul.

"What the hell are they doing, moving you from the wing, Reid? Did you ask for that?"

"Dad," Bastian said. "We're trying to eat here."

"How many Cups do you have?"

"One," Bastian said, then added cockily, "Two by the end of this year."

"Come back to me when you have four." He addressed Reid. "And that team's not going to win another Cup playing *you* at center. God knows you've done well with what you've got. You're a decent right wing. You'll be lucky if they keep you on the second or third line after the novelty wears off. And you need to keep above 50 points to guarantee they'll offer you a contract next year. Center won't get you there."

Durand Senior was getting mighty agitated. "This is what happens when women are put in charge."

"Coach Calhoun is a man last time I looked," Reid said, which made Bastian laugh.

"Don't get smart with me. Guy's a hack. They should have put him out to pasture years ago."

"Henri …" Nadine tried to soothe him.

"Maybe goals aren't everything," Kennedy said. "Isn't hockey about teamwork and brotherhood? Does it really matter who scores the goals as long as the team wins? And from what I can see, Reid's contribution, whether on wing or at center, has immense value. So maybe cut him a break?"

Henri's lip curled in disgust. "Let the adults talk, cherie."

"Don't talk to her like that," Reid said.

"It's okay, I can handle it."

"You shouldn't have to." Reid skewered his father with a look, and like all bullies when challenged, the man reddened and backed down.

But when she reached over to squeeze Reid's pillar-thick thigh, he flinched. Damn. This was going to be trickier than she thought.

31

Reid parked in the resident space outside his apartment building and turned off the engine. On the way home, he had remained silent, shutting down any attempt by Kennedy to talk to him.

"So, that was kind of intense. Is he always like that or was that the special version he brings out for guests?"

His hands gripped the steering wheel, his knuckles straining through the skin. She was being flippant, mostly because she had no idea how Reid truly felt about this man who cared only about winning. No other subject at dinner gained traction. Every word from Durand Senior sucked the life out of the room.

"Listen, I'm sorry if I made things difficult between you and your father, but frankly, the man is a dick."

"C'est vrai." *It's true.* She knew that much French. She knew that much Reid. "I'm sorry he ruined your dinner."

"He didn't. I mean, that sticky toffee pudding was amazing. But I think he ruined something. I think he's made you miserable and it hurts me to see how much he hurts you."

He shook his head. “Kennedy, you don’t have to defend me to him. It’s not your job.”

Then whose job was it? Bastian had tried but even he couldn’t make any headway. Nadine just rolled her eyes as if her husband’s cantankerousness was a joke instead of truly harmful. As far as Kennedy could see Reid was all alone here, bearing the brunt of familial pressure to succeed.

“You’re solid gold, Reid, you know that?”

He turned sharply, his lips parted in shock. “Kennedy—”

“You are! You completely undersell yourself. You know what I see?” She didn’t give him time to answer. “A guy who would rather hide his decency behind a scowl, who thinks his kindness puts him at a disadvantage and his big heart is a weakness. I will always defend you, Reid, because you won’t take the time to do it yourself.”

His big chest heaved with emotion. He looked baffled, those gorgeous denim-blue eyes soft and shining. “That’s not me,” he said faintly. “I’m not decent at all.”

“Push the seat back, baby.”

“The seat?”

“The seat,” she repeated as she leaned over, pressing her breasts against his arm and pushing the button that moved his seat back. In one swift move, she straddled him. “I don’t think I’ve truly demonstrated how flexible I am.”

“Kennedy, you don’t have to—”

But she stopped him with a kiss which had him responding with so much hunger, so much heat. A complete knee-melter. Good thing she was sitting over the thickest thighs in hockey.

Big hands pushed her dress up around her hips. Clever thumbs got to work, kneading, pressing, creating a sensuous friction. Eager to keep up, she unbuttoned his dress pants and unfurled the hard, beautiful length of him.

What a sight. Fully-aroused and all hers.

She mentally chided herself for that *hers* thinking. That would not do.

She needed to keep her wits about her. This was what she'd been telling herself for weeks: don't get sucked in by the dog or the man or the rootedness of it all. Keep it to the realms of pleasure, maybe a stretch to friendship. That's why she defended him against his father's verbal blows.

She was being a good friend, nothing else.

She started to stroke but he was already hard and perfect.

Despite the circumstances—the front seat of a car, the aftermath of a bad night, the desperation in that kiss—there was a reverence in how he touched her. How he slipped her breast out of her borrowed dress and brought it to his mouth. She arched off him, her head touching the roof of the car.

Unable to stand the pleasure, she moved her hands down, touching, mapping, loving this beautiful, pent-up, hurting man.

He was less closed off these days, but still bound by his upbringing. By the lessons his father had taught him. That only through a rigid self-control could he be worthy of that man's love.

He needn't exercise that kind of restraint here. She was determined to rattle Reid's cage.

While he was clearly determined to destroy hers.

She suspected he could hold out all night, could demonstrate that control, to make a point. To himself, perhaps. He had nothing to prove to her.

She curled a hand around his neck and nudged his mouth away from her breast.

"I need you inside me."

His hand trailed down her stomach, over her mound, his palm encouraging her thighs to part further. Gladly they obeyed his silent order.

"You're ... wet."

Of course she was. This was Reid. "Now."

The crinkle of foil, the quick adjustment to secure their protection, then he lifted her like she weighed nothing and brought her down to sheath him, the push excruciating in its deliberateness, exquisite in the pleasure wrought from her inner walls.

Both the ones at her core and the ones surrounding her heart.

"Ohhhh." Her moan didn't sound like her. Each cell had come to life and was now tingling with the stretch of thick, glorious fullness.

He closed his eyes, but if she had to feel it, she needed to see everything from him as well.

"Reid."

His eyelids snapped open, and in those pools, she saw relief, pleasure, maybe even affection. Dangerous to think it. Even more dangerous to rely on it. She recentered herself, drawing on her seduction skillset. On that detached version of herself that loved sex without entanglement, life without roots, the present without a thought to the past or the future.

"Hi," she whispered. "Stay with me. Talk to me."

"You want to talk?" The words sounded strangled, which made her feel more in control. She was seductress and healer.

"Yes. Tell me what you're doing. How good it feels."

"Of course Kennedy wants to talk. Of course she wants a blow—" He lifted her body and thrust up into her slowly. So slowly. "... by-blow ..." He pushed deeper, with a stroke that consumed. "... account of how I'm fucking her."

"Yes. I want to hear all of that."

He clasped her hand and held it over his heart, intertwined with hers.

"You want to hear how you've been driving me mad? How I've had to stroke one out twice a day just so I won't embarrass myself in front of you? How I hate when my brother and every single guy on my team talks to you and takes your attention? How I despise the smiles you give them because it's one less for me?"

This wasn't what she had meant at all. She wanted him to verbalize his desire; she wasn't even expecting it to be focused on her. After all, any woman in the roommate situation would have made him break. *Because it was there.*

Wouldn't they?

But now he'd started, she wanted to hear everything.

"Those smiles for them ..." He stroked a special spot and oh, that was good. "... aren't the same as what I give you."

He moved inside her, finding another untested point of pleasure. "They're not worthy to look at you, Kennedy."

Her heart liquefied. She knew her self-worth but in a general "I am woman—hear me roar" sense rather than a Kennedy-is-awesome sense. No one spoke to her like this because she didn't allow them to get close.

She would never have expected Reid to be the first. Surly, rude, irritable Reid.

She craved his voice. Not just to hear him say nice things about her, but to hear him speak. To hear what was going on inside his head. His heart. His soul.

"More," she murmured, meaning the words and the hands. Meaning Reid.

He rubbed his nose against hers, and it shouldn't have been a turn-on but it was. A turn-on for her heart.

"You want to hear how I've wanted you since the minute you walked into my apartment? Longer than that. Since the first day I saw you at the coffee shop. You were talking to someone and you laughed at something they said, and my pulse went boom. And believe me, I have the steadiest fucking pulse on the planet."

All this time? Surely, this was just the heat of the moment. Her ability to smart-ass her way out of this conversation failed her.

"You know what you are, Kennedy?"

She might have responded with a *what*, but it came out as a moan.

"Five foot two of chaos. You waltz in, disrupt everything, turn my life upside down, and make everything crazy." He stroked deeper, making her moan.

Making her feel.

Now that he'd started, he wouldn't stop. All these words, made for her and her alone. "I belong here." His hands tightened on her ass, fusing their bodies and souls together. "You're mine and I'm yours."

"Reid, I—"

He sucked on her lip. "Just let me imagine, ma belle. Laissez-moi rêver."

She didn't need to understand French to know what he was saying.

Stay with me. Love me.

It wasn't her intention to change up his life but that's what happened when atoms collided, chemical reactions occurred, and new substances were created.

This was what happened when you let yourself fall.

32

Reid opened up the computer to check on an idea he had for Kennedy's Christmas gift.

Last night, his roommate had been amazing, and that was before she had climbed aboard him in his car. She knew exactly what he needed. Her. Only her.

Something was different about the sex, too.

It wasn't just that she called him decent, kind, and big-hearted—labels he would never have slapped on himself in a million years.

It wasn't just her defense of him, though that was soul-wrenching in itself.

It was how she clutched him when she came, like she never wanted to let go. Like he was the one person who could hold her heart safe and give it the care it deserved. Kennedy needed him as much as he needed her.

But he was still worried about scaring her off. He had almost said something he couldn't take back. He had almost begged her to stay.

As if she couldn't figure that out with his desperate sweet nothings. She knew. He'd felt her body melt as he told her she was his and he was hers. He wanted to take care of this woman, cherish her so she didn't work so hard, give her a reason to stay still.

It was what you did for people you loved.

Usually a phone call from Henri would dampen his spirits, but when Reid saw his name flash on the screen, he didn't tense up. He didn't even wish the call away. All this progress!

"Hey, Dad."

"You ready for tonight?"

"Sure, you'll get a good fight."

Henri cleared his throat and seemed to take a moment, which was in itself so rare that Reid's heart missed a beat. "You know I've only ever wanted you to succeed, Reid. Do even more with your talent than I could with mine."

Huh. That was the first time Henri had ever mentioned the word "talent" in reference to Reid. Maybe Nadine had said something.

"You push hard because you want the best for us." Reid knew there was love in Henri's action, but it was a fucked-up version where he called the shots and dictated the terms. Reid was beginning to think he should distance himself from his father's "love."

Surround himself with people who were less obsessed with perfection.

He had placed too much emphasis on self-denial, on his harsh regimen. After all, sex hadn't suddenly dimmed his focus. A raspberry brownie wasn't going to send him on a rocketing descent to the AHL. If anything, Kennedy and Bucky and this home life gave him something to look forward to.

A reason for striving that wasn't tied to his dysfunctional relationship with Henri.

"I know you think your old man doesn't have much to offer. I still think you had a better chance of staying with that team when you played the wing. You can make more of an impression that way. With this center business, don't be surprised if they trade you out."

Another move, another team. If someone wanted him.

"No one has said anything. Coach seems happy with my play once I settled into the groove." Once he had opened himself to possibilities.

To Kennedy.

"Well, no one's gonna give you a heads-up. They'd prefer to blindside you so they can squeeze every last drop out of you. Listen, put up a good fight, show them you can go toe to toe with the best, and you might be in with a shot at the contract. No holding back now. I'll see you after the game." The twisted pep talk at an end, he ended the call.

Reid's mind rebelled against the black seed Henri had planted. He was playing well, his best season in the NHL. Sure his brother would always be the star winger and Reid would always be in his shadow. That was the trade-off he made by switching to center. By becoming more of a team player. The Rebels management would recognize that. They had to.

Fuck you, Henri. Fuck. You.

Distracted, he turned back to the laptop. Something on the screen caught his eye. He clicked on it, then wished he hadn't as the breath clean left his body.

A folder labeled: Travel Docs. Inside was a PDF of a travel itinerary for Chicago to Bangkok on New Year's Eve.

One way.

He checked the date. She bought that ticket weeks ago, probably with the money he gave her for the first time looking after Bucky. Reid had effectively bought her a one-way ticket out of his life.

There was something else with the file name: Visa.

She had said there was some paperwork delay but not according to this. According to this, her path was clear, the visa issue resolved, and her start date at the new job in Thailand was January 2.

Twelve days away.

All that spirit he'd summoned in answer to Henri's negativity a moment ago wavered in the face of this reminder. She hadn't promised a thing. She had been crystal about her intentions: save money, chase the sun, erase the memories.

After everything he assumed was growing between them, after her defense of him, after offering the sensual harbor of her body, she still remained on this course she had set.

Away from Reid and the life he was building here.

Henri was right about one thing. If Reid wanted that contract, he had to give it his all tonight. Prove that he was worth the shot and not even his more talented brother could stop him. No one could. Then it wouldn't matter that he didn't have Kennedy.

It wouldn't matter at all.

BOND CAME off and tapped Reid's stick. "Don't go easy on him now."

That almost made Reid laugh, except he wasn't in a laughing mood. His skin felt too tight, his usually normal pulse pounding.

It seemed like the whole world had been waiting for this showdown, and finally it was here.

He jumped the boards and moved into position. The electricity in the arena was a breathing charge passing from fan to fan, streaming through the players like a live current.

The first fifteen seconds of the shift went by so fast that Reid was barely aware his brother was on the ice.

Lie. Of course he was aware, but he was doing his best to not let it get under his skin.

Bast had to be nervous. How else to explain why he turned over the puck the second Reid got close? Reid passed to Foreman, skated forward, took the pass back. No room to move, then he felt a resounding force to his side. A standard check. Not enough to make him part ways with the puck, but hard enough to send a message.

He pivoted to find his brother staring him down.

Allons-y. *Let's go.*

THE FIRST PERIOD ended and Mia turned to the party assembled in one of the Rebels' private suites with what Kennedy could only describe as a look of oh-shit.

"That was intense."

Kennedy had thought so, too, but maybe hockey was like this all the time? Something about the pre-game interviews and commentary indicated it might be outside the norm. *Blood in the air*, someone had said. Reid and Bast had blown it off as nothing, but Kennedy sensed that this clash was years in the making, fueled by Henri's pugnacious personality and his unreasonable demands of both his sons, but especially of Reid.

Seeing it from above like this gave her the sense of gods watching mortals in battle.

"Are there usually that many hits and …"

"Penalties?"

"I'd say that set some sort of record for the first twenty minutes of a game," Casey said. "Those guys are going all out."

Sadie sipped her wine. "I hate it when they get hit like that. Gunnar had a concussion in the early season and it scared the bejesus out of me."

"Concussion?" Kennedy tried to keep the worry out of her voice. They wore helmets and enough padding to protect a matchstick model. "Does that happen a lot?"

"God, yes," Tara said. "Some of it's terrifying. Broken bones, split lips, skates to the neck—"

"Maybe don't scare the newbie, T." Mia glared at Tara. "Reid seems to be playing more aggressively tonight. Almost like he has something to prove."

"His father's in town," Kennedy said. "Apparently, watching his sons face off gets him hard."

"Yeah, I've heard stories. This guy I knew in college was on a Bantam team with Reid, and Henri was so pissed at a result that he went off at him in the locker room. Had to be told to leave by the coach."

"He seems really anxious to make him proud. It's pretty toxic."

"Well, we've all been there," Tara said. "The people who are supposed to love you unconditionally are often the ones trying to drain your life force."

Kennedy exchanged a glance with Mia. She didn't know Tara all that well, but their interactions rarely touched on anything deep.

Casey nodded wisely. "Best to cut them out with the sharpest implement you can find." Said with feeling. "We need more Chex Mix." Said with even more feeling.

"Okay," Mia murmured, watching Casey head over to the

snack counter to replenish the bowl. This suite was something else—big TV screens, a help-yourself bar, cupcakes. (Cupcakes!)

Tara turned to Kennedy. "Ken, have you succeeded in your mission?"

"What mission is that?"

"To keep poor Reid on the straight and narrow ... into your vagina!"

"Tara!" Mia mimed shock then grinned at Kennedy. "You may as well tell her."

Tara screeched. "It's happened? But shouldn't I have felt a disturbance in the force?"

"I guess it wasn't that good," Kennedy said, trying to remain serious. "Nothing all that earth-shattering."

"Liar," Mia said. "You should have seen them at brunch a couple of weeks back. Even dared to be cuter than me and Cal!"

"Aw, you guys are double-date brunching already?" Tara sighed wistfully. "Livin' the dream right there. So, he's definitely off the market?"

Sadie threw up her hands. "Are you really that desperate to snag a hockey player?"

Mia grinned. "She's just looking for love wrapped up in a multi-million-dollar contract. Eight-pack preferred. You know, Reid seems to be in a better mood these last couple of weeks. Even Cal commented on it."

"I think being kinder to himself has opened him up," Kennedy said. "Don't get me wrong, he's still intense, but maybe not as tunnel-visioned as before. There's more to life than hockey."

"Sure, there's puppies," Mia said, counting off on one hand. "And hot sex. And too-hot curries. And whatever else you're doing to keep him satisfied."

"Bucky *is* good for him."

"So are you." Mia's words were sweet but painful. "I know he might be a hard guy to love."

"Why do people think that? If you took the time to—"

Mia, Sadie, and Tara stared back at her with obnoxious smiles.

"Oh, shut up."

They had her number and so did Reid. She didn't want to dwell on the past, when a burning ball of fire ushered in an era of darkness. She wanted more afternoons in blanket forts and nights watching a game she knew nothing about and bingo with Edie. She wanted to embrace possibilities, not just with a man, but with her life.

She had decided to decline the job in Thailand, refund her ticket, and tell Reid how she felt.

Mia eyed her over the neck of her beer bottle. "You're thinking of sticking around, aren't you?"

"Possibly."

She needed to talk to Reid and see if they were on the same page. After last night, she thought that maybe ...

It might be easier if she got her own place and separated the employer/landlord aspect from the personal. The dog-walking business might be sustainable, but would be even better if she could expand it to concierge services. So much to think about. So much to do.

"Sadie, Kennedy's thinking of starting up a personal assistant business with the Rebels as her primary client base." Mia winked at Kennedy. "Any tips for her?"

"God knows they need it," Casey cut in before Sadie could respond as she sat down with a giant bowl of Chex Mix that was apparently only for herself. "You know Erik Jorgenson once asked me to buy his clothes for him. I told him that's not the job of the CEO's PA!"

Everyone stared at Casey, who seemed pretty riled.

"Well, it's not," she insisted faintly, slightly less riled.

Mia pointed her beer bottle at her. "Do you have something against Erik? Because he's the sweetest guy on the planet."

"Yeah, *sure* he is. The *sweetest*."

Everyone shared baffled glances, wondering what Erik had ever done to Casey beyond asking for some assistance at Big n' Tall. As far as Kennedy could tell he was a doofus man-child with great hair. The flow was strong with that one. (Look at her, learning the lingo!)

At the risk of incurring Casey's wrath, Kennedy mentioned how she had been running errands for the Rebels goalie. "He's been paying me to do some things. Dry-cleaning, research. Some of the other guys, too."

"You should do that!" Tara said. "Like a business."

Uh, yes, Tara. That's what I've been trying to say for the last five minutes.

Kennedy wanted to pick Sadie's brain some more, but the second period had started ...

... and then it all turned to absolute shit.

33

COACH CALHOUN CAME INTO THE PLAYERS' lounge. It must be the second intermission.

"Any word, son?"

Reid shook his head. The medics had rushed Bast off the ice ten minutes ago and no one had come out of the medical room. If it were more serious than that, surely he would be in an ambulance to Riverbrook Memorial by now.

"Sorry I fucked up."

"You went hard. Too hard. The ejection was the right call."

The words were abrupt. Angry. Exactly what Reid deserved, a nice warm-up to the verbal beat down he would surely receive when Henri got some face time.

The first period had been messy, and not just because of the Durand boys facing off on the ice. Crosstown rivalries often took on an even more adversarial vibe. The fans smack-talked, the press bayed for blood, the players got caught up in it.

It was a routine play at the beginning of the second period, a standard chase for the puck. Bast got there first and while usually it was Kershaw's job to defend, Reid forced himself into the mix. His elbow came up and found a soft landing right under Bast's visor, the chaser to a full-body check of his brother against the boards.

On any other day Bast would've picked himself up in seconds. Not tonight. Tonight, he stayed down.

This might blow Reid's shot at that Rebels contract. Why the hell would they want a guy who couldn't control himself on the ice, who let his emotions get the better of him when faced with his more talented brother? Who let his problems with a woman bother him like this?

Because as much as he wanted to think he could separate the personal from his work, it turned out he was no better than Cal Foreman or any of the other players who let their sex lives affect their play. Except those guys were all better players and deserved their spot on the team.

"I know you have to get back out there but could you see how he is?"

Coach nodded and squeezed his shoulder. "I'll check on him."

A minute later, Henri came flying through the door and got up in Reid's face.

"Is he okay?"

"I don't know."

"What the fuck were you doing out there?"

That was rich. "What you taught me. Trying to win."

"At all costs? You can't win clean so you have to win dirty."

"Henri, don't." Nadine put her hand on her husband's arm. "Not now."

"This is what you wanted, Dad. Both of us going at it until no one's left in the cage. Don't act all surprised when someone gets hurt."

His father stared at him, his gaze thick with disdain. "You think this is what I want? All that talent out of the game for the rest of the season?"

No, he wouldn't want that. No one would. When Reid went hard enough at Bast to knock him out, he wasn't even thinking of besting his brother to win Henri's approval. He was thinking of making his mark, separate from the Durands. Forging a path that won him a contract, a team where he could belong, a home with his dog and the woman he loved.

He no longer cared what his stepfather thought, not really.

All he cared about was Kennedy.

Kennedy, who was already packing her suitcase and turning her face to the sun. Away from the darkness that was him.

The medic came out and Henri pounced on him. "Is my son okay?"

"Sure. He's concussed but awake. Busted nose. Wrist fracture."

Henri's expression turned even darker. "His wrist? But that's eight weeks, minimum."

The medic looked sympathetic. "Yeah, usually he would have been able to brace himself but he probably lost consciousness first and fell badly on it. Give the docs a few minutes. They'll be transporting him to Riverbrook Memorial for X-rays and to set the fracture."

Henri turned to Reid and jabbed a finger in his shoulder. "His wrist, Reid. You know what that means? He's out of the Olympics. Probably the rest of the season."

Reid's heart plummeted to a new personal hell. "Dad, you know I didn't intend for that to happen. I would never want to hurt him."

"Sure. You think I don't remember how rough you were on him as a kid? Still jealous, I see." Henri shook his head in disgust. "Just stay away. He doesn't need to see you right now." He headed out to see his son.

Nadine squeezed his arm. "Just give him time, Reid. You know how invested he gets."

Sure, with one of them.

Alone, Reid collapsed on a sofa in the lounge, every bone and muscle in his body suddenly giving out at once. On the ice, he had played hard and rough, determined that no one would come away thinking Bastian Durand was the only talent in the family. If he could take it to his brother, he would prove he was in the right place with the right team. He wouldn't need Henri or Bast or Kennedy because he was here where he deserved to be.

Instead he had acted like a barbarian.

He had become Henri.

His phone buzzed with a message from Kennedy. She'd already called three times.

Is he okay?

When he didn't respond, she called again, her pretty face flashing on the screen. He had freeze framed it one night when she was FaceTiming him, a moment that captured her mid-laugh, a ball of sun in his dark world.

He pressed ignore.

She would want details, maybe even to talk to Bast. Reid was sick of himself and speaking to Kennedy would only highlight everything that was wrong with him.

A screen in the lounge broadcast the game on mute. The third period was starting, the Rebels already down by two, owing to the power play the Hawks got when Reid was ejected.

Reid turned away, repulsed, only to find Kennedy standing at the door.

HER ROOMMATE WAS HERE, looking about as dejected as she had ever seen him.

"Is Bast okay?"

He met her gaze, his pain a shockwave that hit her hard. "Who told you I was here?"

"Mia found out." She closed the door behind her and came closer. "Is it serious?"

"A concussion and a wrist injury. He's conscious. Or so I hear."

Thank God. "You haven't seen him?"

"Henri is with him. He won't want to see me. Not after what I did."

"I doubt that." That sounded like Henri talking. "I imagine he'll be out for a while but—"

"He'll miss the Olympics."

Oh, poor Bast. This game was so much more dangerous than she had imagined. Seeing Bast stretchered off the ice tonight had sent her down a Google rabbit hole.

Tara had not been kidding about hockey's propensity for horrific accidents. Listicles abounded detailing skate blades to the hand, the neck, the head. One guy had received so many stitches after one incident his face looked like a football. Even Isobel Chase, one of the Rebels owners, had suffered a career-ending injury when 37 minutes into her first professional hockey game, a skate blade sliced through her skull and almost killed her.

Bast was hurt tonight, all because his brother had something to prove to an asshole who shouldn't be allowed to raise children. Next time, it could be Reid. A gash to his neck, a concussion that shook his brain loose. An injury that killed him.

But even knowing that, she was prepared to take a chance on him.

On them.

"That was scary. Seeing him knocked out like that."

"By me."

Sitting close, she placed a hand on his arm. "Yeah, by you. Why did you go at him so hard?"

"Because I'm an asshole."

"No, you're not." Sports seemed to bring out certain personality traits, though. "These things happen."

"Yeah, they happen. Usually because one person makes them happen. We're professional skaters, y'know. Most everything that happens on the ice is planned."

Grumpy, difficult Reid throwing up fences. She wasn't falling for that. Of course he didn't mean to hurt his brother —not like that—but the situation had blown up. She wanted to soothe him, do anything to help him through this.

"Maybe you should talk to him. Tell him you didn't mean to go so overboard."

"I'm the last person he wants to see. I just fucked up his Olympics, the rest of his season, his shot at another championship." He stared at her. "And how do you know I didn't mean it? You don't know what's in here." He pointed at his head.

Oh, but she did. She knew how years of brainwashing had held Reid captive to one man's vision and how in the last few weeks he'd emerged from that dark place to become his own man.

"Because I don't believe you'd hurt anyone deliberately, even in the heat of battle. Especially your brother."

"That's where you're wrong. I want a place on this team, and it looks like I was prepared to do anything to get it. Guess there's more of the old man in me than we all thought."

"You're not like him."

His eyes had turned dark, the blackness evicting all trace of blue. "I'm *just* like him. And I don't need your hippie-yoga-let's-all-get-along new age shit to tell me I'm not. I'm out there on the ice, kicking ass and taking names. I'm so on top of my game that I'm slamming my own brother into the boards and dealing out concussions and fractures like candy."

"Reid, I get that something happened tonight with your brother. Something that's been a long time coming and is rooted in the toxic relationship with your father. All your life he's manipulated you into thinking everything is transactional and that you can't have a real friendship with your brother or even your teammates because they're your competition for, well, everything. It doesn't have to be that way. You could step back from that. Just say no more."

He shook his head. "Why? This is who I am. It's who I've *always* been. You know Bast, my brother, nicest guy in the world? You know how I treated him growing up? I was an asshole to him. I pushed him around because I was jealous of his talent, his charm, how goddamn easy he had it. I wanted what he had with Henri. I wanted to be the favorite son. And tonight I made sure that I'll be the only one playing for a while. By any means necessary."

His pain broke her heart. She had known the relationship between the brothers was complicated, but she had no idea of the extent. Reid still carried this guilt about how he had treated Bast all those years ago—but Bast had clearly forgiven him. She saw the love shining between them.

"Bast loves you, Reid." *I love you.*

She would have said it but his self-loathing was on fire, eating up all the air between them. "Well, he shouldn't! I just stole his spot on the Olympics team. Took something that rightfully belonged to him. My teammates think I'm a fuckup and the fans love to hate me and my brother has been knocked off Team Canada, but hey, I'm here. Reid Durand, the alternate, the NHL's biggest asshole. Did you think I was going to become a different person because I got a dog?"

He sounded so hurt, like the bargain he had made with the universe had turned around and punched him in the face. But she saw how far he had come and tonight's events, though painful, were a temporary setback. A gentle creature like Bucky would only bond with someone who already had a heart as big as Reid's.

"Not because you got a dog. Because you are a good man who wants to be a better one. You'd rather buy into your father's messed up worldview than accept you've made a ton of progress? You took a step back. It's not the end of the world."

His expression reeked of disgust. She knew it was with himself, not her.

At least that was her fervent hope.

"Kennedy, you might have landed here like Mary Poppins, sprinkled some magic fairy dust, fixed a frightened dog, and made an asshole hockey player 5% less asshole. Good for you. In a couple of weeks you'll be on a plane to somewhere warm and sunny and you won't cast a backward glance to me or Bucky. Just off to the next assignment."

Wow with the dismissal. That stabbing pain in her chest

couldn't be good.

This was why you shouldn't get too close. She had thought this might work—she and Reid might work—but no. He was too entrenched in his jerk persona and maybe he was right about her: the soles of her shoes were nonstick.

"That—that pretty much says it all." She took a shallow, useless breath. "I'll be packed and out of your hair by the morning."

"No, you won't. Because you still work for me, remember? You'll stay here and do the job I hired you for—looking after my dog. Then you can run back to Asia just like you planned."

Okay, then. The job. The plan. Back to basics, to where it all began.

Maybe it was better that this was ending before it started.

Which was funny because they were way past the point of starting. They were in the middle. The painful, messy, fucked-up-in-love middle. Or at least she was.

Tell him. Tell him you love him. Even if it's the last thing he wants to hear.

She tried to find the words but they wouldn't come, not when she knew he would only ball them up and throw them in the trash. He stared, burning those midnight-dark eyes into her until something clicked in him and he walked out of the lounge. She let him go because she wasn't brave enough to put her fear aside and love all his many shades, the asshole and the hurting man.

For all her claims to being a free spirit, Kennedy was nothing of the sort. She was caged. By memories. By fear. She might have fluttered outside it for a while but she could feel the whoosh of wind as the door slammed on those silly dreams.

34

REID WOKE up with a weight on his chest. A pair of deep-set brown eyes above a stubby little snout met his sleepy gaze. Sleepy, because he'd managed about three hours of shut-eye.

He picked the bundle of fur up and sat, his hands still embedded in the Pom's warm body.

He missed his dog.

The door to Foreman's guest room cracked open. "Reid?" Mia put her head in. "Gordie Howe, leave Reid alone! I'm sorry, we had the door to our room shut so he found you, the next best victim."

"It's okay. I'm sorry for butting in. When I stopped by last night, I didn't realize—"

"That I practically live here now? It's not a problem. Did you get any sleep?"

"Enough," he lied.

She nodded. "I'm about to make coffee, so join us in the kitchen when you're ready. Come on, Gordie Howe! Give Reid some peace."

The dog jumped off Reid and followed her out. Reid lay a forearm over his eyes and thought about the unthinkable.

Kennedy would be leaving soon.

She had that plane ticket and an assurance that he was an asshole. Last night he'd laid it all bare.

Witness my envy and greed. Look at what a fuckup I am.

Think you can pit your sun against my dark and win? Ha, nice try!

Reid didn't have it in him to make her happy so it was better to quit now before he fell too deep.

Sure. *Before.*

His chest hurt—and not because that damn dog had been camped on it for the better part of the morning.

He picked up his phone from the nightstand. Several texts from Bast had come in during the night.

Where r you?

Need to tok.

Talk.

I'm texting with one fucking hand here.

Where the fuck r u?

Hmm. He didn't sound as pissed as he should have, just Bast's version of annoyed, like a baby wasp.

He texted back:

You OK?

No response. Must be asleep. He checked the GPS tracker for Bucky and was relieved to see he was safe at home, though the tracker wasn't sophisticated enough to be able to pinpoint the exact spot. Probably in Kennedy's room.

Five minutes later he appeared in the kitchen to find Foreman and Mia being vomit-inducing cute while they made breakfast. Their heads were close together and they were whisper-smiling something unintelligible.

"Reid," Mia said. "How do you take your coffee?"

"You don't have to do that."

"Let her, Durand." Foreman turned and folded his arms. "Checked in with your brother yet?"

"He's been texting, so still alive." Last night, Foreman had given him the usual teammate spiel about shit happening and it would look better in the morning. Well, it was the a.m. and improvement was nowhere to be found.

"What about Kennedy?" Mia asked, setting a cup of coffee down in front of him.

"What about her? Have you talked to her?"

Mia's look Foreman's way affirmed she had.

Foreman snorted. "Maybe *you* should talk to her."

"I'm not her keeper. And she's not mine." At Foreman's speaking look, he went on. "I'm giving her some space and it's just easier if I'm not in the same apartment."

"Because you might have to deal with your problems in a productive manner?" Mia pushed creamer and sugar toward him. "Skim? That's all we have."

"That's fine. We've already discussed it. She thinks I'm a jerk, which is true, and I think she never planned to stick around, which is also true. We're pretty much back to square one, so no harm, no foul."

He had always prided himself on his no BS truth-telling. Look at how easily those words flowed from his lying tongue now.

"Can I interest you in some bacon and eggs?" Cal held up an egg in one hand and a bowl in the other. The bacon was already crisping and Reid was starving. Surely if his appetite was unaffected, he must be absolutely fine with this Kennedy business.

"Let me guess, it comes with a side of folksy Masshole wisdom and straight-from-the-heart girl-power talk."

That snarky outburst yielded a condescending hand pat from Mia. "Now, you're getting it. Foreman, crack those eggs."

An hour later, Reid stood outside his brother's place, having first stopped at home, changed his clothes, and grabbed an overnight bag. Knowing Kennedy's schedule almost as well as she knew his, he planned it around her being out of the apartment. Cowardly, to be sure, but neither did he want to make it awkward for her. That was her home until she had to leave the country.

Leave the country. The words were cuts to his soul.

This was the logical endpoint to what had happened here, yet he couldn't quite believe it. Apparently, during these last few weeks he had bought into his own bullshit.

I've fallen in love with a dog and a woman and it somehow makes me a better person.

Had he really thought that was possible? Well, it clearly wasn't. Deep down he was the same dick he had always been, only now he was so good at it he knocked the competition—his own brother, no less—out of the game. *Achievement unlocked.*

Maybe he didn't even deserve Bucky.

Taking the self-pity a little too far, perhaps. He might be a miserable worm but there was no way he was giving up that dog.

He had to find someone to care for the little guy, preferably someone who wouldn't mind taking the puppy into *their* home. No more inviting anyone into his for a while.

Despite the factory reset to Reid's default programming, it had actually felt good to spend time with Mia and Foreman. Most likely they cared about Kennedy, and Reid was just a by-product of that concern, but nevertheless these people were doing a fine impression of feigning interest in his well-being.

Did that mean he had to start caring about theirs? Friendships were all sorts of complicated.

This much was true: he had no plans to go easier on Foreman in practice.

He headed up to his brother's place. If necessary he could whip out the spare key—which he *never* used behind Bast's back unlike his brother's crap. The door was ajar and a raised voice, unmistakable in tone and identity filtered through to the hallway.

"I can't believe you let him get the jump on you. You're better than that."

"I didn't. He's been putting in the work—and it shows with my broken nose, fractured wrist, and the thumping pain in my head."

Reid winced. Even now, his brother was playing the peacekeeper. He pushed open the door.

"How goes it, mon frere?"

Bast was sitting on the sofa, his nose bruised and bandaged, his left wrist plastered and in a sling. His lips hooked up at the corners ever so slightly.

"Connard."

That was fair. Reid *was* an asshole.

"Don't think I've ever seen anyone fall so quickly when checked," Reid said, aiming for a lightness he did not feel. "Like a sack of potatoes."

"You are such a fucker. Why you want to go at me so hard?"

Reid had no excuse for how he had played. He had gone into the game pissed about Kennedy and the fact she was leaving. But mostly about the fact he wasn't brave enough to ask her to stay. Lay it all out there. Once on the ice the battle had taken on a life of its own, fueled by anger and desperation.

"I'm sorry. I don't know what came over me."

Bast shot a look at their father who, for once in his life, was keeping quiet. That look said what they both knew to be true: *you became Henri. That's what came over you.*

"It's okay, Reid."

Henri exploded. "Are you kidding? You're out for the rest of the season. No Olympics. No Cup. And if it doesn't heal right, you can say goodbye to your career."

"Dad, it's a full-contact sport and injuries will happen." He turned to Reid. "Kennedy called to check on me. Said you guys had a fight."

"Been sniffing around, has she?" Henri sneered. "Probably trying to work out which one of you will have the longer career."

"Not now, old man," Reid growled.

Henri cocked his head. "Sounds like you're pussy-whipped, son. Is that what has you coming after your brother on the ice? Some piece of ass?"

The man didn't see it coming—one second his lips were slanted in mockery, the next they were parted in fear. As strong as Henri was, he no longer possessed the resilience of youth. With Reid's forearm crushing his windpipe, his eyes bulged and spittle flecked his lips.

"What the f—?"

"Don't talk about Kennedy like that."

"Who the hell do—?"

Reid pressed his forearm harder against Henri's Adam's apple. "If I hear you breathe another word about her again, I will snap your neck."

"Bro," Bast called out lazily. "He doesn't know any better."

"He does. Being a dick is always a choice." If anyone knew that, it was Reid.

He let go, mostly because the thought of any more violence made him ill. Henri rubbed his throat, something like admiration in his eyes. "You would have made a decent enforcer."

"I'm too good for that. Haven't you heard? I'm front-line material now." Though he wondered for how much longer.

His father shot his cuffs. "You've got me to thank."

Reid looked him squarely in the eye. "I suppose I do. Don't think I'm not grateful. You trained me, pushed me, made me as good as I am. But you also made me feel like shit. You pitted me against Bast so every interaction between us was tainted. There was no such thing as friendly competition between us. It was cut throat because that's what you wanted. Guess what, Henri? I'm not dancing to your tune anymore. I'll play my game the way that works for me and you can take it or leave it."

Henri scoffed. "Chiot ingrat. After all I've done for you, taking you in—"

"Taking me in? You married my mother when I was two years old and I fucking worshipped you because you were all I knew. The father I never had, the legend who saw something in me. But I'm not going to beg for scraps of affection anymore because even when you give it, it's poison."

Reid faced Bast who was looking at him, wide-eyed, his

color high. His brother had always hated being in the middle and Reid didn't want to hurt him any more than he already had. "You and I need to talk. I'll wait outside until you're done here."

Bast shook his head, sending Reid's heart into a hard plunge. He understood. It killed him not to have his brother on his side, but he understood.

Except when Bast spoke, the words were unexpected. "You need to apologize to Reid, Dad."

"What?" Henri was aghast. "For what? Making a crack at his woman?"

"For a start. Then you can say sorry for making him feel like shit and treating him like a second-class son and being a general all-around jerk."

"I—" Henri spluttered. "Anything I did was to toughen him up. Toughen you both up. It's the reason you're both so damn good!"

Bast had never looked so stony. "We're good because we work hard. Because we're talented. And because we're fucking Durands. Now say sorry or leave." He pointed with his uninjured hand. "No, say sorry and *then* leave."

Reid opened his mouth to say this wasn't necessary and got the Medusa treatment from Bast. Holy shit.

Henri looked hurt, which pretty much confirmed where his priorities lay. "You—you're serious?"

"Yeah, I am. Reid and I need to talk. If you can't figure out how to apologize then you need to think about that and how you want this family to heal because Reid's right. It's toxic."

Henri's lower lip shook. "This is the thanks I get?"

But Bast held his ground. When the door closed on Henri's back, Reid let out a juddering breath.

"You don't have to fall out with him on my account."

"I should have done it a long time ago. As he was being an asshole to you he wasn't being one to me, so I let it pass. I should have done more."

To hear his brother take on some of the blame lightened Reid's heart a touch, but this wasn't his fault. Reid was responsible for his own actions in that game. For long before that.

"Bast, last night—I went too far. I was upset about ... something. Something else. And I was tired of being perceived as second-best. I needed to prove I deserved to be there. On that line, in that rink, with that team." With *her*. "But, all that anger... I was just like him."

"What, like Luke and Vader?"

"More like Vader and Palpatine." *Let the hate flow through you ...*

"You're not, Reid. You never could be."

Reid looked up, surprised at his brother's heartfelt words.

"You're not like Henri," Bast went on, "no matter what you might think."

Hearing his brother being so kind when he didn't deserve it killed him.

"You've always had these fond memories of when we were kids. Or you've chosen to forget the bad ones. Not sure if you did that for my sake or yours." Reid struggled to push the words from his throat, tied to memories that shamed him. "But you know what I was like. How I bullied you. I was older and I was supposed to protect you—"

"You did. Tommy Gunderson, remember?"

Reid swiped at his eyes. "I beat him up because he hurt you but I wasn't much better, Bast. I was jealous of how Henri loved you more. I wasn't a good brother and I haven't become a decent man."

Kennedy had said he was solid gold. Sold gold prick, more like. Last night he had reverted to that angry kid. He had hurt one of the people he loved more than anything and he needed to put it right.

"I'm sorry for harming you, brother, years ago and last night."

His brother smiled, his emotion waving off him and enveloping Reid in a warm fraternal embrace. "I forgive you. I forgave you years ago, or I thought I had. But then I pulled my own shit and never stood up for you. Bystander revenge, I suppose. With Dad constantly on our backs, we somehow forgot what matters. You and me, the Amazing Durand Brothers!"

Reid choked out a wet laugh. "That makes us sound like fucking carnies."

Bast chuckled. "Trapeze artists, bro. Now give me a hug without hurting my nose or wrist and tell me what the hell happened with Kennedy."

REID WAS IN DETROIT. Kennedy knew this, not because he had told her, but because one of his color-coded schedules said so.

They hadn't spoken in two days. He hadn't even come to see Bucky, though she knew he had stopped by while she was out because he emptied the dishwasher and took some clothes (she had gone into his closet to sniff his Henleys like a loser and noticed one of his suits was missing). Apparently he hated the idea of being in the same place as her so much that he was willing to ignore his dog. Only Reid would deny himself something he loved to avoid dealing with something he hated.

Well, she didn't have to play by his rules.

Bucky lounged on the end of the sofa, looking his usual ugly-adorable self. She held up her phone, snapped a shot, and before she could second-guess the instinct, texted it to Reid with the caption: ***Ruff! I miss my daddy!***

The team would be at the hotel by now, maybe getting ready to head out for something to eat. Reid might be in the shower. For better or worse, he was a man of routine.

A text came in thirty seconds later:

I miss you, too. I hope you're being a good boy for Kennedy.

Cute. He understood that the message was from Bucky, and not her.

Another one, almost immediately:

And I hope you're looking after her when she takes you outside, especially at night. Bark at all the strangers and anything in the bushes.

Kennedy closed her eyes against the sting of tears. Not cute. That was just ... oh God, why did he have to be such a soft-hearted lug under that jerkish exterior?

She texted (or Bucky did):

I'll do my best

She claims she can kick all the ass but I'm there if she needs me.

I know you are. And yes, Kennedy can take care of herself. But she doesn't have to do it alone.

She swiped at her eyes. The phone rang and Reid's

Chicago Rebels headshot came up. Composing herself, she answered.

"Hi."

"Hi, roomie."

A small thing that filled a large hole. Through all this, she felt like she hadn't just lost someone she loved, but the guy who was also her friend.

"How's Detroit?"

"I'm not there because I was suspended for a game. I'm staying with Bast."

He was in the city? That was even worse. But it was a good sign that he was with his brother. "How's he doing?"

"Okay. He'll be out for a while so that's weighing on him." And on Reid, too, no doubt. "Thanks for sending that pic of Bucky. I've missed him."

"You could see him at any time. I know you don't want to —" *see me* "—because it might be awkward. But he's yours."

Long pause. "I need the space, and you need to be safe."

Space from her. "This is your home, Reid."

"It's just four walls and some furniture." He cleared his throat. "I need a favor."

"Of course."

"I'll be flying with Bast to Toronto on Christmas Eve to visit our mom, but I can't take Bucky on the plane. After how I spoke to you the other night, I know I have no right to ask, but will you watch him over the holiday? I expect to be back on the 26th. That should give you plenty of time to wrap up things."

Christmas was four days away and she'd barely given it any thought. Two days ago she had been ready to tear up her ticket to Bangkok and tell Reid how she really felt.

Instead she was wrapping up things.

Having spent so long chasing the sun, she had forgotten

what it felt like to enjoy it. That's how she had felt with Reid, filled with joy and hope. With him all good feelings rushed in, filling the crevices around her heart with love putty. Reid and Bucky had healed her, yet a sharp word from this man still had the capacity to rip it all asunder. Now all she felt was a cold distance.

If he didn't want to see her, fine. But surely they could act like adults and speak their truths.

Hers? That she loved Reid Durand. It hurt to love him, but she suspected it would hurt more not to.

His? She wasn't sure. There was no doubt he had opened up in the last few weeks. His heart had softened, ready to love a misfit dog, a team of rabble-rousers, and his brother despite the envy. But she wasn't sure that love extended to himself.

Until he figured out how to forgive himself, then he wouldn't be ready to love her.

"I can look after him. But I really should move out so you can live in your own place."

"You're staying there, Kennedy. I want both of you where I know you're safe. Don't argue with me on this. And if you have some recommendations for dog sitters, I'd appreciate it."

Right, she would have to do that. She had promised all along that she would because from day one, she'd had her foot out the door just like Reid said.

"I can do some research."

"Thanks. I should get going."

"Sure, say hi to—" He had already hung up. Some things never changed.

35

THERE WAS a reason Reid wasn't a mixer, and that reason was now banging against his head and telling him that he was currently in the worst place with the worst people at the worst time.

Attendance at the Rebels Holiday Party was apparently non-negotiable.

The team had returned from Detroit with a loss, but spirits were currently being revived with ones of the alcoholic and seasonal variety. The NHL was unique in pro sports, in that they scheduled a mandatory break over the holidays. Their next game was at home on the 27th and the mood tonight was definitely festive because of it.

Reid looked around, noting that every one of his teammates had a date, like they were trying to punk him or something. Well, he'd be out of here as soon as the brass made a speech or two.

As if Reid had willed it into action, someone clinked a glass and Harper Chase's voice rose above the hubbub of the crowd. "Hello, friends and family. Thanks so much for joining us tonight as we celebrate the season with each other. And I mean, both seasons: holiday and hockey. We are doing well, thanks to a great roster, both new and o—"

"Veteran, minou," Remy called out, which made everyone laugh.

"Thanks, darling. Always catching me when I fall."

The look they shared was pure love, kind of like how he felt about Bucky.

"I wanted to welcome some of you to the Rebels fam and your first holiday gathering. Cal, Dex, and Reid—we're thrilled you're here, making the team stronger. Cheers to you all!"

Everyone raised glasses, while Reid gave his usual awkward half-smile. Despite the suspension, no one had given him a hard time or hinted that it spelled the end of his time as a Rebel. Likely someone would call him into the front office after the holiday and tell him he was surplus to requirements.

Harper went on. "And I know there's been some speculation about who would take over chief executive duties and I'm thrilled to tell you that our new GM is here tonight. Fitz, say hi to everyone."

A big-shouldered bruiser of a guy in a suit appeared from behind a potted plant. Hale Fitzgerald, known as Fitz, formerly the assistant GM in Philly. With the previous GM, Dante Moretti, retired as a stay-at-home dad, the Rebels needed new blood at the top.

"Didn't expect to be put on the spot, Harper," he said in a deep Georgian accent. "Well, Rebels, you've had a good start to the season and are on your way. I'm looking forward to the magic we're going to make together. To a winning year." He raised his glass.

Yeah, winning.

Screw this. Toasts done and dusted, Reid headed into

the kitchen at Chase Manor to put his glass in the sink. This shindig was catered but he always felt weird about leaving an empty on a tray or a counter. Now he could leave, having shown his face.

"How's your brother?" That instantly recognizable Cajun drawl announced the arrival of Remy DuPre, Rebels elder statesman, married to the boss.

"He'll live."

"It happens, you know. On-ice meltdowns."

Remy knew all about it. He'd had a very famous one several years ago when he beat up a player who had struck the woman who was now his wife.

Reid studied him, assessing for shade. He and Bast had a good talk yesterday. There would be more of them, and they were definitely on the right road, but Reid couldn't change his personality overnight. He needed time to accept his brother's goodwill and forgiveness.

"Family stuff, it's complicated."

"I know it. Heard you're on the outs with your girl."

Gossiping hens, the lot of them. "Do you have some advice to give me, old man?"

"Old man? You're killin' me, Durand."

Casey, Harper's assistant walked into the kitchen. "Oh, sorry, I didn't realize anyone was here."

"Pas de probleme," Remy said, just as Casey turned and walked into Erik Jorgenson. She jumped back and held up her hands.

Jorgenson was always so good-humored and laid-back, but this minute looked about as agitated as Reid had ever seen him.

"So that's it?" Erik said to Casey. "We're not even going to talk about it?"

"I have nothing to say to you." Casey walked back out the way she had come.

Reid didn't need to know the specifics to feel Erik's obvious pain. "You all right, Fish?"

Erik merely shrugged and walked through the kitchen in the opposite direction to Casey.

Reid turned to Remy. "And that's why relationships and hockey do not mix. Too many distractions."

Of course it would help if the *absence* of Kennedy wasn't providing the ultimate distraction. Once she had left the country or the planet or the galaxy, he might be able to return to his usual Zen calm.

"Yeah, I probably could have done with fewer distractions in my playing days," Remy said. "But, hey, it's life—one long distraction. And it worked out."

Reid wouldn't usually bite, but DuPre was one of his favorite players and he hadn't had a chance to talk to him much since he was acquired by the Rebels. "You mean the Cup win in your retirement year?"

"Yeah, I sure did cut it fine." Remy chuckled in fond memory.

Cut it fine? There were a million reasons why the Rebels shouldn't have won that year. New ownership by three half-sisters who barely knew—or liked—each other. The label of second worst team in the league. Led by the man beside him, who was on the butt end of his career. It was a perfect storm of shit yet somehow it all came together for a magical season.

It had Reid curious, though. "Why do you think you won? I mean, on paper it was never going to work. It shouldn't have happened that way."

Reid had studied the tapes of the playoff games that season. Five years had passed since they won the Cup, and while they had been in contention since, they hadn't scaled those dizzy heights again. The team had good players back then, some still on the roster: Burnett, Petrov, DuPre, Callaghan, St. James, Jorgenson. United Nations of Badass, someone called them. But they'd had good players the last couple of seasons, too. What was it about this combination that turned those zeroes into heroes?

"I guess it shouldn't have," Remy said, stroking his chin. "In fact, that year was personally momentous for most of us. It should have thrown us off, screwed us up, messed with our minds, but instead it made us stronger. We were all finding our soul mates while we discovered the recipe that worked to form a winning band of brothers." He smiled that pirate's grin. "You're too young, maybe, to be thinking about settling down. But me? I was ready during that season. Had my sights set on some imaginary little homemaker who would bake cookies, fix me a bourbon, and let me fill her with babies."

Remy smirked. "Yeah, I know, I know. I was pissed at being traded to this shit team. I felt my last shot slipping away. And I had a chance to trade out just before the deadline. We were getting better but not that much better. I could've had a shot with a different team but I'd fallen for the team owner and when I say fallen, I mean flat on my beautiful face. This woman had me, body and soul, and I knew there was nowhere I'd rather be. I'd already won the prize. The Cup was just gravy."

Reid hoped his face was as blank as he wished it to be. Inside, his organs were gallivanting, moving around, swapping places. He read a lot of sports memoirs and psychology treatises. He watched game after game, searching for the clues to what produced a winner. Talent wasn't enough.

Graft helped, but even that was just another string to the bow rather than the whole damn weapon.

It was something indefinable. Some *it* factor that Reid had been grasping for.

He had always viewed a player's personal relationships as a liability, especially romantic ones. Sure some players were happily settled with kids, a stable home life that evened them out. But the journey there was usually momentous, filled with potholes and detours that threw a player off his game. It was why Reid had ruled it out as a contributory factor to being the best. The dip in his play wasn't worth it because he didn't see that the end would ever justify the means.

He refused to believe he could ever be as happy as the man before him. He glowed with it. Yet Reid *recognized* that look, the emotions that accompanied it. He'd had a glimpse of it in his own life these past few weeks ...

"Good thing it worked out. You picked right."

Remy shook his head. "No, that's the thing. I didn't pick, the team picked me. Or I should say the woman did. C'est tout." *That's all.*

"It sounds ... random."

"It does, doesn't it?" Remy laughed, like it had just occurred to him. "But it's a powerful force, that surprise when your best laid plans disintegrate before your eyes. It doesn't always have to be so rigid, mon ami. You can enjoy a trip or two down those side roads."

But to let chance or happenstance have such an influence on the outcome of your life? Reid didn't buy that. He'd tried it and look at where it had landed him: alone and hurting.

And Christ, it did hurt. More than he would have

thought possible. The high … he wasn't sure it was worth feeling this low.

"I control what I can. It's the only way I know how to do it." It was about as honest as Reid had ever been about his drive to succeed.

"Sure, I see you doing that. We all *think* we're doing that. But I also see that good things have come from Coach switching you to center. Bet you never thought that would be where you ended up heading into the new year?"

Reid shook his head.

"Just sayin' be open to another viewpoint. And never underestimate the power of positive emotion to make you perform."

"Just running on my competitive streak."

"Oui, sure you are. I think you're happy, Reid. Keep it up and it might be enough to get you a contract."

A contract? Was Remy clueing him into something he'd heard behind closed doors at Chase Manor or during pillow talk with the boss? He opened his mouth to ask only to be interrupted by a new arrival.

"Duracell!" Kershaw bounded in like a puppy. "Where's Kennedy?"

"Why do you want to know?"

Theo flicked a look to Remy, then back to Reid. "She said she might be able to help me with some business stuff. But if she's not here …"

"She's my roommate, that's all, so why would she be here?"

"Leave him alone, Superglutes." Cal waltzed in and put his beer bottle in the recycling bin.

"Don't need your defense, Foreskin."

Cal burst out laughing.

"What's so funny?"

"You, acting like you don't care about anything but your damn dog. So you had a fight with your girl. We've all been there."

"All been where?" Gunnar Bond appeared, chewing on a cookie.

Theo pointed. "Is that gingerbread?"

"Yep, there's a tray of it in the other room."

Theo left the kitchen faster than the first line on a breakaway, shouting over his shoulder, "Don't start Duracell's intervention without me!"

"There's no ..." Reid arced his gaze over the remaining group, feeling very dumb and very much the center of attention. "I don't need an intervention. Kennedy and I are not a couple."

"But you want to be. She's a nice kid, great with Cooper who, believe me, is no picnic. Sadie likes her, too," Gunnar said around his cookie chewing. "Damn, I hope Kershaw brings back more than one."

"I don't need—listen, that's not the point. If one person is all in and the other is not, you can't make it happen."

"So, who's all in here?" Remy asked.

He shifted against the counter and muttered, "I am."

Remy sniffed. "Just checkin'."

Foreman looked amused. "What's the problem, then?"

"She's not. All in, that is. She's not even somewhat in. She's got one foot on a plane somewhere because she's a commitment-phobe who refuses to settle. Which is fine. She would never choose me anyway."

"Why not?" Petrov's deep, accented voice made Reid jump. He shrugged unapologetically when Reid turned. "Heard we were doing an intervention."

"We're not—"

"I got a selection." Theo placed a tray of cookies on the

counter and all but Reid went to town on them. "Remy, it looks like you've run out of the snickerdoodles. What'd I miss?"

"Durand didn't expect Kennedy to choose him, for some reason." Foreman took a bite out of a chocolate-chip cookie that looked soft and chewy, and moaned a little. "Go on, Durand. Your captain wants to know why."

Reid scowled at him, slid a glance to Petrov, and took a breath. "Even if she was inclined to stick around, I'm not the kind of guy she would go for. Sure, in some ways, we work—"

"Sex, I'm guessin'," Theo mumbled, his mouth full of gingerbread cookie.

Reid ignored him. "We're not compatible. She thinks everything can be fixed with a smile and a nice chat about our feelings. But nothing is that simple. There are personalities involved, conflicting personalities. I'm not the kind of guy who can make her happy."

Or stay.

Gunnar frowned. "Did she say that?"

"Not in so many words."

"So that's what *you* think," Remy said in a tone that said it wasn't up for discussion. "Which is good because that's half the battle right there. Knowing you have a problem." He turned and pulled—ah, fuck—a bottle of tequila from a cupboard. "Grab the glasses from that cabinet over there, Vad. We've got work to do here."

Reid had been on his way out. He had a flight to Toronto at 9 a.m. so he could see his mother and have her fuss over him and feed him something not in his diet and tell him he was her co-favorite son. He sent a longing glance at the kitchen door, which looked about as far away as his peace of mind right now.

Someone put a gingerbread cookie in one hand, a shot of liquor in the other, and one, two, three, bombs away ...

Thirty-four minutes later ...

Remy had trooped them all into his study, which was really just an office with comfortable leather sofas, a TV, and his many trophies. Over the last half hour, the guys had all offered their own takes on Reid's situation. Bond was of the opinion that Reid might need to work on himself (no shit). Remy thought that Reid should make a grand gesture—apparently everything was solved with a grand fucking gesture. About ten minutes in, Jorgenson appeared, looking no happier than he had during that exchange with Casey. His solution: food. Always food.

"I think we need to look at this from Kennedy's point of view." Theo held up his empty shot glass as if he expected the tequila fairy to fill it. "Hockey is fucking dangerous, man. Maybe she's freaked out by Duracell's elbow-to-the-face action. We could have done with you on the ice last night, by the way."

Reid didn't have time to enjoy Kershaw's compliment because Petrov was weighing in.

"You think that's why she won't fight for Durand? You don't think that maybe she's just doing it to make him suffer?"

Petrov's Law said that women enjoyed making men miserable and it was men's fate to endure until their women came around. Weirdly Russian and not helpful at all.

"Making him suffer, maybe for something he didn't even realize he did," Erik said morosely. "That could be the case here."

Gunnar squinted at him. "Except Duracell knows what he did. Don't you?"

Reid had done the opposite of what Edie had advised: *You have to fight for her.* He knew Kennedy was leaving and assumed that was all she wrote. Assumed that she wouldn't upend her life for someone like him.

To hammer the point home and put a big red bow on his insecurities, he told her he was a bad bet, showed her he was one, and then pushed her out of his life. All so he could maintain control over an uncontrollable situation.

Theo grabbed the tequila bottle and filled his glass because no one was doing it for him.

"It sounds like Kennedy's an independent sort. Kind of like my Ellie."

Reid considered that. "Yeah, she's lived this life where she doesn't want to rely on anyone since her parents died when she was a kid. I guess she feels it's ... safer? I understand that." Even though she had Edie, she had created a life that kept her detached from deeper connections.

"We all do," Cal said. "Self-preservation is the default setting of every guy here. And every girl and guy out there." He pointed behind him to the party that was going on without them. "She's worried about losing someone she cares about."

"Because she already did." Hale "call me Fitz" Fitzgerald, the Rebels new GM, had wandered in five minutes ago, pieced it all together from several drunk and half-wrong updates, and was now weighing in with his own brand of Southern wisdom. "No wonder she's jumpy as all get out."

Cal nodded. "So she's erected this wall with a big ass "No Trespassing" sign. Reid, you're going to have to trample all over that sign. But first you have to accept you're worthy of this woman."

Trampling wasn't really his style. As for being worthy, how the hell was he supposed to come around to that way of thinking? It was one thing to unravel years of knots in his relationship with Bast, it was quite another to apply the lessons learned to a love that had barely bloomed.

"I can't force her to love me, Cal."

"She already does, dummy."

He sounded so sure and God almighty, Reid wanted to believe him. "You can't know that."

"Listen, Reid, you need someone to pull that hockey stick out of your ass and show you there's more than that one track you've been stuck on forever. She needs someone to ground her and make her feel safe. These are the gaps you fill for each other, and you've already figured it out because we just fucking told you and we are right. So convince her you're the man for the job."

"Grand gesture, mon ami." Remy puffed on his cigar and grinned like a wise old king. "Grand fucking gesture."

36

THERE WAS a particular cruelty in visiting a familiar place and finding that it hadn't changed one iota. That it had the audacity to carry on without you and didn't miss your presence. As if you never existed.

Dramatic much?

"I'm getting wistful in my old age, Buck." Her faithful companion for the two-hour drive to the past perked up at the mention of his name. Reid would probably have a fit if he knew she'd taken him across state lines—but as Reid had chosen not to visit his dog and leave custody in her hands, then *his* opinion on the matter shouldn't register.

Except he was why she was here.

His accusation that he was merely an assignment for her and that she should just run back to Asia had cut deep. As if she was trying to escape. She was a traveler, a nomad, an embracer of new experiences. Avoidance wasn't in her vocabulary. Reid Durand, who kept everything close to his chest, didn't know the first thing about it.

She was here to prove him wrong.

Silver Springs, fifteen miles east of South Bend, Indiana,

hadn't changed a jot since she left. The drugstore on the corner of Central and Main was still there, with the slightly off-kilter sign. Her dad used to stop there on the way back from the university to pick up day-old donuts, Midwestern frugality at its finest. The bank, the post office, the florist, all the same. The coffee shop might be new—or that might be a fresh coat of paint. Driving through, she wondered about homes—and hearts—frozen in time.

Had she placed the past on a pedestal? Well, clearly she had. But so much so that she shut herself off to all possibilities? Over the last six years, she'd certainly had opportunities to open herself up. Start anew. Yet she even kept her distance from Edie because it would make it easier when her gran moved on to the great bingo hall in the sky.

That's what she had been searching for all these years. A path to minimize the potential for heartbreak. She was no risk-taker—not in the slightest! Not like Reid.

This man was willing to work on himself, make all these small but crucial changes to widen those cracks in his armor. Loosening that grip on his control took effort, but that was Reid: the hardest-working person she knew.

People said that about her. *You're so busy. You work so much.* But unlike Reid, she wasn't working toward something. She was working to keep the past at bay, the present in stasis, and the future from evolving.

She kept driving, past the Congregational Church where her dad used to embarrass her by sing-shouting the hymns. He would wink at her and draw her smothered giggle.

God wants you to express yourself, Ken. He doesn't care how you do it, as long as you do it with joy.

The Kennedy of old would claim wholeheartedly that she was doing just that. With every stamp in her passport, with every bite of a new cuisine, with every sunrise over a foreign hill. But she wasn't sure she knew true joy until she had run around a park with Reid and Bucky or listened as he patiently explained to her the game of hockey or lay in his arms surrounded by a blanket fort dressed with pillows and bed linens.

She almost missed the turn to her old street—the horn of the car behind her told her she took the corner too suddenly. Someone else had built a new structure in the ashes of the old. The only thing that was recognizable was the cherry blossom tree, now naked and frost-flecked.

"Mom loved that tree, Buck. That's why she and Dad bought the house. Because the tree was in bloom and she could see the future under it."

Bucky raised his head, angling for a rub, so she gave it to him because he was a great puppy and deserved all the love in the world.

She headed to her final stop. The cemetery wasn't big enough to drive around, so she parked, grabbed the potted plant, and brought Bucky out on his leash. After a couple of hours cooped up in the car he was clearly excited, even if it was colder than the lake they'd pulled him from.

"Just up here a bit, Buck. Not too far."

The headstone stood tall, unweathered marble that would be here long after she was gone.

Libby and Benjamin Clark
Beloved parents, teachers, and humans.
Death cannot part them.

The pastor wouldn't allow Peanut to be buried with them, which seemed all wrong. Her dad had loved Peanut.

"Sorry it's been so long. I've been away for a while."

Bucky strained at his leash, then relaxed and sniffed at

the grass. She placed the potted calla lily near the headstone. The flowers would wilt and start to die the moment she left, and she tried not to see an analogy for her own heart in that.

"I've been doing okay. Or at least, I thought I was. Faking it around the world. I came back for Edie, but I think I was just tired as well. Tired of having to pretend this was the only way to be happy."

She hunkered down because she needed the warmth of her furry friend to say the next part.

"There's a boy. Now, Dad, I know you won't approve because that's your job. But I think you'd like him. He's serious and quietly funny and he has such a big heart. He doesn't know how big. I think I screwed up because I worried about the joy I felt with him, if it was counterfeit, if it could last. He thinks I don't care when really I care so much it fucking hurts." She sniffed. "I know, language. Sorry, Mom."

"I don't think that."

Shocked at the sound of another voice—Reid's voice—she lost her balance and landed on her ass. Bucky abandoned her and lunged at his master, who hunkered down and hugged him hard, all while keeping his eyes on Kennedy.

"And I thought you yoga experts had better balance than hockey players." He grasped her hand and pulled her upright in one fluid move. "Hi, roomie."

"Hi." He still held her hand or maybe she still held his. Either way, neither of them seemed inclined to let go. "How did you find me?"

"Bucky's GPS. I didn't think it would work so far out but here I am. Stalking my puppy, not you." He pulled her close, giving the lie to those words. "I stopped by the apartment to pick up stuff for my trip to Toronto. You weren't there and curiosity got the better of me. The tracker only has a ten-mile range but you must have just left, so I've been behind you all the way. I should have waited until you were finished just now but—I—I didn't want to wait any more."

That cracked open something inside her. Reid, behind her, supporting her on the road, and she hadn't even realized he was there. But maybe he was here because he was worried about Bucky.

"Don't you have a flight to Toronto to catch?"

"I sent Bast on his way. He and I have sorted things out and this is more important." Reid was doing the dark-eyed intense thing again. "You were right about standing up to my father. I've put up with it, let it affect my relationship with Bast, let it rule how I run my life. I got into it with him. Told him how I felt, how it hurt."

She had checked in with Bast and had the broad brushstrokes of what went down, but hearing Reid say it checked her heart. "That was really brave of you."

"Don't know about that. I told him that how he treats me is toxic and I wasn't going to let him do that anymore. I was mostly worried about how Bast would take it."

"He took your side."

Reid smiled, just that flash she adored. "You know him better than I do because you're a good judge of character. Yeah, he took my side. Told Henri that he wasn't welcome. All this time I've been holding my breath, mostly worried about damaging my relationship with my brother. Or doing more damage to it. I don't have a lot of friends, so I—I need him."

Tears stung her eyes. "And he needs you. Also, you have more friends than you think, Reid."

He shrugged. "Maybe. I have you, I hope. I think we've

become friends, even if I ruined it by doing my grouchy, heart of darkness bit. Now here I am, your asshole friend, intruding on your moment."

"No, not at all." Reid was meant to be here, meeting her parents. "Can I introduce you?"

"Only if you're sure."

She was sure. Even if she and Reid could never be more, she wanted him in her life any way that could happen.

"Mom, Dad, this is Reid Durand, aka Hot Jerk, aka NHL's most amazing center, aka a total cinnamon roll sweetheart." She snuck a look at him to find his eyebrow in the Reid quirk of amused. "They're detail-oriented people."

"Figured as much."

"And Reid, this is my mom and dad, aka Libby and Benjamin Clark, aka the best parents a girl could have."

He nodded with his usual Reid gravity. "Good to meet you both. You did a great job with this girl. She's kind and generous and doesn't understand how special she is. Maybe that makes her humble, but I think it also makes her a little bit clueless."

"Oh, Dad will like that. He always thought I wasn't ambitious enough." The enormity of the moment reared up and threatened to choke her. Reid must have sensed it because he turned her into his hard chest and let her weep softly.

No arms had ever felt stronger. No body had ever sheltered her so well. No heart had ever called to her so clearly.

A few minutes later, they walked hand-in-hand back to the cemetery entrance.

"Would you sit with me for a moment in my warm car with its heated seats?"

"I'd love that."

He opened the passenger door for her and the back door

for Bucky. When he got in on the driver's side and closed the door, he pulled something from his pocket.

"As well as stopping by to see Bucky and get stuff for my trip, I also planned to leave a gift for you." He placed a wrapped box on the dash.

"Reid, really?"

"Yes, Kennedy, really."

With shaking hands, she took it and removed the wrapping. It looked like a jewelry box and she opened it with a held breath. It was a key. It also looked familiar.

"What's this to?"

"The apartment. I know you have one already but this is a spare, one you can keep in a special place in case you lose the other one. I want you to have a key so you know you'll always have a home to return to. With me and Bucky."

He reached in back and petted his dog. "I can't clip your wings, Kennedy, and I'd never expect you to stick around for me—"

She sniffed. "Why not?"

"Because I'm not the kind of guy who inspires devotion. I'm not a fan favorite or a flashy star. I'm a worker, a grinder, and when my career is over, I'll be remembered as a journeyman who scrapped his way out of the AHL and cobbled a career together with spit and sneers and time in the gym and miles on his skates. People respect that guy but no one loves him."

He was so, so wrong, and she hated Henri Durand for ever making him doubt his lovability.

"You listen to me, Reid Fucking Durand. *That* guy is the backbone of the team. The center who directs traffic and controls the ice and makes the game hum. That guy might be a grinder but that doesn't mean he's unpopular or unlovable. Bucky loves that guy and so do I."

Reid's swallow was audible in the close confines of the car. "You mean, like a friend or something?"

"Bucky, do you love Reid like a friend?"

Their good doggo—and he was as much hers as Reid's—gave a quick bark and raised his head for a rub. Which he got, of course.

"Bucky adores you, no friend zone for him. These last few weeks, I've seen you change and open your heart to this little guy who needed you so badly. There is nothing but slavish devotion from that quarter."

"I needed him, too." He reached for her and cupped her cheek. "He wasn't the only one I needed. The only one I *need*. Present tense, future, now and always. If we're talking slavish devotion, I have a serious case of that for my roomie."

"Reid," she whispered, as the tears fell freely.

"I love you, Kennedy. I love you so fucking much. And though my natural inclination is to be a total dick and demand that you stay with me and Bucky, I won't do that. That's how much I love you. But you have my key—to my apartment, to my heart, to my soul—and I hope that one day you'll return and use it."

This guy. She shouldn't be nervous, not after a declaration as beautiful as that. But she was. Her heart thumped like a wild beast.

"And what if one day is ... this day?"

He closed his eyes for a moment then opened them again. "Is that something you might consider?"

"While you were doing the work and becoming an awesome dog daddy, team player, and roommate, I was making some changes of my own. Or my heart was doing it for me."

"Tricky things, hearts."

"So tricky. I've been terrified of standing still because it would force me to think, force me to feel. I've been caught up in this pretense of free-spiritedness when really my spirit and my heart have been in a prison, one I made for them. But with you, I can be open. I feel free. I feel seen. You have my heart, Reid. It's all yours. *I'm* all yours and I love you so much."

"Ma coeur," he whispered as his mouth found hers and settled it once and for all. They belonged together, and Kennedy would be going nowhere without Reid and Bucky at her side.

But first she would be heading away from Silver Springs, where a little piece of her heart remained, toward the next adventure, one that required she stop moving for a while.

The lines of Walt Whitman's "Song of the Open Road" came back to her, more precious to her now that she finally understood.

Camerado, I give you my hand!
I give you my love more precious than money;
I give you myself before preaching and law:
Will you give me yourself?
Will you come travel with me?
Shall we stick by each other as long as we live?

She no longer needed to go around the world to travel the pathways of the heart. She just needed someone to stick with her through it all, as long as they lived.

She had found him at last, and he came with a cute dog. How lucky was she?

Gazing into the eyes of her camerado, she spoke the three little words she had yearned to say for so many years.

"Let's go home."

EPILOGUE

Four months later ...

THE WATER RIPPLED and licked the jagged rocks, looking much less treacherous than it had six months ago.

Reid peered down at his dog. "No swimming for you today, Bucky. Kennedy doesn't want to get wet." Before she could respond, he pulled her close and kissed her open mouth.

"Hey, you set up an awesome sex joke and then ripped it from under me! What kind of straight man are you?"

"One who would rather kiss his woman than—"

"Get her wet? My attempts at innuendo will not be denied!"

A few feet ahead of them, Bucky trotted along the mix of sand and grass, though his innate survivor skills kept him well back from the rocks fronting the water where he'd almost died that cold day in November.

"You think it's a good idea to bring him back here?" She squeezed his hand.

"I do. It's always best to face your fears. And this place is special for all of us."

"Right, the sopping wet ice clothing is something I'll cherish for the rest of my days." A jest, but he knew from the softness in her eyes that she felt it, too. They had each started a new life on this beach.

The Chicago Rebels were headed to Dallas tomorrow to begin their trek to the Stanley Cup Finals. Reid's play as center had been instrumental in getting them to this point, and a month ago the offer of a three-year contract had come through. He didn't pretend any kind of coyness about it, just signed that baby on the dotted line as soon as his agent passed it to him in the Rebels HQ conference room.

It was official. He was a Chicago Rebel at last.

Bast was over the moon. They made an effort to meet once a week for dinner, cementing their bond and deepening their friendship. As for Henri, Reid was reframing the relationship on his terms with Bast's and Kennedy's help. His father didn't enjoy being told no but hey, it was good for him to get some pushback. Good for them all.

Kennedy's business was growing and she was already looking at taking on an assistant. Her first love was her dog clients, so finding someone to help with the other tasks made sense. The Rebels certainly sent plenty of work her way and Reid tried not to get annoyed at how they fawned over *him* just to get preferential treatment. It would be nice to be popular because he was a good teammate but it was what it was.

His phone buzzed with a text from Edie.

You done it yet?

Edie and a few of her Larkvale cronies had formed a

weird-ass fan club with embroidered jackets, in direct competition to Theo's Tarts, a similar fanatical creepfest run by Kershaw's grandmother. For each home game, he gave Reid's Rebelles—that's what they came up with—all his free tickets. At every intermission there were literal granny-offs in the stands!

Kind of strange to have his own fan club. Only Kennedy suspected how much he enjoyed it.

"Who's that?"

"Edie wondering if we'll stop by later."

Kennedy rolled her eyes. "And she texts you? I've been replaced as the favorite grandchild!"

"You know that's not true. Bucky will always be number one in her affections."

Speaking of being number one ... He whistled for Bucky to come back and after a little more encouragement—he had spotted something in the grass that he had to investigate—he came bouncing over, bright-eyed and full of verve.

Reid hunkered down to hug him ... then decided he liked the view better from here.

Wrinkling her nose, Kennedy looked down at him. "That's—wait—what's happening here?"

He held up the scroll, wrapped with a pink ribbon. "I would think it's obvious. Tell her, Buck."

Bucky barked because even he recognized an important, life-changing moment when he saw it.

"Exactly. But just in case you need more—and my insatiable girl always needs more—I'll tell you. This is it for me, Kennedy Clark. You are it for me. My reason for striving, for living, for loving. You came into my life and stirred things up. I don't know what I would do without you. Well, I'd probably never talk to anyone or eat ice cream or have sex with another person. I'd be Terminator

Reid, the guy with a mission and no one to share the spoils with."

"Oh, Reid," she sighed with a sniff.

"I still have a mission. To win a Cup and be the best, but the true mission is you. And to fulfill that mission, I need to be a better person. That's what you've been doing for me all this time, making me worthy of you. Making me whole. So will you do me the honor of joining my team? Our team. Be my wife and be Bucky's mom, officially."

She fell down on her knees, cupping his jaw as she did so—just like that first day when she soothed his bruises. She had been comforting him every day since.

"Before you answer, I'm going to need you to read and sign this." He pulled on the ribbon and rolled out the single sheet of paper.

She mouthed the words as she read:

Official Adoption Agreement for: Bucky
& Promise to Marry his Human: Reid Durand

I'm Bucky and I'm ready to take on the responsibility of another human. My preference is for one on the shorter side, with blond hair, pink streaks optional. You must have moonlit-silver eyes and a pretty mouth. To be honest, I don't really care what you look like but my other human has his heart set on a certain type and this is it. You should be fit and flexible because I like to run around in the park and you have to be able to keep up. This is a deal breaker!

It's okay if you play with other dogs as long as you remember I'm the one you bring home. If you want to spend time on your computer ordering things for other humans because that's how you pay for my food and toys, then I suppose that's okay. As long as I get fed. You don't have to take me to the man with the needles, though. In fact I would prefer you didn't do that at all and I'm prepared to offer whatever it takes to ensure that won't happen. Bribes will come in the currency of snuggles and wet noses.

My other human asked me to put this part in: he's crazy about you and wants to spend the rest of his life ...

There was more but I got bored and dozed off.

Sign here and let's go to the park and play.

Signature: ___________

"REID, I can't believe you did this."

"Uh, Bucky did."

"Okay. Bucky. Such a clever boy." She met his gaze, her silver-gilded eyes wet with emotion. "And—oh my God, a ring as well."

While she had been reading, he had brought out a box. "It's Edie's. She wanted you to have it anyway and she said she'd be fine with you getting something else for an engagement, but I thought, maybe? I had it resized."

"I love it," she gasped, removing it from the velvet bed. A pear-shaped sapphire that Edie insisted matched Reid's eyes (he had rolled those eyes on hearing that), the ring's vintage setting sparkled in the April sun. Beautiful, but not a patch on the vision before him.

"Let me." He placed it on the third finger of her left hand, relieved that it fit. She didn't wear jewelry so he'd had to measure with a piece of string one night while she slept.

"I can't wait to be your wife, Reid Durand." She gave Bucky a rub. "You know I'm already your mom, Buck, but it never hurts to make it official."

"I like it official," Reid said, knowing he would get her signature on that adoption agreement before they left this beach. He was a bit of a stickler for that kind of thing.

"Love you, Coffee Shop Girl."

"Love you, Hot Jerk."

They kissed, sealing the deal on the patch of land that had brought them all together and watched as Bucky chased an imaginary foe through the dew-dotted grass.

SONG OF THE OPEN ROAD

WALT WHITMAN

Listen! I will be honest with you,
I do not offer the old smooth prizes
But offer rough new prizes
These are the days that must happen to you:

You shall not heap up what is called riches,
You shall scatter with lavish hand
All that you earn or achieve.

However sweet the laid up stores,
However convenient the dwelling,
You shall not remain there.
However sheltered the port,
However calm the waters,
You shall not anchor there.
However welcome the hospitality that welcomes
you,
You are permitted to receive it but a little while.

Afoot and lighthearted, take to the open road

Healthy, free, the world before you
The long brown path before you,
Leading wherever you choose.

Say only to one another:
Camerado, I give you my hand!
I give you my love more precious than money;
I give you myself before preaching and law:
Will you give me yourself?
Will you come travel with me?
Shall we stick by each other as long as we live?

ACKNOWLEDGMENTS

Thanks to Kristi Yanta, editor-extraordinaire, who always manages to take my word lump and figure out what I'm trying to do. I couldn't do this without you.

Thanks also to copyeditor Kim Cannon and Michele Catalano, my cover designer.

To my agent, Nicole Resciniti, thanks for another great year.

Thanks to my ARC readers, favorite bloggers, and especially Kate's Kittens, who have read every book and cheered on the Rebels. Your support means the world to me.

And finally, Jimmie, thanks for everything.

ABOUT THE AUTHOR

Originally from Ireland, *USA Today* bestselling author Kate Meader cut her romance reader teeth on Maeve Binchy and Jilly Cooper novels, with some Harlequins thrown in for variety. Give her tales about brooding mill owners, oversexed equestrians, and men who can rock an apron, a fire hose, or a hockey stick, and she's there. Now based in Chicago, she writes sexy contemporary featuring strong heroes and amazing women and men who can match their guys quip for quip.

ALSO BY KATE MEADER

Rookie Rebels

GOOD GUY

INSTACRUSH

MAN DOWN

FOREPLAYER

DEAR ROOMIE

REBEL YULE

JOCK WANTED

SUPERSTAR

WILD RIDE

Chicago Rebels

IN SKATES TROUBLE

IRRESISTIBLE YOU

SO OVER YOU

UNDONE BY YOU

HOOKED ON YOU

WRAPPED UP IN YOU

Hot in Chicago Rookies

COMING IN HOT

UP IN SMOKE

DOWN IN FLAMES

HOT TO THE TOUCH

Laws of Attraction

DOWN WITH LOVE

ILLEGALLY YOURS

THEN CAME YOU

Hot in Chicago

REKINDLE THE FLAME

FLIRTING WITH FIRE

MELTING POINT

PLAYING WITH FIRE

SPARKING THE FIRE

FOREVER IN FIRE

Tall, Dark, and Texan

EVEN THE SCORE

TAKING THE SCORE

ONE WEEK TO SCORE

For updates, giveaways, and new release information, sign up for Kate's newsletter at katemeader.com